What We Found in the Corn Maze and How It Saved a Dragon

What We Found in the Corn Maze and How It Saved a Dragon

HENRY CLARK

LITTLE, BROWN AND COMPANY
New York Boston

Copyright © 2020 by Henry Clark

Jacket art copyright © 2020 by Mirelle Ortega.
Jacket design by Marcie Lawrence.
Handlettering by David Coulson.
Jacket copyright © 2020 by Hachette Book Group, Inc.

Little, Brown and Company
Hachette Book Group
1290 Avenue of the Americas, New York, NY 10104
Visit us at LBYR.com

First Edition: May 2020

Little, Brown and Company is a division of Hachette Book Group, Inc. The Little, Brown name and logo are trademarks of Hachette Book Group, Inc.

The publisher is not responsible for websites (or their content) that are not owned by the publisher.

Library of Congress Cataloging-in-Publication Data

Names: Clark, Henry, 1952- author.
Title: What we found in the corn maze and how it saved a dragon : a novel / by Henry Clark.
Description: First edition. | New York : Little, Brown and Company, 2020. | Audience: Ages 8-12. | Summary: "When three twelve-year-olds discover there are seven separate minutes a day they can do magic, they must use oddly specific spells to save a dragon, themselves, and the world"—Provided by publisher.
Identifiers: LCCN 2019029634 | ISBN 9780316492317 (hardcover) | ISBN 9780316492348 (ebook) | ISBN 9780316492324 (library ebook)
Subjects: CYAC: Adventure and adventurers—Fiction. | Magic—Fiction. | Farm life—Fiction. | Humorous stories.
Classification: LCC PZ7.C5458 Bc 2020 | DDC [Fic]—dc23
LC record available at https://lccn.loc.gov/2019029634

ISBNs: 978-0-316-49231-7 (hardcover),
978-0-316-49234-8 (ebook)

Printed in the United States of America

LSC-C

10 9 8 7 6 5 4 3 2 1

For Tyler Keren.
Hello, grandson!

Table of Contents

CHAPTER 1

CHANGE

It all started at 12:34 on a Saturday afternoon.

The exact time is important. It couldn't have happened five minutes earlier or an hour later.

It had to be then.

Drew and I were sitting on the grass in Onderdonk Grove, next to the brook that separates the nature preserve side of the park from the picnic area. On the opposite bank, both baseball fields had games going: one with adults, the other with Little Leaguers. Smoke from a barbecue grill rose in a straight line and then broke up and drifted east toward the town of Disarray, where Drew and I live. Our bikes leaned against a nearby tree.

I dug a small stone out of the grass and tossed it into the water.

"Did you tell them it's a bad idea?" Drew asked, continuing a conversation we'd begun during the ride over, when we had stopped at an intersection to watch two moving vans leave town. He pulled his legs up, wrapped his arms around them, and rested his chin on his knees, turning himself into a compact, glasses-wearing boulder with mossy brown hair on top.

"I'm pretty sure they *know* it's a bad idea," I said, looking around for another pebble. A leaf walked by to my left. I lowered my head so that I could see the ant beneath it. The leaf was five times the size of the ant, yet the tiny creature had no trouble with the load.

"The farm stand's losing money," I added, raising myself back up. "My dad says if we have *one* rainy weekend this October, we'll barely break even. If we have *two* rainy weekends, we'll end up owing money."

"So...*no* rainy weekends would mean a profit?" Drew turned his head sideways and stared at me.

"Not a big one." I sighed. "Not like we used to get."

My family owns a farm. This is possibly why I look like a scarecrow. At least, that's what some of the kids at school say. I'm tall and I'm bony, and my clothes sometimes fit and sometimes don't because most of them are hand-me-downs from my brother, Glen, who's six years older and three inches taller. And it doesn't help that my last name is Sapling. My first name is Calvin, which is all right but not something I would have chosen, if anybody had asked. I try not to turn around whenever somebody shouts, "Hey, Sap!"

"But *Elwood Davy*!" Drew muttered. "He owns half the town already." He shifted closer to the embankment, picking up a few stones of his own. He's eight inches shorter than I am, with a rounder face, and he knows how to weave twigs together to make little rafts that float down the stream, while the ones I make break apart and sink.

"His company made the offer." I shrugged. I had seen my dad shrug a lot lately. Maybe it was contagious. "The farm stand makes more money these days off the corn maze and the monster barn than it does from selling produce. And it's not enough. My dad says you can only milk Halloween for six, maybe seven weeks out of the year. He also says the offer from Davy is decent. We have a week to think it over."

We fell silent as we watched one of the adult baseball players run backward to catch a pop fly, crash into another player, and miss the ball, allowing the batter to miraculously make it to second.

"If your parents sell the place, you'll move," said Drew. He sounded the way I felt. "Couldn't they hold out till spring?"

"If there was enough money in the bank," I said. "But. You know." I shrugged again. "The Fireball 50." I forced a lilt into my voice as I said it, as if the words were song lyrics rather than the name of a charred pile of junk I could see from my bedroom window. *The Fireball 50* was something I said whenever I felt the need to remind myself that my family's money problems were mostly the result of something I had done. Usually when I mentioned it around Drew, he knew enough to change the subject.

Usually.

"That wasn't your fault," he said.

The ant with the leaf made it to the anthill. Other ants gathered around and started nibbling the leaf into smaller pieces that could be dragged underground.

"They're selling. They really don't have any other choice," I said, as if *Fireball 50* had never passed my lips.

We watched an empty plastic bottle bob past in the brook. It snagged against a rock, filled with water, and disappeared.

After a while, Drew said, "This doesn't change our sleepover plans, does it? I'm already packed."

"That's not until tomorrow," I reminded him.

"Even so. It'll be bad news if I have to be home."

Drew's parents had arranged for him to stay at my place on Sunday and Monday nights while they tore apart their house's one bathroom and tried to update it into the twenty-first century. The toilet was being ripped out and, knowing Drew's parents' lack of plumbing expertise, might take more than a day to replace. There had been talk of chamber pots.

Out of the corner of my eye, I caught a tiny movement in the grass. I turned my head slightly, expecting to see another leaf on its way to the anthill.

But it wasn't a leaf.

It was a coin.

And it was sliding through the grass faceup, heading for my foot.

So the time would have been 12:34.

"Hey," I said, happy for the diversion. "That's got to be Super Ant. It's actually carrying a quarter."

Drew leaned over to see. The coin wobbled out of the grass and onto a stretch of bare dirt. "Why would an ant need a quarter?" he wondered.

"Maybe it's looking for a soda machine."

The coin hit my sneaker and stopped. It backed up an inch, then came forward and hit my sneaker again. I could have moved my foot, but I wanted to see what would happen. The coin tried three more times to get through the sole of my sneaker, then backed up and started to go around.

I reached down and gently lifted the quarter, expecting to see three or four ants working together or possibly a very muscle-bound ant all by itself.

There was nothing under the coin.

Only dirt.

Really.

"Whoa!" I said, squinting at the quarter.

"It's gotta be some sort of trick," said Drew. "Is there a thread attached to it?"

"There's *nothing* attached to it." I turned the coin from heads to tails and back again. It was tarnished and worn at the edges, and its date was the year my grandfather was born. But otherwise, there was nothing strange about it.

Except that it had been moving by itself.

I put it back on the ground.

It did nothing. Just sat there.

I nudged it.

Still nothing.

I flipped it over and nudged it again.

It didn't budge.

"Maybe it's playing possum," said Drew.

"It's a *coin*," I said. "It can't *play* anything."

"It could play an arcade game if you had enough of them," Drew reasoned. "Toss it here."

I picked up the quarter and flipped it at him. It bounced off his fingers and landed in the grass; he scrambled after it, raking his hands through the grass, but he came up empty.

"Lost it."

Which was all the quarter needed.

It came out of the grass, rolling on its edge this time, and slipped onto the narrow dirt path that led to the wider trail at the top of the embankment.

"It's rolling *uphill*," I said in disbelief.

"We gotta follow it!" Drew jumped to his feet and clambered up the slope.

I was right behind him.

The coin reached the trail and made a right.

"It changed direction," Drew muttered. "That's not possible."

"None of this is possible," I reminded him. "Don't lose it!"

We kept pace with the coin. It showed no sign of slowing down.

A sweaty man in a jogging suit rounded the bend and trotted straight at us, the wires of his earphones flopping like the wattle on a rooster. We split to either side of him, and his right foot stomped down less than an inch from the coin, which wobbled a little, then straightened and accelerated.

"No way!" I gasped, halting in my tracks and catching Drew by the sleeve.

"What?" Drew looked but missed what I was seeing.

I pointed.

A second coin—a nickel—had slid out from under a bush and was tumbling end over end, heading in the same direction as the first. The quarter caught up with it, and they traveled on together. To our left, a faint hissing sound and a disturbance in the grass was either a snake or—

Another quarter tumbled onto the trail, raising a tiny dust cloud as it surfed on its belly.

"It's a coin migration," declared Drew as we both started running again.

"Coins don't migrate."

"They must. That would explain why sometimes I can't find my lunch money."

The three coins skidded to the left and departed the trail, slowing down as they plunged into the weedy meadow that stretched to the trees bordering the park to the west. Two bright copper pennies sailed up a tuft of bent-over grass, became briefly airborne, then landed ahead of the first three coins, taking the lead.

"Fifty-seven cents!" shouted Drew.

"More than that!" I waved to either side. The grass and weeds rustled as small things in a hurry brushed past their stems. "It's a stampede!"

"I wonder what they're running from," Drew said.

"Probably some guy with a metal detector."

At least two dozen coins rolled and tumbled around us as we ran. In front of us, the fastest ones started to funnel into a single line.

"They're heading for that tree." I pointed to an elm at the edge of the park. Beyond the tree was a chain-link fence. "Don't lose them!"

We sprinted, and I slammed into the tree first. Drew came in a close second, and the coins veered to our left.

The two pennies were still in the lead, and as they sped by, I looked around the tree to see whether they would go through the fence to the road beyond.

Not quite.

A girl was crouched in front of the fence holding a bright-yellow beach pail against the ground. The first penny flew into the pail and thumped against the bottom. A moment later, the second penny joined it.

Drew leaned past me, and I caught him before he could draw the girl's attention. Her black hair was pulled back from her face and gathered in a thick bun stuffed with what looked like pencils or pens—or possibly chopsticks. Smudges on her nose and cheeks made her look as though she'd gotten too close to the frosting on a multicolored cupcake.

I recognized her as the captain of the Disarray Dolphins, the school swim team. She wasn't in any of my classes, and she moved too quickly for conversation in the halls. The one time I'd tried to speak to her, she'd been nearby when I said, "Hey, I like your back—" but was thirty feet away by the time I said, "—pack." I'd been trying to compliment her on the very cool hand-painted rhinoceros on her bag, but it had come out as *I like your back*. Talk about awkward. I pulled Drew farther behind the tree.

As we watched, a stream of coins rolled, spun, and tumbled into her pail. Just a few at first, then a bunch, then a trickle. Then none. She looked up, as if to see if any more were coming.

"Modesty Brooker!" Drew blurted, then lost his balance and staggered forward. I stepped out after him, since I no longer saw any sense in hiding.

"Hi," I said, raising my hand in what I thought was a friendly greeting.

She bolted, clutching her plastic bucket. She doubled back to snatch up her rhinoceros backpack, then ran to a break in the fence. She wiggled through the gap, scrambled onto a bike, and was down the road before we'd even managed a step.

"Hey! Come back!" I shouted after her. "We don't want the money! We just want to talk!"

She disappeared around the bend.

"Okay," said Drew. "That was strange."

"*Strange* isn't the word for it," I replied as we walked to the spot where she had been crouching. "Did we just dream that?"

A dime rolled out of the weeds and bounced off Drew's shoe. He picked it up.

"I would say no—we didn't dream it."

"Hey," I said. "She forgot something."

I fished a three-ring binder out of the tall grass along the fence. Its cover was spattered with paint and frayed at the corners. I flipped it open.

Handwritten at the top of the first sheet of loose-leaf were the words:

To Gather Lost Coins

The rest of the page was filled with gibberish. Odd syllables and real words were mixed together in sentences that meant nothing, as if they had been put together for the way they sounded rather than their sense.

I turned the page. The second sheet had the heading:

To Change the Color of a Room

It was followed by the same kind of nonsense as on the first sheet.

"What is this?" I wondered aloud.

"Well," said Drew, scanning the pages as I turned them, "as a guess, and based on what we just saw, I'd say...maybe..."

"What?"

"Maybe it's a book of...*magic*?"

CHAPTER 2

A REALLY WELL-DONE DRAGON

Cal, you can't argue with what we saw," Drew said half an hour later as we sat at one of the farm stand's picnic tables, the binder open between us.

From where we were, I could see cars pulling in and out of the parking lot. Business may have looked brisk, but it wasn't; the overflow parking field on the other side of Route 9 was empty. So empty that I had an unobstructed view of the blackened remains of the Fireball 50 combine harvester in the wheat field beyond. I stared at it just long enough to get my usual queasy feeling, then shifted my gaze to the pumpkin-shaped sign by the roadside, which announced that this year's corn maze, haunted hayride, and monster barn would have their *spooktacular* opening on Friday.

"There's no such thing as magic," I said.

The sound of hammering came from the barn. My dad and the five high school kids he had hired were putting up the walls of the creepy rooms that would soon be filled with weird furniture and monster mannequins. Starting Friday, these same five kids and ten others would dress up as creatures and jump out at anyone foolish enough to pay to walk through the place. I would have helped assemble the rooms, but I was scheduled to work in the stand later that afternoon, and my mom didn't want me covered with sawdust or glue or some sticky combination of the two.

"*You* know there's no such thing as magic, and *I* know it," Drew agreed, "but Modesty Brooker made nickels and dimes jump into a bucket without touching them. And she had this book, with a page that says *To Gather Lost Coins* at the top, with some sort of spell or incantation written on it."

"This is *not* a book of spells," I said, pushing the notebook toward him. "It's a *three-ring binder*. Every kid in school has one exactly like it. A book of spells would be...would be—"

"What?"

"Old, for one thing. And musty-smelling, with a

padlock on it and a leather cover with a creepy pattern that might or might not be a face but suddenly bites your hand if you try to open it." I flipped randomly to the book's middle. The page it opened to was titled *To Brighten Teeth*.

"And the spells would be written in blood with a raven's quill pen, and they wouldn't be about painting rooms or...or—"

"Dental hygiene?" Drew suggested.

"Exactly. And the pages in this book were obviously written with a pencil." I gave the book a quarter turn and read the first line beneath *Teeth*.

" 'Gum puppy stump mucky; foo fee rump yucky.' Does that sound like magic to you? This *can't* be a book of spells."

Drew turned the book back to him and flipped to the front.

"Well," he said. "There's one way to find out. You should probably crouch down on the ground with your hands cupped together."

"Why would I do that?"

"To catch the coins that are going to start flying at us after I read the incantation."

I folded my arms defiantly in front of me and rested them on the tabletop.

"Okay," Drew said, "but some of those coins were moving pretty fast. Don't blame me if you get a dime stuck in your ankle. Or a silver dollar slices off your big toe."

I kept my arms where they were.

But I pulled my feet up.

Drew propped the binder on my folded arms, as if that was why I was holding them there. He pulled his phone from his pocket and took a picture of the page he was about to read from.

"In case it, you know, bursts into flame or something while I'm reading."

He started to put his phone away, then flipped the book and took pictures of the next two pages.

"We don't have time to snap the entire thing," I said. "I have to be at work pretty soon."

"Just give me a sec," he said, adjusting his glasses, then twiddling his fingers on the phone's face some more.

"Now what?"

"Audio recording," he replied, finally placing the phone to one side. "It's what a scientist would do. For future study."

He turned his attention back to the book and, in as deep and solemn a voice as he could manage, began to read.

"'Mully ully goo gafsik hummus, portnoy fidget punko summus; Rastafast interabang gunk embargo, trundleheim thimblewits dum escargot—'"

I giggled. Drew shot me an angry glance, then giggled, too.

"It's not going to work if we laugh," he said, straightening his shoulders.

"No," I agreed, "there's absolutely nothing funny about this," and burst out laughing again.

"You and I both saw the coins move," Drew reminded me. "So there is some reason to think this might work. I'm starting over."

I took a deep breath and held it. This time, Drew didn't stop reciting until he had uttered every silly word and nonsense syllable on the page. It took him about a minute to get through it, but it felt like an hour because I was biting my tongue after the first ten seconds. As soon as he spoke the final line—

"'Bullriggies blefuscu batburgers blintz; purple flirp baby birp conestoga mintz!'"

—we both turned and looked around us.

Nothing.

An acorn fell and hit Drew on the head. We both cringed and raised our hands to protect ourselves in case he had mispronounced one of the words and accidentally turned the spell into one that caused nuts to rain from the sky.

But the acorn was the only thing that fell, and after a moment, we both relaxed.

"This is a kid's notebook," I said, riffling the pages. "There are cross-outs and scribbles, and if these are magic spells, most of them are ridiculous. I mean, *To Open a Door.* How lazy is that? In the time it would take to speak the words, you could get up, open every door in your house, and close them again." I read off the names of more spells as the pages fluttered through my fingers. "*To Walk with Stilts, To Untangle Yarn, To Cast a Reflection, To Repair a Chimney, To Get Chewing Gum Out of a Carpet, To Materialize a Storm Cloud*—"

A shadow fell across the table between us.

"Hey," said Drew, "you materialized a cloud just by saying—"

"*Give me my book back!*"

Drew and I jumped.

Modesty Brooker was leaning over us. Up close, it turned out the sticks in her hair were paintbrushes, and the smudges on her face were paint. It made sense, since she was wearing an artist's smock. She slammed her hand down on the notebook and yanked it away from us. Drew's hand shot out and caught the book by the bottommost of its three rings.

"Let go! It isn't yours!" Modesty said angrily.

"We found it in the grass," I said.

"I thought it was in my backpack." She huffed. "I came back for it the moment I realized."

"Finders keepers?" Drew suggested, then looked like he regretted it as she spun the notebook to the right and twisted his fingers in the ring.

"Owww."

"We were going to return it," I said.

"When?"

"Monday. At school. We figured it was yours. It's not like we stole it."

Modesty locked eyes with Drew.

"Let go," she said.

He released the notebook. She tucked it under her arm and started to walk away. I grabbed Drew's phone, held it up, and called after her, "We took video of the moving coins!"

It was a lie, but I thought it might make her come back.

It didn't.

"You're in it," I added.

She stopped walking.

She turned slowly and came back to us.

"Video of coins moving by themselves could easily be faked using stop-motion photography," she said testily, "so what you've got doesn't prove a thing."

"There are always idiots who think the latest photo of Bigfoot is real," I said. "No matter how fake it looks. If we sent our video to Milton Supman over at Channel Seven News, and he ran it in the Wide World of Weird segment, you'd have people camping out on your doorstep wanting to know how you got coins to jump into a bucket."

18

"Right!" agreed Drew. "Uh…just how *did* you do that? Get coins to jump into a bucket?"

Modesty gave us a sour look.

"If I tell you, will you delete the video?"

"I promise you, no one will ever see it." I held up my hand as a pledge.

A family with three kids plunked themselves down at the table next to us, each of them with a steaming ear of corn from the snack bar, butter already running down their kernel-speckled chins.

Modesty eyeballed them.

"Anywhere we can go where it's more private?" she asked.

I glanced around, considered the abandoned poultry shed where we had once kept prize-winning chickens, then noticed the shadow that stretched across the shed's roof.

"You bet." I nodded. "Follow me."

I threaded my way through the picnic tables, past the vacant goat pen, to the base of the fire lookout tower.

The tower was a single room perched on top of four steel legs, with an open-air stairway that *zigged* four times and *zagged* five until you popped through a trapdoor in the floor of the cab, which is what a fire lookout tower room is called.

I used my key to unlock the gate at the base of the stairs, locked it behind us once we were through, and the three of us climbed the 123 steps to the top.

"Nice view," Modesty said once we got there. She took a moment to turn 360 degrees, which is what most people do, to look out the glassless windows that stretch across all four walls and allow you to see, on a clear day, ten miles in any direction. To the west, it gave a good view of downtown Disarray.

"People pay five bucks to come up here to look at the maze," I said, stepping to the clunky pay-per-view binoculars bolted to the floor atop a green metal post.

My dad said that the tower and binoculars had paid for themselves after only a single Halloween, eight years earlier. He had bought the tower for $900 and spent twice that to move it seventy miles from Tinderwood State Forest to the edge of our cornfield. The binoculars were surplus from a national park. The heart-shaped metal box that held the lenses always reminded me of the head of a space alien. I popped a quarter into the alien's nose, looked into its eyes, and swiveled its head in Modesty's direction. I jumped back when all I saw was her eyeball.

"They study the maze for a while," I continued, stepping aside and offering Modesty a free peek through the eyepieces, "then they head back down, pay their ten bucks to go into the maze, and they *still* get lost."

Modesty ignored my binocular offer and strolled to the east side of the cab. She leaned out the window a little. Then she leaned out a lot.

"That's a really well-done dragon!" she cried, sweeping her head back and forth to take in our cornfield.

I leaned out next to her.

"It sure is," I agreed. "My dad says its name is Phlogiston."

The corn maze stretched out below us in a dozen shades of green. The walkways of the maze formed a picture of a giant dragon curled in on itself with its head in the center. The previous year, the maze had been in the shape of the high school football mascot—a tough-looking anteater—and the year before that, the *Mona Lisa* with crossed eyes staring at a spider on her nose. My mom says my dad's mazes are what Michelangelo would have done, if Michelangelo had owned a tractor.

"We really shouldn't be leaning out this far," I said.

"It's okay; I have perfect balance." Modesty slid out even farther, stretched her arms forward and her legs back as if she were swimming, and teetered on the windowsill on the flat of her stomach. She looked from side to side. "Comes from years of dance class. Why did you paint your harvester black?" She pointed in the direction opposite the maze. "Just for Halloween?"

I didn't want to talk about it. "It's not paint, okay? It's... soot from when the harvester burned. Please come back inside." I caught her by the wrist and dragged her into the cab. "If you fell out of the tower, I would get *so* yelled at."

"Harvester fire, huh? Those are more common than people think." Modesty adjusted her smock. "I've got an uncle in Alberta—"

"So how much did you make?" asked Drew, stepping between Modesty and me, *this* time changing the subject exactly the way he was supposed to.

Modesty's scowl, which had disappeared while she was admiring the view, came back.

"How much did I make?"

"From your coin collecting."

"I haven't counted it yet," she said sharply. "I came straight here the moment I realized I didn't have the note-book. I knew where to go after the two of you popped out from behind the tree, and I thought, *Oh, it's Scarecrow Boy from the farm stand.*"

"You can call me Cal," I said, "and I've only dressed as a scarecrow *once*. Three Halloweens ago as a charac-ter in the corn maze. The past two years, I've been the Grim Reaper. Little kids sit on my lap, tell me what they want for Halloween, and get their picture taken."

"Parents take pictures of their kids sitting on Death's lap?" asked Modesty.

"It's a Halloween thing."

"What do most kids want?"

"Candy."

Modesty walked back across the cab and stared down at the parking lot. Drew and I came over to see what she was pretending to be interested in. I could tell she didn't want to say how she had caused coins to jump into a bucket.

A big black limousine was pulling in to the farm stand, taking up three parking spots. Two guys with matching bald spots and business suits got out. They opened their trunk, lifted out a large cardboard box, and lugged it into the main building.

"Those guys look rich," said Modesty. "Maybe you're going to make a big sale."

"Oh, we are," I said glumly. "Those guys work for Davy's Digital Vegetables. They've got my folks pretty much convinced to sell our land."

"Ick," said Modesty. "I hate DDVs. Their cucumbers are awful. The seeds are completely unconvincing. I hope your parents don't have to sell. At least, not to *them*."

"Maybe they won't have to," I said, "if I, like, knew a way to pick up some spare change...."

It had already crossed my mind that the *To Gather Lost Coins* spell might be a way for me to help my folks. At the very least, it could mean money toward a new harvester.

"It wouldn't help," said Modesty, returning to the table at the center of the cab and plunking the binder down on it. Drew had already left his phone there; Modesty's hand twitched toward it, but then she refrained from grabbing it. "I've never managed to make more than four dollars any time I've tried."

"But the money *does* come to you," Drew said, nodding encouragement.

"Of course it does. I can be downright magnetic when I put my mind to it."

"Is that how it works?" I asked. "Magnetism?"

"No, Scarecrow Boy."

"Cal," I suggested.

"It's not magnetism." She tapped the notebook with her finger. "It's magic."

"I knew it," said Drew.

"The problem is," she added, "*magic only works for one minute each day.*"

CHAPTER 3

SEVEN HUNDRED WORDS PER MINUTE

Think about it," said Modesty. "Why hasn't anybody ever gotten magic to work? Everybody talks about it; everybody would *love* if magic existed; there are a zillion stories about magic, but nobody's ever done it. Why? *Because magic can't be performed at any old time. It can only be done during one particular minute of the day.*"

"When?" I asked.

"Twelve thirty-four in the afternoon."

"That's it?"

"That's it. You've got sixty seconds. Twelve thirty-*five* rolls around, you're done."

"That's stupid," said Drew.

"Stupid or not, that's how it works."

"How do you know this?" I was having enough trouble believing in magic. Magic with conditions was even less believable.

"I figured it out. It took me two weeks. But nobody else has been able to figure it out *ever*, so I'm thinking that makes me smarter than anybody else who's ever lived. Of course, I had the notebook and the bookmark, and they didn't, so I suppose that gave me an edge. I'm not only very smart; I'm also very fair."

"But not modest. Despite your name."

"My sister Patience interrupts people all the time, my sister Serene has a temper you wouldn't believe, and my sister Verity can't be trusted. Mum says our names were supposed to help form our personalities."

"Why would she think that would work?"

"Her name is Hope."

"Bookmark?" asked Drew.

Modesty frowned, as if she had let slip something she shouldn't have. Then she shrugged and pulled a narrow slip of paper from one of her smock's many pockets. She held it up so Drew and I could read it.

If a child had written the pages in the notebook, then an adult using a quill-tip pen had carefully lettered the writing on the bookmark.

IRKSOME'S SEVEN INSIGHTS
Magic is fluid.

Magic evolves.

The three levels of magic are:
Everybody, Somebody, and Very Few.

Dragons are the source of magic—
unless it's something they ate.

The noblest use of magic is to
accomplish household chores.

Magic isn't arbitrary—
it only looks that way.

Popcorn.

"This was in the book when I found it," Modesty explained, "in between the pages marked *To Summon the Forces of Torque* and *To Open a Door*. It's what made me think the things in the book might be incantations."

Drew reached for the bookmark. Modesty tucked it back into her smock.

"How can *popcorn* be an insight?" I asked.

"You'd have to ask Irksome—whoever, or whatever, Irksome is," Modesty replied.

"Where did you get the book?" asked Drew. "Somewhere in that weird old house of yours?"

I glanced at him. Modesty's house was as old as mine. It was the same size and style. Drew had never called my house "weird."

"I found it in my gym locker."

"Your...*gym locker*?"

"Three weeks ago, on the first day of school. Ms. Dalton assigned me the locker, and when I opened it, there was the notebook. I was going to turn it in, but when I searched for a name, I found the bookmark, and that got me interested. I took the book home and tried reading some of the incantations out loud. I chanted them, I sang them, I shouted them."

"What happened?" asked Drew.

"Serene told me if I didn't knock it off, she'd staple my lips shut. That was all right, because I was feeling pretty silly, since nothing magical had happened. But the next morning, after a good night's sleep, it occurred to me: Maybe magic has rules, and I wasn't following them. Maybe I should have recited the incantations outdoors or with a cone-shaped hat on or in the locker room where I first found the book. So I tried those things and dozens of others, including reciting the incantations with a mouthful of popcorn—I *don't* recommend that—and when that didn't work, I finally thought, well, *Maybe magic works better at certain times of the day.*"

"Midnight," I said.

"You'd think. But I tried that, and all that happened was Serene yelling at me for waking her up. So then I tried three AM—"

"Why three AM?" I asked.

"I don't know. There's just something creepy about three AM. I tried the spell that changes the color of a room, because that's a short one, but my room was still aquamarine zebra stripes in the morning."

"Your room is aquamarine zebra stripes?" Drew sounded appalled.

"I painted it myself. It honors all the zebras that have died because their habitats have been destroyed. Anyway, the only other magical-sounding time I could think of was seven o'clock, because seven's supposed to be lucky, but it didn't work. So I was just about to give up, but then I thought, *What about twelve thirty-four in the afternoon?*"

"Why would that be magical?" I couldn't follow her logic. I was pretty sure there wasn't any.

"Two reasons. It's the time of day when I first found the book, and, get this, it's *also* my gym locker combination."

"Your locker combination?" Something in my voice must have told her I didn't believe it. She glared at me. I glared back.

"Yes. *My locker combination.* One, twenty-three, four. I figured that *had* to be more than a coincidence. So I went into Patience's room—she's away at college—and I sat on the bed, and at exactly twelve thirty-four, I started reciting the color-changing spell. I just barely managed to get through it before twelve thirty-five. Suddenly—the room was fuchsia."

"It had a funny smell?" I asked.

"*Fuchsia* is a color. Purplish-red. Not to be confused with *magenta*, which is reddish-purple. The color of the room before I started had been *cerulean*"—she held up her hand to keep me from speaking—"by which I mean, *blue*. My point is—the spell worked. But I tried it again twelve hours later, at twelve thirty-four AM, and nothing happened."

"You mean your living room stayed chartreuse?" Drew said sarcastically.

"No, the upstairs bathroom stayed *yellow*. Who paints their living room chartreuse? So. What did I learn? After only two weeks of experimentation? When it took Madame Curie two *years* to discover radium?"

"You learned"—Drew sighed—"that magic works but only for sixty seconds each day, beginning at thirty-four minutes past noon. You expect us to believe that?"

"Whether you believe it or not doesn't matter. The next day, I went to the Cost-Mart parking lot, sat under the only tree, and chanted the coin-gathering spell."

She stopped and looked at us. I knew what she wanted.

"And?" I prompted.

"And I made three dollars and fourteen cents. That's

how it's done. Now delete your recording, and I'm going home." She snapped the notebook shut, tucked it under her arm, and stood.

"Wait," I said. "The spell only gathered the coins that had been lost in the Cost-Mart parking lot? Nothing from the drugstore parking lot across the street?"

"As far as I could tell. The spell is very picky about geography. If you're in Onderdonk Grove, it only brings you coins that have been lost in Onderdonk Grove. I tried it in the schoolyard on Monday, and I made two dollars and seventy-one cents. I tried it in the same place two days later, and all I got were two dimes and a nickel. I figure those coins were lost after the first time I tried it."

I suddenly had the sinking feeling that the coin-gathering spell wasn't going to solve any of my problems. It wouldn't bring in enough money to keep Elwood Davy from buying our land, or enough to replace the Fireball 50, or even enough to pay a scrap-metal dealer to haul the harvester's remains out of the field so they wouldn't be there to constantly remind my parents—and me—of how I'd screwed up.

"It doesn't bring you every coin ever lost in the whole wide world," Modesty continued, hammering more nails in the coffin, "and it doesn't touch money that isn't truly lost. The second time I tried it, I put some pennies behind a trash can, and they were still there after I read the spell. I knew they were there, so they weren't lost."

"That must be why the quarter we found in the park stopped moving until we lost it again." Drew nodded knowingly, like a scientist discussing lab results with another scientist.

"It's good for a few bucks here and there," said Modesty, "but if you keep returning to the same place, you're going to get less and less. And it doesn't touch paper money. That's why it's not going to get you enough to save your farm." She looked at me apologetically.

"The magic works for *more* than a minute, though," said Drew. "When we saw the coins move in the park, we chased them for a couple of minutes at least."

"Yes, and my sister's room is still fu...uh, purplish-red," Modesty confirmed, "and it took the coins in the park however long they needed to reach me from however far away they were."

"Oh. That reminds me," said Drew, fishing the late-arriving dime out of his pocket. "This came for you after you left. It's a 1963, so it's worth more than ten cents. Closer to two dollars."

"You're a coin collector?" Modesty asked.

"My dad is."

"Keep it, then." Modesty waved away the dime.

"Magic seems awfully temperamental," I said. *And mostly useless*, I thought. A spell that could fetch coins would fetch you only enough to buy a soda. And soda was among the things I had been denying myself ever since the Fireball 50 disaster.

"But," said Drew, "most of the spells in the notebook go on for pages. Nobody could speak fast enough to recite any of them in a minute."

"Ah!" said Modesty, like a teacher pleased with a student's answer. It wasn't a tone I was overly familiar with. "That's just it. There are only two spells in the entire book that are short enough to work. All the rest are more than eight hundred words, and no human being can speak more than seven hundred words per minute and pronounce the words clearly enough to be understood."

"Is that for real?" I asked.

"It's in all the record books. The record holder, Betty Jo Tachylalia, only managed it by speaking nothing but prepositions. As, at, but, by, for, from, in, of, off, on, to—"

"Enough!" I held up my hand. I was trying to work something out.

"*Enough* is actually an adjective," Modesty said. "Sometimes an adverb."

"If no human being can speak faster than seven hundred words per minute," I said slowly, "then that would mean..." I stopped.

"Ye-e-s?" Modesty dragged out the word.

"That would mean...the original owner of this notebook...*wasn't human.*"

CHAPTER 4

PHLOGISTON'S EYE

A car alarm went off in the parking lot, making us all jump. It ended as quickly as it started, with an ear-piercing *yip-yip-yip*.

"I wouldn't go that far," said Modesty. "You've *seen* the handwriting in the notebook. It obviously wasn't written by the bogeyman."

"No," agreed Drew. "More like one of the bogeyman's kids. Bogeyman Junior."

Modesty rolled her eyes.

"I think it's time we erased your video."

She plucked Drew's phone from the table and ran her fingers over it until she found the photo app. She stared at the screen for a moment, then glared at us. "The only video on this phone is somebody squeezing their belly button in different ways to make it look like it's talking!"

"It says some pretty funny things," said Drew, reaching out to turn up the volume. Modesty held the phone away from him. "It's, uh, very upset about smelly sweatbands on underwear...."

"You never took video of the coins moving," Modesty snapped. "You lied, and then you blackmailed me into explaining about the spells. And here I was, thinking how good it felt to finally *tell* somebody, because I couldn't share it with any of my blabbermouth sisters, and I thought Mum might be upset about the fuchsia bedroom, but I thought *maybe* I could trust you two, and we could team up to research the best places to gather coins, and maybe one of you might be fast enough to say the door-opening spell—"

"You have a door you can't open?" I said.

"It's a door I'm very curious about, yes, *but never mind*, because now I know you're a couple of jerks, and I wouldn't hang out with either of you if you were the last jerks on earth!"

She wound up her arm and pitched the phone out of the tower. Drew yelped, and he and I raced to the window to see where it went. It sailed over the corn maze in an impressive arc and fell into the center of Phlogiston's eye. It caught a ray of sunlight, and the dragon winked at us.

"Good throw," I admitted.

"My pitches have been clocked at fifty-five miles per hour," Modesty informed us. "Which is seriously impressive."

"Only for someone who's thirteen," Drew corrected her.

"I'm twelve!" she snapped.

"I'm sorry we lied to you," I said, realizing it bothered me that we had been less than honest with her. "But I don't think sending a nonexistent video of stampeding coins to Channel Seven would be blackmail, exactly."

"No," she said. "*Threatening* to do it—that's when it's blackmail. It's no better than cyberbullying. You wouldn't cyberbully someone, would you?"

"*No!* I would never do that," I said, flustered. I had been cyberbullied by some kids who got a video of me using the hand dryer in the bathroom on the front of my pants after a particularly out-of-control handwashing. The kids had put it on the Internet and made comments that had nothing to do with handwashing. "*We* would never do that," I added to include Drew, who was nodding vigorously. "I apologize, and I mean it. Really." I stared at her. She stared back. "This is where you say, 'Apology accepted.'"

She studied some cobwebs on the ceiling, glanced out the window, then looked back at me.

"No," she said. "Actually, it isn't."

She dropped through the cab's trapdoor before Drew

or I could say anything else. We listened to her furious footfalls thunder down all 123 steps. This was followed by a moment of silence, then the sound of her fist hitting the locked chain-link gate.

"That's going to make her even madder." I sighed and started down after her.

She was waiting with her arms folded and a look on her face that could have caused passing birds to fall dead at her feet.

"I can't believe you locked me in."

"I didn't lock anybody *in*," I said as I undid the padlock. "I locked nosy farm-stand customers *out*. They sometimes wander up the tower if they find the gate open, and if anything were to happen to them—like falling out and landing on their head or, worse, landing on somebody *else's* head—my family could get sued. I wasn't holding you prisoner."

I pushed the gate open, and she stormed past me to retrieve her bike from where it was leaning against a pyramid of pumpkins. A moment later, she left a plume of dust behind as she pedaled furiously out of the parking lot.

"Do you think she was telling the truth?" asked Drew as we watched her disappear over a rise in the road.

"You mean about being mad? Yeah, I'd say so. I hope we never meet Serene."

"No. I mean about finding the notebook in her gym

locker. Why would a book of spells be in a gym locker? That's totally wacky."

"So is money moving by itself," I reminded him. "I'm just sorry she's upset with us. We probably shouldn't have blackmailed her or whatever."

"Yeah," said Drew, pulling me toward the entrance to the maze. "Maybe you can make up with her. I think she likes you more than she likes me. Then maybe she'll let us see the notebook again. I bet if we practice saying tongue twisters, we might be able to speak more than seven hundred words per minute."

We reached the maze's entrance. Drew gave an uneasy glance to the hulking wooden statue of a maniac in a hockey mask holding a chainsaw. My dad had carved it himself out of a single ten-foot-tall tree stump, and he had used a chainsaw to do it. He said that made it art.

So my mother had named the maniac *Artie*.

I led the way into the maze. The corn always whispered inside, even when there wasn't a breeze anywhere else, and the sky always seemed a little bit darker, whether or not there were any clouds. Each year, the cornfield was like any other cornfield until my dad cut paths into it. Then, suddenly, it had its own weather.

"Do we have to solve the maze, or can we cut across?" asked Drew as he started to push aside some of the stalks that lined the path. I caught him by the elbow.

"I know you want your phone," I said, straightening

the stalks he had bent, "but my dad would kill us if we cut through. It's bad enough when lunkheads like Mace Croyden and his friends do it on purpose; it spoils it for everybody else. We have to stick to the paths."

I rearranged the stalks a little more until they looked exactly the way they had before Drew messed with them. I wished all damaged things could be fixed that easily.

"But you *do* know how to get to the center?"

"I know how to get to the *exit*," I said as I led the way to the first intersection and made a left. "But it's possible to get in and out without passing through the middle."

We rounded a bend.

"You really think repeating tongue twisters like *rubber baby buggy bumpers* will help us talk faster?" I asked as we went right, left, and left again.

"It might. There's got to be a way to squeeze those incantations into a minute. I wish I had taken pictures of more of them. And Modesty's bookmark. You think my phone's okay?"

"I don't see how falling from a hundred feet could have hurt it."

We made a turn and passed a seven-foot-tall blue plastic box with a door on it, set back into the corn. A sign on the door said HONEST JOHN'S HONEST JOHNS.

"Toilet?" Drew asked.

"Yup. We always have three of them in the maze. Sometimes people wander around so long, they need one."

"My folks could use one while they're redoing our bathroom," said Drew, then grabbed me by the sleeve. "Hey! You know what you should do? Put one of the high school kids dressed as a zombie inside one of them. Then they could jump out at anybody who comes to use it."

"We tried that once," I admitted. "Turns out, it's not a good idea to scare people when they're looking for a restroom." We reached another intersection, and I turned to see where the fire tower was. "I think...if we make the next three rights, that should get us to the middle."

The walls of corn on either side of us were impossible to see through. My dad always planted a variety of corn called *maze maize*. It was especially dense. We made the next three rights, but instead of winding up in Phlogiston's eye, we found another Honest John.

"We're not going in circles, are we?" Drew wanted to know.

"I...don't...think so?"

"Call my phone. When it rings, we'll know what direction it's in. We can follow the sound."

I fished my phone from my pocket and tapped Drew's number. We both leaned forward, as if this would somehow improve our hearing. From two paths away, a woman's voice said, "Ring, ring."

Drew and I exchanged glances.

"Is that one of your ringtones?" I asked.

"Ring, ring," said the woman again.

"No!" said Drew. "I'd die of embarrassment."

"Ring, ring."

"It's coming from that way." I pointed.

"Then maybe we should go this way," said Drew, pointing in the opposite direction.

"Do you want your phone back or don't you?"

"Not if it's possessed."

"Ring, ring."

I pulled him down a path I thought would take us to the maze's center. We made a right, then a left—

—and, rounding an especially tall clump of cornstalks, found ourselves in the eye of the dragon. Drew's phone lay facedown in the center of the clearing. It said "Ring, ring" again and quivered as if it were eager to be picked up. Drew didn't give it the satisfaction. He nudged it with his foot and flipped it over. A photo of his belly button was on the screen.

"You're getting a call from your navel," I said.

"Don't be ridiculous."

"Ring, ring," said the phone.

"Answer it," I suggested.

"Why? We both know it's you calling."

"What if it isn't? Your ringtone for me is the Darth Vader theme."

"Instead of me answering, why don't you hang up? If it keeps ringing, it isn't you."

"Okay." I canceled the call. We both looked down. Drew's phone didn't move. All was quiet. Then—

"Ring, ring."

"D'oh!" Drew snatched up the phone and shouted, "Hello!"

"Thank you for using the Congroo Help Line," the same voice that had been saying "Ring, ring" announced loudly over the speakerphone setting. "How may we assist you?"

"Who is this?"

"This is the Congroo Help Line. Thank you for allowing us to assist you."

"What's the Congroo Help Line?"

"Sorry. Only one question per call."

Whoever it was hung up. The screen flickered with an odd shade of reddish-purple. Or, possibly, purplish-red.

"I wonder if that's *magenta*?" I said.

Drew shook the phone, and when the screen's weird color didn't change, he switched it off. It took longer to reboot than it should have, but when it came back, it looked normal. Then the screen started to pulse, going from dim to bright and back again. Drew grimaced.

"It shouldn't do that," he muttered, and I watched as he brought up the pictures he had taken of the spells in Modesty's notebook and sent the pictures to my phone, along with the audio file he had made of himself reading the coin-gathering spell.

"This way," he explained, "if my phone goes bonkers, we'll still have the incantations."

"What if I open those files and my phone goes bonkers, too?"

"That's just a chance we'll have to take."

"Thanks."

"How do we get out of here?"

"The same way we got in."

"By getting lost?"

"Follow me," I said, sounding more confident than I felt.

I led him around two corners and grinned when I saw the porta potty again. We were on the right track.

"Wait," said Drew. "I'll just be a second."

He strode up to the portable toilet and reached for the handle.

The door flew open, and a zombie lurched out.

CHAPTER 5

DAVY'S DIGITAL VEGETABLES

We both jumped back. The man who staggered toward us looked like a walking corpse. His face was gray, his lips were blue—possibly *cerulean*—and his eyes were sunk deep into his head. He had a drooping mustache that appeared to have ice in it. Two bony hands stretched out from the sleeves of his hooded robe. One hand groped forward; the other cradled a large glass jar that glowed with a flickering orange light.

Drew fell backward into the corn, and I dodged to the left as the weird figure shambled past. He didn't grab at us or wave his free hand in the air while moaning *braaains* or *kiiidneys* or the name of any other organ zombies supposedly enjoyed eating. He showed no sign at all that he saw us. He dragged one leg behind him in true zombie style, reached the end of the path, and disappeared around the corner.

"Whoa!" said Drew, and started laughing. He retrieved his glasses and hauled himself to his feet. "That guy's *good*."

"You think that was—"

"One of your dad's high school kids. Who else could it have been? He probably overheard my idea about popping out of the porta potty."

I knew the high schoolers weren't supposed to get their costumes until the following day. This guy not only had his costume, but he was in full makeup. I was about to point this out to Drew when I remembered that a lot of the kids who were willing to work for my dad this time of year were a little...obsessed...with Halloween, might have their own costumes, and might even show up for work with their faces painted.

"I suppose," I agreed, not entirely convinced. "Do you, uh, still need to use the, uh—" I waved my hand vaguely at the blue box.

Drew started to reach for the door handle, then pulled his hand back.

"Nope," he said. "I think I can wait."

We stared at the door.

"You think it's like the clown car at the circus?" I asked. "A toilet with a never-ending supply of zombies inside?"

"Of course not," Drew replied. Without moving.

I gathered up my courage and pulled the door open an inch. When nothing jumped out at me, I swung it wide. The box was empty. It was a nice, clean, yet-to-be-used toilet.

"That's odd," I said.

"You mean...that it smells like lemons?"

"No. When that guy came out of it, I thought I saw..."

"What?"

"Stone walls. On the inside. Gray rocks held together with cement."

"*Ohhh...kaaay.*" Drew nodded hesitantly. "That's... sort of what I thought I saw. Like, maybe it was painted inside to look like a dungeon. Your dad loves to paint stuff."

"Yeah, but he wouldn't paint this. Honest John wouldn't like it. Neither would my mom—she's been trying to get him to paint the downstairs bathroom for more than a year now."

The cornstalks around us rustled, and the shadows on the path shifted.

"It could have been a trick of the light," said Drew. "People always talk about tricks of the light. Apparently, light is a big practical joker."

I watched as a faint pattern that looked a little like stacked bricks rippled over the toilet's door.

"Yeah," I agreed. "That has to have been it. A trick of the light."

I turned and headed down the path in the same direction the zombie had taken. I made the only possible turn and faltered. Drew came up next to me.

"What?"

I pointed ahead of us. The rows of corn on either side formed one of the maze's longest unbroken corridors.

"He wasn't moving fast," I said. "I mean—*he was dragging a leg behind him*. Where is he?"

"You think he still dragged his leg once he was out of sight? Obviously he came around the corner and ran like crazy."

"Yeah. You're right," I agreed nervously. "You know, that's not such a bad idea."

"What?"

"Running like crazy!"

I sprinted. Drew came pelting after me. We made a dozen lefts and half as many rights, and a minute later, we shot out of the maze's exit. We crossed the lot, burst into the back room of the farm stand, and slammed the screen door behind us.

My mom turned on her swivel chair from the antique desk where she kept accounts, looked me up and down, and said, "You're taking over from Cindy in fifteen minutes, and you look like you just fell off a hay wagon."

My mom's brown hair was half out of its bun and

hanging down one side of her face, and a sprig of timothy grass was clinging to the bib of her apron, so she might have fallen off the same hay wagon. I considered pointing this out to her, then thought better of it. I brushed dust and bits of straw off my shirt instead. Drew dove into the office's tiny bathroom.

As I ran a hand through my hair and came away with a clump of corn silk stuck to my fingers, I asked, "Are any of the kids working with Dad dressed up?"

"No," replied Mom, coming over to fiddle with my shirt collar. "They're all stark naked."

"No, I mean, dressed for Halloween. Like, I dunno, wearing a monk's robe and old-man makeup?"

"The Robinson boy has on the wrong shade of eyeliner for his color eyes." She flicked something off my left shoulder. "Other than that, I haven't noticed anyone. You haven't been prowling around the maze, have you?"

"Maybe a little," I said, not wanting to go into detail. "Two or three paths. To make sure it's puzzling. Which it is. *Holy cow.*" I looked past her and felt the room reel around me. "You didn't!"

For a moment, I could tell she didn't know what I was talking about. Then she rolled her eyes and gave me a sour look.

"No, I didn't," she said angrily. "But the men from Davy's Digital Vegetables were very insistent. As a token of their gratitude because we're even considering selling the farm to them."

Mom stepped aside, and I got a full view of the big black box set up next to the computer on her desk. It looked like a cross between an oversize microwave and a Kchotchke 3000, which was the janky 3-D printer in the school art department. No matter what your design looked like, the machine always produced a blobby plastic figure that resembled the melting-face guy in a painting by Edvard Munch called *The Scream*. The box on my mother's desk had DAVYTRON ULTRA in raised letters on a silver plaque attached to its front. An upside-down can of tomato juice stuck out of the box's top.

"Wow." Drew came out of the bathroom and stopped dead next to me. "A DavyTron Ultra! Is that model even out yet?"

And yes, we had both just learned that magic was real and that there were spells that could be performed if you talked super fast, and that should have been the only thing on our minds. But this was a *DavyTron Ultra*. No one else in the world had a DavyTron Ultra, except maybe Elwood Davy himself. The machine had been in the news constantly for the past month. It had its own Facebook page, Twitter account, and Zapflutter board, even though nobody had ever heard of a Zapflutter board. That's how new it was.

"I refused to let the men from Davy anywhere near the house," my mom said with a sniff. "They wanted to put it in the kitchen, along with a two-month supply of their tomato juice"—she waved her hand at one of the windows, and I realized it was partially blocked on the outside by a stack of cardboard boxes—"so I told them to set it up here. Apparently, it needs to be near a router."

"That's how it updates," said Drew. "Happens every night to keep the program from getting corrupted. I read that somewhere." He walked over to the black box and peered at a small monitor next to its keypad. "Holy crimolies. You can make pumpkins. *Nobody* can make pumpkins yet. They only announced the upgrade yesterday."

The DavyTrons were 3-D printers that made vegetables. Real, edible vegetables. All you had to do was open a two-quart can of Davy's Deluxe Tomato Juice, jam it upside down over a receptacle at the top of the machine, and type in the code of the veggie you wanted. Twenty seconds later, the door would pop open, and there would be your carrot or potato or—if you weren't careful—asparagus.

"We've got the old, second-generation model, the DavyTron LISA, at home," Drew said as he took a brochure from a stack on top of the machine. "It's much smaller than this, and the only things it makes are turnips, lima beans, and zucchini. *Whoa.*" He pointed at the brochure. "There's a list of codes for eighteen precut jack-o'-lantern faces!" He looked imploringly at my mom. "Can we, Mrs. Sapling?"

"That's one of the worst things about it," my mom informed him. "Once you no longer have very small children trying to carve very big pumpkins with very sharp knives, Halloween stops being a scary holiday. Also, it stops being a creative one. That's *my* opinion anyway."

"Please?" said Drew, waving the brochure.

My mom held up her hands and turned away. Drew took that as a *yes* and rapidly tapped in a ten-digit code on the keypad. The can of DDT Juice went *glug*, and through the DavyTron's glass door, we could see a dozen metal nozzles spraying orange goop that quickly solidified into a perfect pumpkin, which developed the evilly grinning features of a fiend from hell. *Ding* went a bell, the door popped open, and a bunch of roasted pumpkin seeds tumbled down a chute on the side of the device like coins from the return slot of a vending machine.

"This is so great!" Drew said.

"No, it isn't," I said, putting the pumpkin on the table. "First of all, it only works with Davy's Deluxe Tomato Juice. The tomatoes are special—"

"They're genetically modified," chimed in my mom, "and Davy's Digital Vegetables owns all the patents, so they're the only company that can grow the right kind. If you use any other brand of juice in the machine, you get a pile of something that looks like cow manure."

"That's why Davy's is buying up so much farmland," I added. "They need it to grow their tomatoes. My dad says the day will come when nothing else is being planted. Anywhere."

"Well," said Drew, scooping up a handful of pumpkin seeds and popping some into his mouth, "if you can make any kind of veggie you want, you wouldn't *need* to plant anything else."

"It's the reason the farm stand isn't doing well," I said quietly. "It's the reason we'll be selling it and moving away." Even as I said it, I remembered that my destruction of the Fireball 50 hadn't helped. Digital vegetables might be the reason the farm was failing, but the loss of the harvester was making it fail a lot faster than it should have.

"Oh." Drew's shoulders sagged, and a pumpkin seed tumbled from his lips. "Right. I forgot. This actually stinks, doesn't it?"

"The part I really don't like," said my mother, turning the pumpkin so she didn't have to look at its face, "is Davy's Digital Vegetables has only been in business for three years, and yet they say they already have their machines in sixty percent of homes in the country. How is that possible?"

"Hey, wait." Drew brightened. "Maybe you won't have to move, Mrs. Sapling. Cal and I have this great idea for making money!"

"We do?" I said.

"What would that be?" inquired my mom, sounding amused.

"Room painting. We'll go door-to-door and convince people to let us change the color of their rooms."

"That's a lovely thought, Drew," my mom said as she settled herself back at her desk and a spreadsheet reappeared on her computer screen, "but I'm afraid you're not going to find too many people willing to hire two twelve-year-olds to paint. You might have better luck mowing lawns."

"No," replied Drew. "I think the painting thing will work." He gave me a conspiratorial look. "We might have to do the first few for free, to get the word out, but I'll bet people line up to hire us once they find out how fast we work."

My mom tried to stop herself from laughing but failed. She shook her head, looked over at me, and said, "You have to be out front in five minutes."

Drew waved his phone in my direction and said, "I'll call you."

He went home, and I went to work. Over the next four hours, I sold three bags of apples, two pounds of potatoes, and a pot of chrysanthemums. Not good for a Saturday afternoon in late September. Twice I made mistakes giving people change, because I kept thinking about everything that had happened since that morning:

the stampeding coins, Modesty and her notebook, the strange guy staggering out of the toilet—usually, people staggered out only when the toilets hadn't been cleaned—and I had an uneasy feeling things were only going to get weirder.

Magic existed.

Anything could happen.

CHAPTER 6

AS EASY AS
ONE-TWO-THREE

The farm stand closed at seven. I climbed the little hill behind the stand to our house and joined my parents for dinner. Mom shared an e-mail she had gotten from my brother, Glen, who was away at SAFE—the School of Agriculture and Field Engineering. My dad said he missed Glen, especially with the monster barn in the works. Nobody talked about the farm being sold, and I decided against babbling about books of spells and migrating coins. For some reason, I wanted to keep the whole thing between Drew and me. And Modesty.

I finished my usual small plate—I hadn't had much of an appetite lately—skipped dessert, and, after loading the dishwasher, went up to my room on the third floor.

The room shared the top of the house with the storage attic. Its two windows were above the treetops and looked west toward town. I could see three church steeples, the cupola on the town hall, and, only a little closer than all those buildings, the third floor of the old Brooker place, where Modesty lived. A light was on in her attic. I had never been in her house, but it had been constructed by the same builder who had built ours 150 years earlier, and both houses were the same from the outside. So I assumed they were both the same on the inside. Plenty of room for seven sisters.

On the far end of town, on Gernsback Ridge, I could also see the top floors of the Davy Tower, the world headquarters of Davy's Digital Vegetables. Four years earlier, Elwood Davy's parents' house had stood there, with the one-room apartment over the garage, where Elwood had invented the DavyTron. The house and the garage were still there, in the center of the tower's lobby, and the lobby's huge windows enabled the lawn and flower beds to keep growing, despite being indoors. You got to see inside the house if you took the factory tour.

I flopped down onto my bed, took out my phone, and stared at it. The background photo on the screen was of the burned-out remains of the Fireball 50, while it was still smoldering. I had downloaded the picture from the fire department's website. It had replaced one of my family and me that I liked a lot better, but the smoldering hulk had a purpose, and until I figured out some way to make it up to my parents, it would always be the first thing I saw when I looked at my phone.

I didn't text much.

Or do much of anything else with my phone unless it was absolutely necessary.

Now, though, I brought up the three image files Drew had sent me. Each was a photo of a different page in Modesty's notebook. They were too small to be read comfortably on the phone's screen, so I transferred them to my computer, increased the contrast, and printed them out.

The first page was the spell *To Gather Lost Coins*. The second page was *To Change the Color of a Room*. I was disappointed to see the third was *To Untangle Yarn*. The yarn spell was a paragraph longer than either of the other two: It ran at least eight hundred words. There was no way I could speak it in the space of a single minute. Fortunately, I didn't have any yarn I wanted to untangle.

I lay sideways across my bed, studying the coin spell, reading it aloud, trying to improve my speed every time I read it. I said "rubber baby buggy bumpers" over and over, until I fell asleep mumbling "rugby bobby badger baggers."

The sky was full of storm clouds.

They had appeared out of nowhere on the western horizon, darker and angrier than the clouds that had, not long ago, swept a hailstorm across our farm and ruined a prize crop of winter wheat. I hadn't wanted it to happen again. My parents had been ninety miles away at an agricultural meeting in Pratchettsburg—the topic of the meeting was "Digital Vegetables: Threat or Passing Fad?"—and our seasonal workers weren't due to start for another two days, when bringing in the wheat was going to be priority number one.

I'd decided I could do it myself.

Our new Fireball 50 combine had an onboard computer that was smart enough to turn the lumbering forty-foot machine when it reached the end of a field. I had ridden with my dad twice and knew I could handle it. Which I did, pretty well, for almost two full acres of harvested wheat. Then some chaff blew into the engine, caught fire, and the extinguisher I grabbed emptied itself before the fire was fully out. I jumped off just as the flames spread from the engine to the grain carrier, and the whole thing went up like a barrel of gunpowder.

The storm passed to the south.

We didn't get any hail.

Not one bit.

I woke with a start.

The clock on the nightstand said 11:45.

My phone, on the bed next to me, was glowing the weird *magenta* color that had appeared on Drew's phone before he'd restarted it. I squinted at it groggily.

"Ring, ring," it said.

I sat bolt upright and flicked the phone away from me. I wasn't ready to answer it. The last time a phone had said *Ring, ring* and Drew had answered, the Help Line person had hung up on him, claiming she would answer only one question. I didn't want to make the same mistake.

"Ring, ring."

I had no idea what my question should be.

I picked up the phone gingerly between my thumb and forefinger, as if it were a mousetrap with a dead mouse dangling from it, and walked over to my desk. The screen read UNKNOWN CALLER. If it rang two more times without being answered, the call would go to voice mail.

"Ring, ring."

I jabbed the *Answer* button.

"Hello," I said, being careful not to make it sound like a question.

"Hello." The voice was the same woman who had been saying *Ring, ring*. "Thank you for using the Congroo Help Line. Please listen carefully, as our options have changed. They change on a daily basis. And there are always fewer of them. It's getting scary. Press *One* if you wish to ask a question. Press *Two* if you wish to make a statement. Press the side of your head with your index finger if you are thinking."

I self-consciously pressed the side of my head with my finger.

"Press *Three* if you wish to hear the options again."

I pressed *Three*.

"Not really." The voice sounded annoyed. "I refuse to repeat myself. If you couldn't understand the options the first time, you're not the person I should be talking to."

I pressed *One* and asked, "How do I do magic?"

"Ah. Good. Now we're getting somewhere. Listen carefully. This will be in the form of a rhyme. Rhymes are mnemonics."

I started to say "What?" but bit my tongue.

· "Here we go," continued the Congroo Help Line. "Ahem. When the time comes, you will see, a magician you will be—as easy as one-two-three."

I waited for the rest of it. The silence stretched.

"That's it." I made sure my voice didn't rise with a question mark at the end.

· "That's it," agreed the Congroo Help Line.

"That doesn't answer my question."

"Yes, it does."

"It isn't even good poetry."

"It does what it set out to do."

"It's nonsense. 'When the time comes, you will see, a magician you will be—as easy as one-two-three.'" I examined each word as I said it. I was right. It didn't answer my question.

"There," said the Help Line. "I told you it was mnemonic."

"Moronic is right," I agreed.

"*Mnemonic*. Something that helps you remember. Like Roy G. Biv. The letters in the name Roy G. Biv help you remember the names of the first seven rulers of Congroo: Ravenel, Orion, Yolanda, George, Blaine, Irksome, and Viridis. Irksome, Congroo's first-ever oracle, was renowned for her Seven Insights, of which *Popcorn* is perhaps the most infamous. Many scholars believe *Popcorn* was intended for a different list entirely, Irksome being the last of our rulers to do her own grocery shopping. So there may only be Six Insights, but we say seven, because *seven is a very important number in magic.* You might find it beneficial to remember this. Viridis, while not as famous as Irksome, bred racing dragons and discovered, interestingly, that a dead dragon can be reunited with its anima if the anima is given a jolt. But first, of course, you have to *find* the anima, and they're only visible for a short time after the dragon's death. The other five rulers were pretty dull, but then, they *did* live seven hundred years ago, when there was a lot less going on. What's *your* name?"

"Uh." I hesitated, but I couldn't think of any reason not to give my name to a strange woman who was trying to be helpful, even if she wasn't very good at it. "Calvin Sapling."

"Ah. A tree name. Very strong. Very powerful. I am Delleps. Delleps is spelled backward."

"Delleps is what spelled backward?"

"Sorry. Only one question per call."

The *click* told me I had messed up. I shook the phone angrily, then checked the call log to see if I now had the number of the Congroo Help Line. If I could call back, I could keep calling until all my questions were answered. But the log showed nothing more recent than yesterday.

I paced the room, sat back down, and wrote out the awful poem she had given me in answer to the question "How do I do magic?" I also wrote down *"DELLEPS"* in big block letters. She was right. It was spelled backward.

The clock at my bedside said five past midnight. Modesty had said she'd tried doing magic at 12:34 at night but had discovered it worked only at 12:34 in the afternoon. I decided to double-check. Maybe she had mumbled or her clock had been fast or the room temperature had been wrong. Who knew what might affect the way magic worked?

I read *To Change the Color of a Room* out loud and recorded it on my phone. I played it back, caught two places where I'd possibly mispronounced words, and recorded it again, getting my time down from fifty-seven seconds to fifty-one.

After two more rehearsals, I figured I was ready. I watched the clock, and my hands started to get sweaty the closer it got to 12:34. As soon as the clock changed, I read through the spell. I did it in less than a minute, but the walls stayed the same faded wallpaper pattern of cows in a field that dated back to when the farmhouse was new. I was really sick of those cows.

So Modesty was right. Magic didn't work at thirty-four minutes past midnight. I put on my pajamas and crawled under the covers. I was asleep in minutes.

This time, mercifully, I didn't dream.

At 1:20, my eyes popped open, and I scrambled out of bed. I turned on the lamp and reread the note I had made of the Help Line's answer to my question.

"When the *TIME* comes," I mumbled to myself. Then added, "Easy as *ONE-TWO-THREE*."

I looked at the clock.

1:21.

"*TIME*," I repeated. "One...*twenty*-three."

I waited. The clock advanced to 1:23. I read the spell again, keeping it to less than a minute and being careful to say all the words correctly, without slouching in my seat, in case posture had anything to do with it.

I jumped up so fast, I knocked over the chair.

The room had turned purple.

CHAPTER 7

FOUR MORE MINUTES

My entire room was now a shade of purple that Modesty probably had a special, many-syllabled word for. And it was only the walls, not the switch plates or the moldings or the ceiling. It had been done very professionally.

I whooped, danced around my fallen chair, and slapped the wall to see if it was wet. It wasn't, although it did feel a little warm, as if it were running a fever. I set my chair back up, sat down, snatched a pencil, and scribbled:

12:34

1:23

Then I thought for a moment—I pressed my index finger to the side of my head to make it official—and added:

2:34
3:45
4:56
5:67

After a moment, I scratched out *5:67*, since there was no such time. All the rest were real times that involved *consecutive* numbers. *That*, I was guessing, might be the key. Maybe magic was fond of times when numbers appeared in numerical order.

I'd be able to test that idea three times before the sun came up.

The first test, coming in a little over an hour, should have been easy to stay awake for, but I caught myself nodding off after twenty minutes. I tried to recite the yarn untangling spell into my phone, but reading phrases like "Mantong tagalongs shooby-doo nibble; mishegoss double-cross snackie-poo kibble" soon had my eyelids drooping.

I forced myself awake and set my alarm for two thirty. I was grateful that my parents had their bedroom on the ground floor and that Glen was away at school; I didn't need anybody knocking on my door asking what the commotion was. I nodded off again, but the alarm did its job, waking me at two thirty. I got up and paced back and forth with my eye on the time.

2:34.

I started to recite the color-changing spell and tripped

up within the first few seconds, saying "nasty chums" instead of "ghastly crumbs," and then I messed it up again when I started over. I groaned as I realized I wouldn't be able to say the spell within sixty seconds.

Then I realized . . . maybe I didn't have to.

I seized my phone, found my earlier recording of the spell, and played it, sliding my finger along the playback line to speed it up. My recorded voice went up high and became very fast. I sounded like a chipmunk. The recording ended with ten seconds to spare.

The room turned school bus yellow.

Not my favorite color.

But still.

I had done it. I had figured out how to squeeze more than seven hundred words into a single minute. For some reason, we had all assumed a magic spell had to be spoken by a living person. A witch. A wizard. A sorcerer's apprentice. I had discovered it worked just fine with a wizard's cell phone.

I had also discovered there was more than one minute each day when magic worked: 12:34. 1:23. 2:34.

I was betting it would work at 3:45.

And 4:56.

The five minutes each day when time was told with consecutive numbers.

Figuring it out had been as easy as one-two-three.

I didn't see why, if magic worked at these times early

in the morning, it shouldn't work when the exact same times rolled around in the afternoon. Was magic like my aunt Lucy? She called herself "a morning person" and was full of energy before noon, but she fizzled out and fell asleep if she took you to a matinee movie. So maybe magic had more energy in the AM than in the PM. But then, why did it work at thirty-four minutes past noon and not at thirty-four minutes past midnight?

I needed to talk to Modesty.

I tried to find her number on my computer. There was no listing, which was just as well, since I probably would have called her then and there at three AM, a time she thought of as *creepy*. I decided I would have to go over in person once the sun was up.

At 3:45, I played a recording of the coin-gathering spell at double speed, whizzing through it in twenty-six seconds. I sat back and waited.

Nothing happened.

I realized I should have stuck with the color-changing spell. At least with that one, you knew immediately if you had succeeded. Gathering lost coins didn't work if you were in a place where nobody ever lost coins. My family wasn't the type to misplace money. We pretty much knew where every penny was.

I got up, planning to set my alarm for 4:51 and get an hour's sleep before the final Magic Minute of the night, when I heard three tiny taps on my bedroom door.

I froze with my hand outstretched toward the door-knob. The house, as far as I knew, wasn't haunted, but it was 150 years old and maybe, just maybe, somebody doing magic in the attic might have awakened *something*.

Then three coins slid sideways under the bottom of the door, righted themselves, and rolled across the floor to fall at my feet. I relaxed and picked them up.

I was richer by a 1952 dime, a 2012 quarter, and what I assumed was a 1913 nickel because the back of it said v CENTS. I knew *V* was the Roman numeral for five. That one, I figured, must have been stuck between floorboards for a century or so. My jeans were hanging off a knob on my dresser. I slipped all three coins into the pocket where I kept the rest of my change.

At 4:56, I turned my room bright pink.

I cringed. The color was so intense it hurt my eyes, and it would probably be even worse once sunlight started streaming in. I pulled down the window shade, climbed into bed, dragged the covers over my head, and slept.

Five hours later, Drew and I were standing on Modesty Brooker's front porch.

CHAPTER 8

SEVENTH DAUGHTER

The Brooker house wasn't completely identical to my family's place. It was dark green while ours was gray, and their porch didn't wrap around to the back. But otherwise, the house was the same size and shape and had the same arrangement of windows. I had never been closer to it than the street. For some reason, standing at the front door now made me nervous.

I had bicycled over to Drew's first. He hadn't answered my calls, and it turned out his phone was messed up. The words FATAL ERROR 678 were the only things that appeared on its screen. Falling from a hundred feet hadn't done it any good.

"You're going to Modesty's?" Drew had grabbed

a hoodie and pushed me out the door. "She owes me a phone. Let's go."

I didn't tell him anything about what I had discovered the night before. It wasn't that I didn't want to—I was bursting with it—but I figured it would be better if I waited and told him and Modesty at the same time. All I said was that I had something important to discuss with them both.

I rang the Brookers' doorbell. A dog barked off in the distance, and one of Disarray's many church bells announced a Sunday service. But the house itself was quiet. I rang the bell again. I was about to knock when Drew and I heard somebody coming downstairs. I expected Modesty's mother or one of her sisters. Instead, Modesty opened the door. She was wearing her baggy smock with many pockets and splotches of paint on it. A blue smudge on her cheek was possibly *cerulean*. She didn't look happy to see us.

"What do you two want?" she asked, gripping the door as if at any moment she might slam it.

"A new cell phone," Drew chirped before I could stop him.

"No, we don't," I said, putting a hand in front of Drew's face. The door wasn't open as much as it had been a split second earlier, and the gap was getting narrower.

"We're here to apologize again," I said, sounding like a sped-up voice recording, "and I've found out there's more than one minute each day when magic works."

The door, which was almost closed, reopened the width of Modesty's frown. I nodded encouragingly. The door opened another inch.

"You'd better not be joking," she said darkly.

"We're not. We really do want to apologize. I'm sorry we tricked you yesterday, and I admit threatening to use video of you without your permission was wrong, maybe even bullying, even though the video didn't exist, and I'm hoping you can forgive us and we can be friends."

"Mmmphff," Drew added, my hand still across his mouth.

"That's not what I meant when I said you'd better not be joking." Modesty reset the door back to frown width, which seemed to be the default.

"There are *five* minutes each day when magic works," I said.

The door opened wide enough for Modesty to take a small step forward and join us on the porch.

"Oh...*all right*," she said grudgingly. "I accept your apology."

"You broke my phone," Drew announced, holding it up to her.

Modesty scowled. "What's wrong with it?"

"What's wrong with it? It's—" Drew turned the phone around. The screen showed the correct time and Drew's usual background photo of Myron, his pet hamster.

"Oh," he said, deflating. "It got better."

Modesty sat down in the center of her porch swing and stretched out, placing one hand on each of the swing's arms in a clear invitation to us to find someplace else to sit. Not that next to her on the swing would have been my first choice. Drew plopped into a wicker chair. I leaned against the porch railing.

"Which five minutes?" asked Modesty.

I described everything I had done during the previous night, from my conversation with Delleps—"turns out Irksome's this woman who lived hundreds of years ago"—to my first successful experiments in magic—"my room's still this hideous, eye-burning pink"—and by the end of a very dramatic presentation—I did a particularly nice job acting out the scene where the three coins showed up like little round ghosts at my door—Modesty was sitting on the edge of her swing. Her eyes were bright.

"So this means," she said breathlessly, "not only can we try out every single spell in the book, but we've got four more times each day when we can do it!"

I liked that she was saying *we*. It meant she had actually forgiven us and was thinking of us as friends. Or at least fellow researchers in the growing field of magic.

"It's just too bad four of the Magic Minutes are in the middle of the night," I said.

"Hey!" Drew jumped up. "What about nine ten? Or ten eleven? Eleven twelve? Twelve thirteen? Those are all clock times, and they're all consecutive numbers. Are they Magic Minutes?"

Modesty looked at her watch. "It's ten oh eight now. We've got three minutes until ten eleven. C'mon!"

She bolted from the swing, and we ran after her as she shot through the front door. The rug in the entry hall skidded sideways as we galloped over it, and we managed to go up four steps on the staircase before she halted, turned, and caught us by our sleeves.

"No." She spun us around and faced us back the way we had come. "Wait for me in the parlor. I'll only be a sec."

We obediently trotted down to the space that, in my house, we called the living room. A central table had a half-finished jigsaw puzzle on it, and the pile of ash in the fireplace had a few glowing embers. There was no TV, no radio, no computer. No video games. It didn't surprise me she didn't call it the "living room."

"Holy cow," said Drew, looking at a photograph on the mantel. "She's got six sisters."

"I'm the seventh daughter of a seventh daughter," Modesty said, sweeping into the room with the three-ring binder. "Do you know what that means?"

"You can't get a word in edgewise?" Drew guessed.

"No. And that's sexist, even if it happens to be true in this case. Being the seventh daughter of a seventh daughter means I'm specially gifted when it comes to unseen forces."

"What unseen forces?" I asked.

"I don't know. I've never seen them. But that's what the legend says. I'm assuming it means *magic*. We can't do this here—Mum will kill me if she comes home and the parlor is puce. Quick—into the pantry!"

We followed her around the corner, through the kitchen, and into a cramped room next to the stove. She yanked a chain to turn on an overhead light and pulled the door shut behind us.

"I assume you brought your phone," she said, giving me a look that said if I hadn't, she might brain me with one of the jars of peach preserves on the shelf next to us.

"Yeah," I was relieved to say. I fished the phone out of my pocket. The time was 10:10.

"Quick," Modesty instructed me. "Cue up your recording of the color-changing spell. Play it the second I give you the signal."

I found the file and hovered my finger over the screen.

"If we're using my phone, why'd you waste time getting the notebook?" I asked.

"In case you, or your phone, screw up. There still might be time to read the spell from the book."

The time advanced to 10:11. Even before Modesty poked me, I started the playback. I even sped it up a bit to make sure it finished before 10:12.

The walls of the pantry remained the dull yellow they'd been when we first crowded in.

"Well." Drew sighed. "It was worth a shot."

Modesty wasted no time popping the door and striding out.

"I think it may have something to do with the numbers not really being consecutive," I theorized as I followed her. "If you write out 'ten eleven' in numerals, it's one-zero-one-one. Not the same as 'twelve thirty-four,' which is one-two-three-four. More, you know, *numerical*."

"Maybe." Modesty wasn't happy. "But we'll try again at eleven twelve and twelve thirteen, just to make sure. And we definitely have to check out the PM versions of one twenty-three and two thirty-four and the rest. In the meantime, I have a project for us." She let the notebook fall open on an island in the center of the kitchen. The island's hardwood countertop sat atop a cabinet that, surprisingly, had an antique safe in the middle.

Modesty popped open the binder's three rings and lifted out the pages. She divided them by eye and handed a third of them to me and a third to Drew.

"Here's my idea." Modesty jogged her third to make it even. "You go out on the porch"—she nodded at Drew—"and you stay here in the kitchen"—nodding at me—"and I'll go up to my room. We've each got seven or eight incantations. Read them aloud, record them on your phone, and speak slowly enough to get each word right.

Label your recordings so we know which is which. Then we'll meet back here, speed up the recordings so they all play out in less than a minute, and we'll make new recordings of the sped-up versions. If we work quickly, we'll have an audio library of all twenty-three spells by the time twelve thirty-four rolls around. Then we can try out whichever one of them we want...." She paused. "As long as it's the door-opening spell."

Drew and I took a few moments to absorb all this. The plan was pretty much the same one I had worked out while eating breakfast, and I was a little upset I hadn't been given the chance to suggest it.

"Why the door-opening spell?" asked Drew.

"Most of my life, I've wanted to know if there's anything in the safe." Modesty pointed at the squat metal box beneath the counter. "My folks bought it at an auction back when my dad was still alive. Mum thought it would look good in the kitchen. Dad built the island around it."

I gave the safe a second look. The door had fancy pinstriping in faded red paint that crisscrossed at the corners and did curlicues down the sides. Above the worn combination dial, a tarnished medallion declared THE OSO SAFE COMPANY.

"It's never been opened?" Drew asked, kicking it gently, as if that might do it.

"Mum says it isn't likely there's anything valuable

inside, otherwise it never would have wound up in the same auction as plastic flamingos and a life-size cardboard cutout of Elvis Presley. But I'm not so sure, *and I've always wanted to know.*"

"Drew and I will only do what you ask under one condition," I said, putting my handful of pages down on the stove and folding my arms across my chest.

"Right," agreed Drew, then turned to me and silently mouthed, *What?*

"We each get a copy of the recordings for our own use," I declared. "Otherwise, there's no point in us helping you."

"Right," Drew repeated, this time with more confidence. "That way, we'll be able to brighten our teeth at three forty-five in the morning whenever we want!"

"I suppose that's fair," Modesty admitted. "It's not like I'd be giving you the power of invisibility or levitation or mind reading or anything dangerous like that."

"Yeah, why is that?" Drew wondered. "Why are all the spells in the book so boring? They don't do anything you couldn't do yourself with only a little effort."

"The noblest use of magic is to accomplish household chores," said Modesty. "That's Irksome's Fifth Insight. And you know what it tells us?"

"What?"

"Irksome had kids. Otherwise, why go on about how good it is to do chores? The really cool magic, Irksome probably kept for herself." Modesty picked my pages up off the stove and jammed them back in my hands. "We're wasting time. Let's get to work."

She caught Drew by the sleeve and started out of the room with him.

"Wait," I said. "What if somebody walks in on me?"

Modesty paused in the doorway.

"The triplets," she said, "are away at college. The twins are at a sleepover and won't be back till late. And right now, Mum's sitting in the ER with Prudence. The only one who might walk in on you is the cat."

"Emergency room?" I asked.

"She was skateboarding with a machete."

"Skateboarding with a machete!"

"Is that anything like running with scissors?" asked Drew.

"It's faster and more dangerous," Modesty informed him. "Prudence doesn't like to duck for low branches."

"Is she all right?" I asked, imagining doctors reattaching an arm.

"Eighteen stitches. They're on her face, so Mum's demanding a plastic surgeon, but the doctor she wants is playing golf. It'll be a while. The cat, if you see her, is named Grimalkin."

She tugged Drew through the door, and I had the room to myself.

CHAPTER 9

SAFE CRACKERS

As a kitchen, Modesty's couldn't make up its mind whether to be modern or old-timey. Cabinets that looked at least a hundred years old surrounded new appliances, and the floor had dark bumps where knots stood out like islands in a sea of worn wood. The one wall without cupboards had a poster of a fog-shrouded jungle with critters peering out of the mist, above block letters saying SAVE THE RAIN FORESTS. An ironing board on a hinge stuck out below the poster. The board was ancient, but the iron on it looked like a spaceship about to blast off. Hanging under an antique cupboard was a fancy-looking microwave.

I was happy to see there wasn't a DavyTron.

I spread out the spells I was responsible for. Modesty had given me seven:

To Sop Up a Spill
To Get Chewing Gum Out of a Carpet
To Repair a Chimney
To Cast a Reflection
To Summon the Forces of Torque
To Walk with Stilts
To Tidy a Drawer

She was right; most of the spells seemed to involve housekeeping or manual labor. The only one that sounded close to what I thought was true magic was *To Summon the Forces of Torque*. That had a real ring to it. I imagined reciting it and an army of skeletons rising out of the earth in full battle armor to do my bidding. I'd finally be able to get back at Mace Croyden, this kid at school who always called me "Sap." We'd see who the sap was when skeletons were chasing him down the hall.

So that was the spell I started with.

It was the usual collection of gobbledygook. I rehearsed lines like "Widdy foo calla shoe gastropod fiddles; twickenham marjoram multihued skittles" a few times, then set my phone to *Record* but messed up halfway through. I didn't go back to the beginning, though. I just backtracked a little and recorded over my mistake. I didn't see how doing it that way would make much difference. We were, after all, going to speed up the recordings until we all sounded like cartoon mice.

I recorded the first four of my spells while keeping an eye on the clock. At 11:12, I stepped into the pantry and tried to change its color. No go. Even the green labels on the pickle jars stayed green. I came back out and recorded the remaining three spells, jumping in the air once when something brushed my leg. It was Grimalkin, who was chubby, green-eyed, and gray except for white mittens. She sauntered over to the refrigerator and stared up at it.

"Done?" asked Drew, poking his head around the corner.

"Just finished. Now I really need to speak something other than gibberish."

"You're in the wrong house for that," he said cheerfully, putting his phone next to mine on the counter. "One of my spells was *To Remove Unwanted Nose Hairs*. I always thought magic would be more..."

"Magical?"

"*Glamorous*. I don't even have nose hairs."

"Older people do," I said, studying his phone. He had come up with short file names for his spells the same way I had. *Teeth. Cloud. Warm. Intensify. View. Egg. Nose Hairs*. The color of his screen was still a little off.

"What's *View*?" I asked.

"*To View Things More Clearly.* I'm betting it's a spell that washes windows."

"What about *Egg*?"

"*To Empty an Egg without Breaking the Shell.* Maybe so you don't get bits of shell in your omelet."

"And *Intensify*?"

"Now, *that* one might actually be useful." He opened a cupboard, didn't see anything interesting, and closed it. He opened another. "The full name's *To Intensify an Enchantment.* Sounds to me like it might make another spell more powerful. Like, maybe expand the coin-gathering spell so it pulls them in from a greater distance. We have to try that. Have you checked out the cookie jar?" He lifted the head off a ceramic pig.

"Those cookies were made by my sister Fidelity," Modesty announced, bustling in and adding her phone to ours. She dropped the loose-leaf binder onto the counter and started putting our pages back in. "Fidelity wants to be a chef when she grows up, so she keeps practicing, but she never follows recipes exactly. Eat at your own risk."

"Why are the chocolate chips green?" Drew held up a cookie.

"Because they're peas."

Drew dropped the cookie back in the pig.

"If you're hungry, the saltines are safe." Modesty nodded at a tin that presumably held little square crackers. Then she started shuffling the three phones around like she was playing the card game where you have to guess where the queen is. She paused, looked at me strangely, and pointed to my phone.

"Why that picture?"

The last thing I wanted was to discuss the Fireball 50. I shrugged and pretended to be interested in the ironing board.

"That's how he beats himself up for burning down the family harvester," Drew said, and I whirled on him.

"*You* did that?" Modesty leaned forward and studied the picture more closely.

"We don't talk about this," I said to Drew in the fiercest whisper I could manage.

"You and I talk about it all the time," Drew protested. "We need a second opinion."

"How did it happen?" asked Modesty.

"There was a storm coming," said Drew, "and nobody else was around. He was trying to save the barley."

"The wheat," I corrected him.

"I'm changing up the story. Trying to keep it fresh."

"You're *bored* with it?"

"A little."

"Harvesters catch fire," said Modesty. "All the grain dust blowing around. I'm sure it was an accident."

"When other kids have accidents," I said, "they have to pay for a broken window or fish their homework out of the toilet. This"—I tapped my phone—"is a *one-hundred-thousand-dollar* accident. It's why my parents are selling the farm."

"They're selling the farm," said Drew, "because digital vegetables are putting farm stands out of business."

"The harvester wasn't insured?" asked Modesty.

"It had been," I admitted. "But my folks cut back when business started to go bad."

"Were your parents furious?"

"No." And that was the part that bothered me the most. "The main thing they were concerned about was that I was all right." My voice cracked on *all right*, a dead giveaway that I wasn't. I turned toward the fridge and swallowed the lump in my throat.

"He voluntarily gave up his weekly allowance," said Drew, who had, for some annoying reason, become a fountain of information.

"How long before he gets it again?" asked Modesty.

"Two hundred and eighteen years," said Drew. "He's got a countdown calculator on his phone—"

"You were about to do something with these?" I turned back and gathered the phones together on the countertop.

Modesty finally sensed the mood.

"Yes. Right." She pushed me gently aside and spread the phones back out. "Okay. Everybody, quiet."

She played my recording of the coin-gathering incantation, sped it up, and recorded the sped-up version on Drew's phone. Then she sped up the sped-up version and recorded it on her own phone. The incantation whizzed by in less than two seconds. You couldn't make out a single word. It sounded like *blippity-blip*. Then she started to do the same thing with all the rest of the spells.

"Aren't you making them *too* fast?" I asked when she paused at 12:13 so Drew could go into the pantry and try to change its color. "You can't make out *any* of the words."

"I'm betting that doesn't matter. I'm making sound bites. Actually, I'm making *Magic Bites*. If we can get each of the incantations to play in two or three seconds, we should be able to cast more than one spell during the same minute."

"That would be great," said Drew, coming back from the pantry. "We could untangle yarn while walking on stilts. Oh—your pantry's still the same yucky yellow."

"So twelve thirteen *isn't* a Magic Minute." Modesty frowned. "I didn't think it would be, after ten eleven and eleven twelve weren't. Too bad."

Drew stopped to study the animals on the SAVE THE RAIN FORESTS poster. "Man, that is one sad-looking monkey!"

"It's a uakari," said Modesty absently as she set up the next recording. "Practically extinct. When it dies out, probably something else that depended on the uakari will die out, too. Then a third and a fourth thing. And so on. Everything's connected. That's what my dad always said. He once wrote an article about the uakari."

"Your dad was a writer?" I asked, feeling that everything she had just learned about the harvester and me deserved some information from her in return.

"He sure was," she said, and stopped fiddling with the phones. She turned to the ironing board, removed the iron, and raised the board on its hinges so it stood upright against the wall, partially obscuring the rain forest poster.

On the underside of the board was another poster, this one reproducing a book cover. It was a collage of three photos: a huge machine—ten times the size of the Fireball 50—crushing a swath of trees in its path, a whale floating belly-up amid garbage, and a group of men sawing the horn off a dead rhinoceros. The title of the book was *Life's a Web...Beware the Spiders*. It was by Homer Brooker.

"That was my dad's first book. He said he regretted the title—that it was unfair to *real* spiders. But it was a runner-up for the Rachel Carson Prize. He was in Kenya researching his next book, about a certain type of honeybee that'll go extinct if strip-mining continues, when a game warden friend of his learned about poachers killing elephants for their ivory, and my dad joined the posse to go looking for them. That was the last we ever heard from him."

She pressed the ironing board until something went *click!* When she stepped away, the board remained standing, flush to the wall. The uakari was still visible. The ironing board next to it looked like a tombstone.

"That was two years ago."

She went back to our phones.

Drew and I goggled at each other.

"That's terrible," I said. "Modesty, I'm so sorry—"

She raised a hand. "Everybody, hush—we're recording."

She turned the four remaining incantations into Magic Bites, then made a big show of transferring all the files she had just made to our phones.

"That's fair, right? Nobody can say I'm not fair. I'm the fairest of them all."

"Did your mirror tell you that?" I asked, trying to lighten the mood.

"No, my mirror just grins at me; it's *so* happy to be my mirror." She saw the way I was looking at her and added, "My dad's been gone for two years now. Somehow, I'm going to continue his work. All the coins I've gathered with the coin spell, I've donated to a group that defends wildlife. I figure that's a start. And that's all I want to say about this right now. Find another subject."

"Why is your cat staring at the fridge?" asked Drew.

Modesty looked past Drew to where Grimalkin squatted, and she shook her head. "Fidelity made ice cream yesterday. That cat loves anything with fish in it. Hey, it's almost twelve thirty-four! Stand back. We're going to get this safe open!"

She pushed us away from the counter, and Drew and

I crouched so we had a good view of the safe's door. She tickled her phone until she had the door-opening spell cued up, slid the playback volume to *High*, then waved the phone around as if it were a wizard's baton. She aimed it at the safe's combination dial.

"Have you ever tried the coin-gathering spell here in the house?" I asked.

"Last Sunday. I made thirty-eight cents, including a Mercury dime."

"Did you hear any rattling from the safe, like money was trying to get out?"

Modesty's outstretched arm drooped a bit.

"I didn't recite the spell in the kitchen; Fidelity was in here making croutons. She wouldn't have heard anything over the sound of the blender."

"Twelve thirty-four," Drew announced.

Modesty raised her arm and thumbed her phone.

Blippity-blippity-blip.

We stared at the safe. I expected the dial to start turning, going through the long-lost numbers of the combination, and then the door to pop open.

It didn't.

The dial didn't turn; the door didn't budge.

Modesty checked the screen of her phone, frowned, then extended her arm again, her thumb poised to play the Magic Bite once more.

From behind us came the sound of two glass bottles clinking together, followed by a soft mechanical hum.

Drew and I straightened out of our crouches. Modesty dropped her arm, and her shoulders sagged. The three of us turned slowly, knowing full well what we were going to see.

We had used a magic spell to open the door to the refrigerator.

"Is that carrot cake?" Drew asked.

"Turnip cake," Modesty muttered, then raised her voice. "What good are these spells? What's the point of changing the color of a room if you can't pick the color? What's the point of a spell that opens a door if you can't specify *which* door—"

A hurricane wind blew out of the fridge. The icy blast was strong enough to push the three of us back against the counter. Grimalkin's fur stood on end, and the cat shot out of the room. All three of us gasped.

The turnip cake had vanished. The glass shelves, and everything on them, had vanished. The inside of the refrigerator was suddenly lined with blocks of stone. It looked identical to what I thought I'd seen inside the portable toilet in the corn maze the previous day.

And surrounded by the stone walls, a figure wrapped tightly in a snow-covered gray cloak teetered, then pitched forward and sprawled on the floor at our feet.

CHAPTER 10

PREFFY ARROWSHOT

Nobody moved. The figure on the floor lay facedown, blanketed under the hooded cloak. Suddenly an ice-cold hand shot out from a baggy sleeve and clutched my ankle.

I yelped, and the figure rolled over, the face framed by the hood. I expected the old guy we had seen in the maze, but this was a boy's face. His lips were blue, and frost dusted his cheeks. Two dark-brown eyes stared briefly at the ceiling, then closed, and the hand on my ankle lost its grip.

Modesty threw herself to her knees and lifted the stranger's head. A boy falling out of her fridge didn't seem to faze her. I made an effort to be just as cool as she was.

"That's a—It's a—Wh-wh-what?" I stammered, pretty

much blowing *cool* right off the bat. Drew had climbed up on the counter, as if the floor might be covered in snakes, so he wasn't doing any better.

Modesty pressed a hand to one side of the stranger's face.

"Freezing," she said. "Quick. Second shelf, yellow bowl—zap it!" She gestured at the fridge. The shelves had returned, along with everything that had been on them. I recovered myself enough to step over the body and get the bowl. Drew dropped down beside me and popped open the microwave. The bowl sloshed as I put it in, so I decided it was soup. I loosened the plastic cover and punched in three minutes on *High*.

"Help me get him out on the porch."

Modesty lifted shoulders, Drew grabbed feet, and I caught the droop in the middle. Together we maneuvered the body out of the kitchen, down the hall, and into the warm sunlight that was flooding the front of the house.

We put him on the porch swing, and while Modesty chafed his hands, Drew and I pulled off snow-dampened moccasins and tried rubbing some life back into a pair of frozen feet.

The microwave beeped.

"Sit him up." Modesty twisted the stranger around on the swing, then ran into the house. The stranger's eyes fluttered open but didn't focus.

"I shouldn't have skipped breakfast," he mumbled.

"It *is* the most important meal of the day," Drew agreed.

"I gave my porridge to Master Index." The stranger looked imploringly at Drew.

"Of course you did." Drew nodded approvingly.

"There's something…I have to…do…" He squinted, as if trying to remember.

Modesty returned, bearing the bowl.

"This is chicken soup," she said, holding it to his lips. "My sister Fidelity made it, so there may be a little too much peanut butter in it. But it will warm you up."

The stranger took a sip, then another, then reached up with two trembling hands, grasped the bowl, and gulped down the steaming liquid. Modesty took the empty bowl, and we watched as the boy's shoulders straightened and his eyes went wide.

"You didn't close the door, did you?" He grabbed Modesty by her elbows and looked at her imploringly.

"Wh-what? The refrigerator door?" Modesty stuttered. "I kicked it out of my way when I was leaving the kitchen—I'm not sure whether it closed or not."

Our visitor jumped up and stumbled through the door to the house. He stopped in the hall, not knowing which way to go. We crowded in behind him.

"Where?" he shouted, his restored strength a good advertisement for peanut-butter-chicken soup.

Modesty darted past and led the way to the kitchen.

The refrigerator door had stopped an inch shy of closing. The stranger flung it open, and two water bottles flew from the door rack and went skittering across the floor.

He turned to us and pulled the cloak's hood away from his head. The skin of his face was no longer frosty. Its normal color appeared to be...green. A pale green, not sickly and only noticeable when the light hit it just right, but *green*, no argument about it. He was shorter than Drew, thinner than me, and his cheeks were a little sunken, as if he had been missing meals. Curly hair was gathered in a frizzy ponytail.

He reached into the fridge, his arm passing through a jar of mayonnaise and vanishing.

"Good! It's still open. If the connection had been broken, we'd never get back."

"We?" asked Drew.

"*Who are you?*" demanded Modesty.

"Third apprentice librarian, second class, Preffy Arrowshot. Preffy is short for Preface, which I don't really like—it sounds so formal. You could also call me 'Pre.' And you are?"

"Uh...first-class swim team captain and, uh, friend to animals Modesty Brooker. Don't call me 'Mod'—I hate that."

"Cal Sapling," I said.

"Drew Higgins."

"You have my notebook!" Preffy lunged at the loose-leaf

binder lying open on the countertop, snapped it shut, and hugged it to himself. "Of course you'd have to have it; otherwise, I wouldn't be here. You must have figured out the door-opening spell—it has to be incanted from both sides of the door; otherwise, the door won't open. *Oh!*"

Pre froze with an expression of horror on his face. The notebook slipped from his hands and hit the floor.

"I am such a *coward*!" he wailed. "Master Index told me to hide, but I should have stayed with him! Instead, I went out on the seventh-floor balcony, in the wind and the snow, and I didn't think they were there to arrest him, but he thought they might be, and they might be after me, too. I was growing numb; I found myself incanting the door-opening spell to stay awake—I've incanted it at least twenty times a day, ever since I put the notebook in the gniche—but I must have fainted. The next thing I knew, you were pouring that strange fluid down my throat. Was that something scientifical?"

"My sister's s-soup?" Modesty sputtered. "Scientifical? It's barely edible."

"Master Index hasn't come looking for me. Maybe they *did* take him away. But how could they arrest somebody just for writing letters to a newspaper? They weren't even his letters. They were mine, but he signed them. *How could I have been so spineless?*"

"We're not following a word of this," I informed him.

"Sorry. Sorry." He snatched up the notebook from

the floor and returned it to the counter. "I have to go back. But they may still be in the tower, so we'll have to be ready to defend ourselves."

"Who is this *they* you're talking about?" I asked.

"The Quieters." In reply to my puzzled scowl, he added, "What you would call, I think, *police*?"

"So," said Drew, "on the other side of the refrigerator, there's a place where the police arrest people...for writing letters to newspapers?"

Pre nodded a little too quickly.

"The letters were highly critical of the Weegee Board," he added, as if this would clarify things.

"The Ouija board...hasn't been contacting the right type of ghosts lately?" I said, feeling it made about as much sense as anything else he was babbling.

"The Weegee Board is our governing council. Named after Regina Weegee, who started it in the seventh year of the reign of Panacea Irksome. Seven hundred years ago. Lately, the board's been a bit touchy when it comes to criticism." He snatched a blender from the counter near the stove. "Is this a weapon?"

"Only if you hit someone over the head with it," said Modesty.

"Does it possess scientifical powers?" Pre held the blender between himself and the overhead light. He peered up at it quizzically.

"It, uh, whizzes around," Modesty answered.

"It whizzes around!" Pre hastily put the blender back. He looked at his hands as though they might be contaminated. "That won't do—I need something more controllable. What about this? Is this a weapon?"

He snatched a spray can from a shelf near the ironing board. The label had lightning bolts on it and the words:

CLING-BE-GONE

ANTISTATIC

"*No,*" Modesty snapped, grabbing the can. "This-prevents-a-black-sock-from-sticking-to-the-seat-of-your-pants-without-you-knowing-it-and-causing-kids-at-school-you-*thought*-were-your-friends-to-not-tell-you-about-it-while-they're-laughing-at-you-behind-your-back-and-posting-pictures-that-make-it-look-like-you-had-an-accident. Leave it alone." She jammed the can into one of the pockets of her smock. Drew and I looked at each other and blinked.

"Accident? What kind of accident?" asked Pre, foolishly trying to make sense of Too Much Information.

"We don't talk about it," muttered Modesty.

"There must be something here that will help." Pre sounded desperate. "But—maybe just yourselves will be enough. You have to come with me. I'll feel so much braver if you do. You must be very clever scientists to have figured out how to open the door. If they've taken away Master Index, that means I'm alone in the tower, and I can't do this on my own. You should put on warmer clothing. Where are my shoes?"

"They're soaking wet," I said. "They're out on the porch, drying in the sun. Why don't we all sit down and discuss this?"

"*There's no time!* I have a dragon to feed! May I have these?" He jammed his feet into a pair of fuzzy pink bedroom slippers that were below the ironing board.

"Those belong to Serene," said Modesty. "If you take them, she'll hunt you down, and you won't be able to walk again for a week." When Pre looked alarmed, she added, "Go ahead. It's fine."

Pre snugged the backs of the slippers over his heels, then flipped up his hood.

"Are you coming?" he asked.

"Did you say...dragon?" inquired Drew.

"Dragon, yes. One of the only two surviving, and we have only twenty-eight days of dragon food remaining, so you can see how serious this is. We lose either dragon, it will be the end of life as we know it in Congroo. A world is hanging in the balance."

"Congroo," I said.

"Yes. Have you heard of it?"

"As a matter of fact, I have." I was pleased to be on top of things for once. "The first seven rulers of Congroo were, uh, Roy, Orion, Yo-yo...uh, Green, B-something,

Irksome, and Veranda. Irksome had Seven Insights, and Veranda did something with dead dragons."

"*Viridis*," Pre corrected me. "She found a way to *resuscitate* dead dragons. But you have to be quick about it. How do you know this?"

"A woman named Delleps told me. Delleps is spelled backward."

Pre looked stunned. I assumed it wasn't because he hadn't known Delleps was spelled backward.

"Delleps is the greatest of all our oracles," he said, a touch of awe in his voice. "She is also the most eccentric and most difficult to get in touch with. Her crystal is booked up for *decades* in advance. How were you able to consult with her?"

"The Congroo Help Line. I didn't find it very helpful."

"If Delleps used the Help Line to contact you three," said Pre, "then you are, without a doubt, vital to the survival of Congroo. That means I've found the right people. We should get going."

"Wait!" Modesty caught him by his robe as he took a step toward the fridge. "Did you say…you have a species on the brink of extinction?"

"More than one, actually."

"What's dying out other than the dragons?"

"First the dragons, then the rest of us. Everything's connected."

Modesty's head snapped up at the words *everything's connected*. She looked from Drew to me. "Okay, then. We're in. We're coming with you."

"You gotta be kidding," I informed her.

"You have something better planned?"

"Uh, no, but—"

"Then, it's settled. Let's get some coats."

Modesty spun on her heel and left the kitchen. Drew and I exchanged looks and followed her into the entrance hall, where she pulled open a closet and began rummaging. Preffy came up behind us.

Modesty thrust a light-blue winter coat at Drew and threw a scarf and a wool hat at him. She started to hand a large red plaid jacket to me but began a tug-of-war when I tried to take it.

"This used to belong to my dad," she said. "Don't do anything to mess it up." She released the jacket, and I shrugged into it as respectfully as I could. I caught my breath when I realized that by doing so, I was agreeing to jump into a refrigerator with her. It seemed completely insane, but then I also realized I had been preparing myself for completely insane stuff from the moment I had seen the first moving coin in Onderdonk Grove.

She handed me mittens, and I stuffed them into the jacket's pockets; then she pulled an annoyingly long stocking cap—it had a pom-pom—down over my ears.

The hat she'd given to Drew turned out to be the shape of a cooked turkey, a woolly drumstick on either side pointing skyward like Viking horns.

"This is a joke, right?" he asked.

"My sister Joy wears it every Thanksgiving. You'd think it would make her smile, but nothing ever does."

Modesty shrugged into her own bright-green coat, then bent down and fished a pair of fur-lined boots from the back of the closet and handed them to Pre.

"Put these on," she commanded. "You don't want Serene as an enemy."

Pre kicked off the pink slippers, sat down on the floor, and pulled on the boots.

"Something's wrong," he said after a moment. "These boots are loose, and I just envisioned the final three syllables of the *To Alter Clothes to Fit* spell, and they didn't adjust to my feet."

"That's because magic only works here for five minutes each day, and this isn't one of them," I explained, amazed by how quickly the explanation had come out of my mouth—and how normal it felt. "The next Magic Minute won't be for another twelve hours or so. Are you telling me it only takes three syllables of a spell to make it work?"

"Only if you've said all the other words and syllables of the spell completely at an earlier time. Everyone in Congroo has a few of the more useful spells prepared in advance, with only the final three or four syllables left unsaid. You never know when you might need a spell in a hurry." Pre got to his feet. "These are only a little loose anyway. Are we ready?"

"Are you trying to tell me," said Modesty, "there's a spell called *To Alter Clothes to Fit*?"

"It's one of the first ones we're taught," said Pre, stepping past her and heading for the kitchen. "We find it fairly useful."

"*Fairly* useful?" Modesty grinned. "It's a game changer! Can you teach me that one later?" She fell in behind him.

We arrived back in the kitchen. Drew adjusted his turkey hat in the black glass reflection of the microwave and turned away from it, frowning.

"I can do this, now that I have the three of you," Pre said gratefully. "Promise me you'll follow?"

"The boys and I wouldn't miss it," Modesty assured him, giving each of "the boys" a look that dared us to contradict her.

"Okay. Good. Here I go." He set his jaw, strode forward, and vanished into shelves filled with almond milk, avocados, and string cheese.

"Are we really just going to plunge in after this guy?" I asked. The harvester fire had taught me caution. Or I thought it had.

"He asked for our help," Modesty said indignantly. "We opened the door for him *using magic*. In a way, we started this. We have a responsibility. Plus, we just *promised* him."

"I have to be back at the farm stand by three," I said.

"I'm sure that won't be a problem." Modesty whisked a chair away from the wall and jammed it under the dairy shelf on the inside of the door to prop it open. "Besides," she continued, "he says it's dragon-feeding time. You'll kick yourself later if you pass up your one opportunity to see that."

"What if it turns out," said Drew, "*we're* the dragon food?"

"That's a chance I'm willing to take," Modesty snapped. "My dad would have. If I can help save an endangered species, I'll be doing something he'd be proud of."

With that, she threw herself at the fridge and disappeared the same way Preffy had.

Drew and I looked at each other.

"I really hate this hat," he said. And dove in after her.

I took a last look around the kitchen, for one split second making eye contact with the soon-to-be-extinct uakari in the SAVE THE RAIN FORESTS poster; then I ducked my head, plunged through the fridge—

—and found myself in another world.

CHAPTER 11

THE VIEW FROM
THE FIRE TOWER

I staggered into six inches of fresh snow that concealed a sheet of ice and slid across the width of a balcony. I hit a stone wall at the balcony's edge that was a little too low for a kid who was a little too tall, and I almost fell a hundred feet to my death.

Welcome to Congroo.

I flailed my arms like windmills, got my center of gravity back over the building, and was able to backpedal a step. No one had seemed to notice my plight. Modesty and Drew were forty feet to my right, and Preffy was ten feet farther, his ear pressed to a door at the far end of the balcony.

I pulled the mittens Modesty had loaned me out of

the pockets of her dad's jacket and wiggled into them. If Pre had been hiding on this balcony for more than a few minutes, I could see why it had taken an infusion of peanut-butter-chicken soup to revive him. The cold drilled its way into your bones.

I spun and faced the wall, expecting to see the back of the refrigerator. Instead, I saw solid-looking stone with snow clinging to it, and my heart began to race. I reached out, and the tip of the mitten vanished. I leaned forward and found myself staring into Modesty's kitchen. The cat, who had returned to her spot staring up at the fridge, took one look at my face peering down at her from the center of a cabbage and ran for her life.

"Door's still open," I announced as I pulled back and watched refrigerator shelves disappear behind solid rock.

I slid along the ice until I reached Drew and Modesty. Drew immediately turned to me and said, "It's the view from the fire tower."

I looked out.

The landscape was gray, as if all the life had been sucked out of it. The trees for miles around appeared dead and withered. Brown grass stuck up out of dirty snow, and the sky was crowded with the darkest clouds I had ever seen, even darker than the ones that had tricked me into trying to save the wheat crop from a nonexistent hailstorm. On a hill in the far distance sat the rocky ruins of what might once have been a castle, and a little closer, poking above the trees, were the spires of three gloomy buildings and possibly a house, all made out of the same dismal slate-colored stone.

"It's the view looking west," he added as he pulled the turkey hat farther down his head.

"Don't be ridiculous," I said.

"I can't help it—my ears are cold."

"That's not what I mean. This isn't..."

I faltered. It wasn't, but it *was*. It was the view from the west side of the fire tower, which was also the view from my bedroom, only drabber and much more wintery. The spires matched the locations of the church steeples, the rocky ruins stood where the Davy's Digital Vegetables tower now stood, and the slate-gray house squatted in the same spot as Modesty's place. I leaned out as far as I dared and looked straight down. Beneath a fresh blanket of snow, crumbling foundations marked the locations where my house, the barn, and the farm stand would have been.

"It's like some weird, dying version of Disarray," I admitted, feeling a chill run up my spine that had nothing to do with the wind.

"This is the town of Dire," Pre whispered as he came up behind me. "The ruins on that far hill are the remains of the Abbey of Legerdemain, and that spire on the left is the Wizened Wizards Home."

"In our world," I replied, keeping my voice just as

low, "that's the Unitarian church, and the ruins on the hill are the location of a company called Davy's Digital Vegetables. And this stone tower we're standing on is in the exact same place as a forest-fire lookout tower my family owns."

"Your family likes to watch forest fires?"

"It's...part of an alarm network. Or it was."

"Master Index believes our two worlds share the same geography, right down to buildings and streets, even though the details differ from place to place." Pre stepped away from us and once again pressed his ear to the door at the balcony's end. "I don't hear anything," he reported. "I'm hoping it's not a trap, but we really should find out what's become of Master Index. He would have come looking for me if everything was all right. Maybe he did, but I wasn't here."

He glanced around. A hefty icicle was dangling from the overhang of the tower's roof. He snapped it off and held it in the air like a club. Then the icicle broke, and the biggest chunk bounced off his head. He was left holding a useless stub.

"I *knew* I should have brought my baseball bat," said Modesty.

Pre tossed aside the ice and pulled open the door.

"They're probably gone," he said, "but until we're sure, we have to go quietly."

The door led to a landing and a corridor that doubled

back the way we had come—it was obvious we were now behind the windowless wall that ran along the back of the balcony—and then a side corridor took us to a spiral staircase. Its steps were thick slabs of stone that curled straight down the center of the tower, passing perilously through the middle of each level without any handrails, making us completely visible—and vulnerable—to anybody who might be waiting in the areas we descended through. Fortunately, there was no one.

There were, however, an awful lot of books.

"It's a library!" declared Modesty, in nothing like a whisper, when we had reached the bottom floor and it had become obvious the place was deserted.

The walls of each level we had passed through had been lined with books, dimly lit by candles flickering in floor stands. The window shutters had been tightly closed, presumably to keep out the cold, but the interior of the tower was barely warmer than the balcony. Free-standing bookcases had been arranged in odd patterns in the middle of the rooms. One of those patterns, on the third floor, had looked a little like Stonehenge.

"Of course it's a library," muttered Pre as he poked his head under a long stone counter that faced a massive pair of doors at the library's entrance. "Master Index and I are librarians."

"You're not magicians?" asked Drew.

"Well, *everybody* here is a magician, of course." Pre

walked briskly past aisles of books, glancing down each. "The three levels of magic are Everybody, Somebody, and Very Few. We can *all* do some degree of magic. I can get gum out of carpets, heat a teapot by holding it, and make sense of the Dewey decimal system, but the really big stuff is done by specialists." He reached the end of the aisles, then tilted his head back and bellowed at the ceiling, *"Master Index! It worked! The door opened! I brought back scientists! Hello?"*

He held up his hands to prevent us from speaking. We listened to the sound of books sitting on shelves. I glanced around, wondering where the scientists were.

"They got him," said Pre, his shoulders drooping. "I was hoping they were only here to give us a warning like the last time."

"The Quieters," I said, to prove I had been paying attention.

"Yes," he agreed. "The government agency charged with keeping the peace."

"Of course," said Modesty. "Librarians can be *so* noisy. The other day, Ms. Bowen shushed me so loudly, you could hear her out in the parking lot." She folded her arms across her chest and raised an eyebrow at Preffy, clearly challenging him to explain.

"I was hoping Master Index would be here to do this," said Pre glumly. "But now I guess it's up to me." He stood a little straighter and squared his shoulders. "Put as simply as I can, the world of Congroo is coming to an end. Your world is destroying it. Only you can save us." He blinked rapidly a couple of times. "I can't believe I just said that. Half the books in the adventure section have somebody saying, *Only you can save us*. I never expected to say it myself. To tell you the truth, I always imagined somebody saying it to me. As if I had the courage." He looked down at his feet.

Modesty opened her mouth to say something— possibly *Librarians are weird*—but before she could speak, a mournful moan came from outside the building. It was long and drawn out, and it sounded like the half-hearted roar of a very depressed lion.

"Fazam!" said Pre. "I forgot about Phlogiston!"

CHAPTER 12

FLYER-FRIES

Pre bolted for the back of the building. We followed him through a door that returned us to the ice and snow of the outside world. A cobblestone courtyard separated the library tower from a high stone wall with an arched opening in its center; he plunged through the arch, and when we caught up with him, I wasn't surprised to discover we were in a maze.

"This is exactly where our farm's corn maze is," I told him as we threaded through the stone passages. "Behind our fire tower. My father cuts the corn into a different pattern each year. This year, from above, the maze looks like a dragon. My dad says the dragon's name is Phlogiston."

"That's no coincidence," Pre acknowledged without

breaking stride. "Sometimes, when conditions are exactly right, people in one Adjacent World can briefly become aware of things in another. Labyrinths can be focal points. So can lakes. Phlogiston is a common name for a female dragon."

"Not where we come from."

"Nevertheless, our maze isn't in the shape of a dragon—it has an actual dragon in the center. They like living in the hearts of labyrinths. People in Congroo build mazes in their backyards in the hope of attracting a resident dragon. They're good luck."

"We planted special bushes in our backyard," Drew piped up. "To attract...um...butterflies."

"The dragons can fly in and out of the maze as they please," continued Pre, apparently unimpressed with Drew's comparison, "but for some reason, they like it when visitors have to follow a convoluted path to get to them. Fazam!"

Pre stopped short. Drew crashed into him. We had rounded a corner and discovered a wooden door hanging off a single hinge, partially covering an opening in the wall.

"What have they done?" Pre gasped. He swung the door on its lone hinge—which snapped, and the door fell away—and the four of us looked into a small room with empty shelves on three of its walls and an overturned coal stove in its center. The glowing coal had spilled and fanned out across the floor. The tiny room was beyond toasty.

"Watch where you step," Pre warned as he eased himself gingerly inside. The rest of us solved the problem of navigating a floor strewn with hot coals by peering in from the edges of the doorway.

"I can't believe this." Pre shook his head in dismay. "There were twenty-eight jars of dragon food being kept at exactly the proper temperature in here, and they took them *all* and kicked over the stove! I think they took a section of stovepipe, too! Quieters don't do that kind of thing."

"Maybe they weren't Quieters," I suggested, having seen way too many TV shows where bad guys masqueraded as cops.

"Without dragon food, Phlogiston will be dead in a day!" Pre said desperately. "And with no Phloggie, there's no saving Congroo. Nobody in their right mind would do this!"

He turned to leave but then paused and stared at a spot just inside the door.

"They missed one!" he shrieked, stooping to pick up a large glass jar that was glowing with a familiar orange light. He stepped out of the storage room with the jar clutched protectively to his chest. "But this will buy another day, maybe a day and a half, for Phloggie."

The moaning roar we had heard while in the tower came again—much closer but noticeably feebler.

"No time to waste!"

Preffy darted past us, and we ran the twisted paths of the maze with him until we rounded a corner and—

The center of the maze was full of dragon.

The creature was curled tightly in on herself, golden wings folded like a tent around most of her body, her head resting on one cushioning forearm. Judging from the farm machinery I was familiar with, she might have been—if stretched out—about a hundred feet long. Her scales were the size of skateboards. The creature's color shimmered between gold and green, except her thinner parts, like claws and eyelids, which were possibly *cerulean* but definitely some shade of blue.

"Phloggie!" Pre shook the food jar, and it started buzzing like a drop-kicked beehive. "Num-nums!"

The dragon raised an eyelid the size of a garage door and looked blearily at us. Pre lifted the jar to make it more visible. The dragon sighed—a yellow mist formed around her nostrils—and the eyelid sagged shut.

"*No!* No. Don't give up. This is a really tasty batch." He twisted the top off the jar, and the buzzing got louder. He turned the jar upside down and shook it. "Fazam! It's too cold. They won't come out. I hate it when I have to break the glass!" He raised the jar over his head.

"What's in there?" demanded Modesty.

"Flyer-fries," said Pre.

"You mean fireflies," said Drew.

"No, *fireflies* are harmless. Flyer-fries, on the other hand, can scorch the hair right off your head!"

He smashed the jar against the dragon's leg and released a huge cloud of angry, brightly glowing insects. They swarmed wildly for a moment, then got their act together and flew straight at us. We all had the presence of mind to scream like four-year-olds.

Pre ducked. Drew fell back against Modesty, who fell back against me, and the three of us went down like a very short line of dominoes.

The insect swarm dove at us.

And disappeared as a scaly chin passed over us, followed by a long reptilian neck. Phlogiston's head had darted out, lightning fast, jaws wide open, and scooped most of the frenzied bugs from the air. The few flyer-fries that remained fluttered aimlessly here and there, and the dragon's head darted to and fro, snapping them up, until only one remained, struggling upward into the cold air with rapidly dwindling enthusiasm. The dragon nosed up under it, inhaled, and it was gone.

Phlogiston's head drew back on her arched neck, and she eyed the four of us without much interest. Her eyelids drooped, her head sank back on the cushion of her arm, and she became motionless again.

"She used to be so lively." Pre sighed and straightened up. He kicked aside some broken glass from the jar.

We had gotten to our feet. Modesty put a comforting hand on his shoulder.

"She's beautiful," she said.

"Three years ago, there were eight *thousand* dragons in Congroo." He reached out and patted Phlogiston's nose. "Today there are just Phlogiston and her mate, Alkahest. He lives in Bleek, the next town over. This area used to be the largest dragon breeding ground in all of Congroo. Now it's dwindled to nothing. Remember I showed you the ruins of the Abbey of Legerdemain?"

We nodded.

"That was once the home of Viridis, seventh ruler of Congroo. She was our greatest dragon expert and kept a stable of racing dragons. Until it burned down. She would have been so sad to see this."

"So," I said, "what happened?"

Pre wagged his head glumly from side to side.

"The only thing dragons eat is flyer-fries. The only thing dragons *can survive on* is flyer-fries. Three years ago, there were such vast swarms of the insects, they would sometimes block out the sun for days at a time. They actually gave us more light than the sun. People were disappointed when the swarm passed, and we went back to dim, old sunlight. Then...our magic started to get sucked away." Pre looked at us as if he thought we were personally responsible. "The temperature dropped, and almost all the flyer-fries died off over the course of a single week. The streets were covered with them. We had to shovel the sidewalks. The dragons started dying off right after that."

I had forgotten how chilly I was, listening to this awful story. Modesty looked appalled. Drew appeared slightly nauseated.

"The terrible thing is," Pre continued, "dragons are the source of magic. When they breathe out that stuff that looks like fire, it's not really fire. It won't burn you. It's what magic looks like before it dissolves in the air, spreads out, and gets used for doing work."

"Work?" I asked. "Like all the chore spells in your book?"

"Exactly," Pre said. "And much, much more, of course. The dragons take something pre-magical that the flyer-fries have and turn it into the energy that powers Congroo. True magic. And all of it's going away."

"It's a disrupted ecosystem!" Modesty exclaimed. "Exactly the kind of thing my dad kept warning everybody about. How can we help? What will happen to the people of Congroo?"

Pre hunched his shoulders. "Oh, most of the Congruents will probably survive—for a while. But they won't be able to use magic anymore. And Congroo will be a lot colder. The climate-control enchantments, which have been shutting down one by one as the magic has drained, will be gone completely. We'll be back in what we call the Dark Ages, the way we were before the Renaissance, when we learned to use the magic that was all around us. Warlords will probably rise to power again, and there will be wars, and *then* most of the Congruents will die, and everything will be terrible."

DINK-bingle-BONK!

An odd musical sound came from the direction of Pre's chest. He reached up, plucked at a leather cord around his neck, and drew out a crystal pendant from under his robe. It looked like an emerald and glowed with a faint greenish light. He dangled it in front of his face and said, "Excuse me—I have to take this."

He stepped away from us and spoke to the crystal.

"Hello?"

"Third apprentice, second class, Preface Arrowshot?" inquired a woman's voice.

"Yes."

"Please hold for Hemi-Semi-Demi-Director Oöm Lout, sixty-fourth assistant head of the Weegee Board."

A moment later, a disembodied, greenly glowing head materialized in front of us. It frowned beneath a tsunami wave of combed-over hair and had a squint like the flame on my dad's welding torch.

"Arrowshot!" snapped the head. "What's going on there? My perceptor spells inform me somebody has a door open between Congroo and one of the Adjacent Worlds. If this is true, *it must be closed immediately*!"

"Hemi-Semi-Demi-Director Oöm Lout." Pre touched his forehead in something that might have been a salute. "Yes, there's a door open—but it was opened from the World of Science by three powerful scientists who are here with me now. I'm hoping we can work with them to find a way to stop the magic from draining out of Congroo. This could mean our salvation."

The floating head expanded. Its tiny, puckered mouth looked like the tied-off part of a toy balloon, and its suddenly swollen cheeks suggested the balloon might be about to burst.

"We have already settled this," Oöm Lout hissed, letting a little air out of the balloon. His head contracted. "There is no 'draining of magic,' as you gullible fools call it. Only a rising and falling cycle of magical power that is now at its lowest point and will begin rising again within the next day or two. You have but to wait, and the magic will return. I've been saying this ever since you and that idiot Index brought in your ludicrous weather calculations. The man's pie chart was half-baked!"

Oöm Lout's shaggy brows lowered, and his squint intensified.

"Who's that standing behind you?"

"Those are the scientists I was telling you about."

"Is one of them some sort of high priest?"

"Uh...not that I know of."

"Why is he wearing a bird on his head?"

"It's a hat. In the shape of a cooked turkey."

"Does it have scientifical powers?"

"No," Drew volunteered. "It's just that I have a cold head."

"Hemi-Semi-Demi-Director Oöm Lout"—Pre put himself between Drew and the director—"Master Index has been taken!"

Oöm Lout drew back. "What's that supposed to mean?"

"Three Quieters were here. They took Master Index with them when they left, and they also took our remaining supply of flyer-fries. I think they would have taken me, too, but I hid. Phlogiston will be dead within two days if we don't get more dragon feed."

Oöm Lout gave Pre a calculating look.

"This is a serious accusation, Apprentice Arrowshot. Quieters don't behave the way you describe—"

"They may have been impostors."

"I will make inquiries," Oöm Lout purred in a distinct change from the way he had begun the conversation. "I'm sure if Master Index has been detained, it was the result of a simple misunderstanding. In all probability, your head librarian will be returned to you by the end of the day. In the meantime, I will arrange to have some of the flyer-fries from Alkahest's labyrinth in Bleek transferred to you. It would be a tragedy if either of Congroo's two remaining dragons was to die."

"Oh, thank you, sir!" Pre sounded genuinely relieved. "I had no idea what I was going to do. This will give the scientists and me time to come up with a plan."

"Yes, about that." Oöm Lout looked as if he was putting some effort into smiling. "I would very much like to meet these scientists personally. Several of my staff and I can be there within the hour. In the meantime, make your guests comfortable. Discuss whatever you wish with them. *Just don't leave the library.* I would hate to have gone on a fool's errand because the four of you decided to go out for lunch."

"All the local lunch places have gone out of business," Pre reported.

"Wonderful. I'll see you shortly."

Oöm Lout's head disappeared. Pre dropped the pendant down the front of his robe.

"Who'd like some tea?" he asked brightly.

CHAPTER 13

ADJACENT WORLDS

It turned out, Preffy *could* heat a teapot with his bare hands. Modesty could, too, as she was quick to point out, but when she did it, the teapot warmed only to the temperature of her hands. When Pre did it, steam immediately came out of the teapot's spout, and the tea inside was ready to drink. He did this little trick after we had returned to the library. The teapot was in the shape of a dragon, its tail the handle and its snout the spout.

We were sitting at a circular oak table in front of a fireplace on the second floor. Pre had passed around mugs. His mug had lettering on the side that declared CONGROO'S GREATEST LIBRARIAN. My mug said OUR LIBRARY'S ROCK! Which, once I thought about it, was perfectly true.

"Drew and I both saw a jar of flyer-fries yesterday," I informed Pre. "It was in the hands of a zombie who popped out of the door to a porta potty in our corn maze. The zombie had gray hair, a mustache, and was dragging one leg behind him."

"Was the leg his or somebody else's?" inquired Pre.

"His. Attached to his hip."

"It sounds like you saw a vision of Master Index. He's been limping lately, ever since his bursitis started acting up. He went out to feed Phlogiston yesterday shortly after midday."

"That was right around when it happened," Drew confirmed.

"As I say, under the right conditions, people in one Adjacent World can briefly become aware of things in another. They usually dismiss what they've seen as a dream or hallucination. The door your zombie came out of is probably in a location similar to the location of our dragon-feed bin. What's a *porta potty*?"

"It's a bathroom," said Drew.

"You take a bath in it?"

"No. Of course not." Drew made a face. "It's a restroom."

"It's for napping?"

"A comfort station?" I suggested.

"You go there for sympathy?"

"N-no," sputtered Modesty. "It's where you—well—*you know*!"

Pre stared at us blankly.

"You can't possibly mean..." He blinked several times in rapid succession. "Oh. That *is* what you mean. Well. We don't do that."

"What do you mean, *we don't do that*?" Modesty asked.

"We haven't done it in, oh..." Pre looked up at the ceiling. "Eight hundred years."

"You must be awfully uncomfortable," said Drew.

"Eight hundred years ago, our ancestors evolved the magical ability for Intestinal Teleportation and Bladder Remote Broadcasting: IT and BRB. Essential parts of day-to-day life." Pre spoke matter-of-factly, as if he were talking about the weather. "Since then, it's an instinct we're all born with. It requires even less magic than heating a teapot. And it's a real time-saver."

"You teleport your..." I didn't know how to finish the sentence. Pre finished it for me.

"We call it euphemera, from the word *euphemism*, which means 'an acceptable word used in place of an unacceptable word.' We teleport our euphemera to another place before it has a chance to...leave on its own."

"Where does it go?" squawked Modesty.

"Jupiter."

"What? The *planet* Jupiter?"

"Yes. Do you have a planet Jupiter in the World of Science?"

"Yes," said Drew. "It's what our scientists call a gas giant."

"That definitely sounds like Jupiter."

"So...you're not cutting down your forests to make toilet paper," said Modesty thoughtfully, "and you don't have diapers, because babies already know how to get rid of their...euphemera. This is all very good for the environment."

"So...there are no bathrooms in this building," I said.

"There are no bathrooms in this *world*," Pre informed us. "Except in the Museum of Plumbing, where the exhibit always makes the smaller children giggle."

"Then...we won't be staying long," Modesty said decisively. "I had a big breakfast. We should get this meeting started."

"Any reason that fireplace isn't lit?" asked Drew. The grate was piled high with logs and kindling, but it could have been a Jenga stack for all the heat it gave off.

"*To Ignite a Fire* utilizes many more ERGs— Enchantment Resource Granules—of magic than *To Warm a Teapot*," Pre said in apology. "I'm trying not to be too wasteful of our dwindling resources."

"I can understand that," said Modesty as she got up

from her chair and bent down over the hearth. Within moments, tongues of flame were licking through the wood.

"How did you do that?" asked Pre, awestruck.

Modesty tossed him the lighter she had used. He caught it, then held it between two fingers as though it might explode.

"You carry a lighter?" I asked Modesty.

"I'm always taking them away from Prudence. We live in a wooden house."

"Is this a scientifical fire starter?" Pre asked.

"I'm pretty sure *scientifical* isn't a word," said Drew.

"If *magical* is a word, why wouldn't *scientifical* be?"

"I have no idea." Drew shrugged. "I'm sure there's a scientifical reason."

Modesty took back the lighter, flicked it, then waved the flame in front of Pre's face. She released the catch and returned it to him. He fumbled with it, figured out the trick, and a flame shot up.

"I just did *science*!" he declared, as if it was the most wonderful thing ever. "Being a scientist must be so great! Ouch!" He dropped the lighter and shook his fingers to cool them.

"That's the downside," Drew pointed out.

"But it's *science*." Pre's enthusiasm was undiminished. "The things you scientists do are the sort of things only our writers of fantasy would ever dream of. Flying through the air in metal tubes. Putting bread in a box to turn it into toast. Sawing a volunteer from the audience in half and then putting them back together again."

"That last one is magic," said Drew.

"No, it isn't. We can't do it. Not without making a mess."

"How is it you know so much about our world?" I asked, since we knew absolutely nothing about his.

"We have a few gifted seers who get glimpses of the World of Science from time to time. They're encouraged to write down what they see. And what they hear. Which I'm pretty sure isn't all that accurate, but we take what we can get."

The fire started giving off some heat. Modesty, Drew, and I jostled our chairs around the table so our backs were closer to the warmth. Pre stayed where he was, facing us from the other side, possibly out of guilt from not wanting to start the fire in the first place.

"Master Index and I were the first to figure out Congroo was getting cooler," he said, staring down into his mug. "This was three, maybe three and a half years ago. And actually, *I* was the one who figured it out. I used to go up on the roof of the tower each day and take temperature measurements."

"I suppose there's a spell *To Gauge the Air's Temperature* or something equally exciting," said Modesty a bit sarcastically.

"No, there isn't," Pre surprised us by saying. "When I was eight years old, I made a little doodad, a skinny glass tube with some quicksilver inside it, and put markings along the tube—I called the markings 'increments'—and it seemed to reflect how hot or cold the air was by how high or low the quicksilver was. I noticed the temperatures were getting progressively lower at a time when they should have been growing warmer. That could only mean something was wrong with our environmental-control enchantments. And that implied our magic might be thinning out. Master Index agreed with me, and we made a special trip to present my findings to the Weegee Board."

"You went to see these people when you were only *eight*?" I asked. When I was eight, I was afraid to raise my hand in class, even on the rare occasions when I knew the answer.

"By that time a year had passed and I was *nine*, and Master Index pretended the discovery was his—they would never have listened to a kid—but I helped with the presentation, and I answered most of the questions. We used bar graphs and a pie chart made from an actual pie, because we knew the board members were more easily swayed by visual aids that also doubled as refreshments, and we did our best to prove to them that Congroo had sprung a leak and that our precious magical power was draining away into one of the Adjacent Worlds."

"Adjacent Worlds?" said Drew.

"Your World of Science is an Adjacent World, and you're practically next door, so we told the board your world was the most likely place our magic was draining away to. *The board members laughed at us.* Oöm Lout was there, and he laughed the loudest. He asked us what could we, as lowly librarians, possibly know about the mechanics of environmental magic? According to him, the cooling was only temporary; it was being caused by a massive pod of space whales passing between us and the sun, and temperatures would return to normal once the pod had passed. As if a few space whales could account for the fluctuations in my temperature measurements. We were thrown out of the boardroom, *and*"—Pre rapped his mug on the tabletop—"*they kept the pie!*"

He got out of his chair and started pacing back and forth.

"A year later, when it became obvious to everybody that the world was getting colder, it was too late. Had they listened to us, there still would have been enough magic left to create barriers to stop the leak. But now, our magic reserves are down to only eight percent. I've been writing angry letters to the *Dire Inklings*, our local paper, pointing out how shortsighted the council has been. Master Index signed the letters, since, again, nobody's going to listen to a kid."

"You think someone from our world is draining the magic out of yours?" I asked.

"Haven't you been listening? Yes. Is it you? Are you engaged in some research project that's using a tremendous amount of magical energy?"

"I turned my sister's bedroom fuchsia," said Modesty.

"You made it smell funny?" asked Pre.

"Fuchsia is a color!"

"Changing the color of a room uses almost zero magic," Pre said. "Some of our research magicians theorize it could even be done with some sort of liquid pigment and a fuzzy roller on a stick, using no magic whatsoever. *No.* The amount of magic that's been drained from our world would be obvious when it showed up in yours. For instance, has anybody in your world recently built an invisible city?"

"How would we know?" asked Drew.

"You'd see people walking around in the middle of the air."

"No."

"Brought to life an army of forty-foot-tall statues made out of clay?"

"No."

"Sent an ocean liner to the moon?"

"No."

"Rearranged mountains so they're in alphabetical order?"

"No."

"Changed lead into gold?"

"*Nooo*...wait." We had been alternating saying "no," and it was my turn. But something occurred to me. "Did you say you started losing magic *three* years ago?"

"Three years, four months, ten days ago. According to my temperature charts."

I looked at Modesty and Drew.

"Isn't that..." I said hesitantly, "about the time they started selling DavyTrons?"

"You think turning tomato juice into asparagus is the same as turning lead into gold?" Drew made a face.

"Isn't it?"

"It certainly is." Pre's eyes went wide. "It's what we call 'transmutation.' It requires more energy than any other kind of magic. I mean, it's messing with the fundamental structure of the universe. Have you really been turning tomato juice into asparagus?"

"Not us personally," said Modesty. "We have machines that do it for us. Doesn't that make it science?"

"Not necessarily," said Pre. "Are your people especially fond of asparagus?"

"It's not just asparagus," I said.

"Rutabagas?" Pre looked horrified.

"Mainly lettuce, carrots, and potatoes," I said.

"And precarved pumpkins," Drew reminded me.

"*That's it.*" Pre stopped pacing and gripped the back of his chair. "That's where our magic's been going. You're killing us off...so you can have salad!"

CHAPTER 14

THE GIRL FROM STITCHEN

It's not like we're doing it intentionally," Modesty protested. "I hate salad."

"It's actually being done by a company called Davy's Digital Vegetables," I said. "A guy named Elwood Davy started the company around three years ago, and now it's this big international corporation. But its headquarters are in Disarray."

"It's poorly managed?"

"Disarray is the name of our town," said Modesty. "Our founder named it after his wife."

"He had a *wife* named *Disarray*?"

"Désirée. But neither of them could spell. The original Désirée was an ancestor of mine," Modesty said proudly.

"Davy's Digital Vegetables makes these machines called

DavyTrons," I said. "There are, like, *millions* of them. They're putting farm stands out of business. The DavyTrons turn tomato juice into practically any vegetable you want."

"Then the solution is obvious," said Pre. "You must go to this Elwood Davy and tell him to stop."

"He's...not an easy person to see," I said.

"Invisibility? In addition to transmutation? No wonder our magic is draining," Pre muttered.

"That's not what I meant," I said, pulling off my stocking cap as the room grew warmer. "Elwood Davy's a busy man. He's not somebody who's going to meet up with a bunch of twelve-year-olds."

"I'm not so sure about that," Modesty chimed in, pushing her chair back and getting to her feet. "I've seen photos of him with kids. They usually have food they've made with his digital veggies, and they're presenting him with a sample. Last week it was a brother and sister giving him a broccoli soufflé."

"You really think we could see him? And somehow talk him out of making DavyTrons?" I couldn't help the hopeful tone of my voice. We could save Congroo. And no more DavyTrons would mean people buying vegetables that were grown in the ground again.

"Maybe we could make him some potato pancakes," I said, suddenly on board with the plan. "Or a pumpkin pie." I thought of Modesty's sister Fidelity. "Or asparagus ice cream!"

"There," crowed Pre. "You're working on a plan already. I knew the moment you told me Delleps had contacted you that you were genius-level scientists. You should return to the World of Science immediately."

"And you should come with us," said Modesty, retrieving her lighter from the table. "You'd be a big help convincing Elwood Davy that Congroo exists."

"No, I have to stay here and wait for Hemi-Semi-Demi-Director Oöm Lout." Pre pushed in his chair and looked down at it, refusing to make eye contact with any of us.

"Why would you wait for him?" I asked. "It's obvious he can't be trusted."

"Why... obvious?" Pre looked up, sounding hopeful.

"Because one minute he's telling you he knows there's a door open between the worlds and it must be closed immediately, and the next he's being way too helpful about Master Index's abduction and your stolen french fries. I mean, *flyer-fries*. He wasn't consistent; that's usually a sign someone's hiding something."

Pre looked, for a moment, as if he might be getting ready to pack an overnight bag. Then his shoulders slumped, and he said, "No. Oöm Lout is an elected government representative. I have to respect that." His eyes darted around the room. "But... I'll come with you to the balcony and see you off."

Preffy led the way up the spiral staircase. We were

halfway to the top when Drew detoured on the fifth level and ran over to one of the bookcases.

"There's no way I'm leaving a library in a world of magic without checking out the books," he said over his shoulder. He ran his fingers along the spines. "These are all probably full of ancient wisdom and great feats of wizardry and, and—*What the heck?*" He leaned closer and started reading off titles. "*The Mystery of the Old Library. The Librarians Take a Holiday. All's Well Where There's a Library. Franklin Gothic: Ghost-Hunter Librarian.* What *is* this?"

"Oh," said Pre, coming up behind him. "That's the li-fi section."

"Li-fi?"

"Librarian fiction. A few years ago, one of our authors realized that any book that has a librarian as a main character is much more likely to get recommended by real librarians. Ever since *Cooper Black, Pirate Librarian* became a big hit, other authors have been churning out books about librarians who are also detectives or spies or super wizards or costumed crime fighters or stunt unicyclists. Most of our libraries now have li-fi sections. One of my own favorites is *The Adventures of Biblio Baggins.* Librarian by day, dabbler in the scientific arts by night."

"So this isn't a tower full of books on how to do magic?"

"No, but we do have a few of those. They're in the basement."

"*This* looks like a book of magic over here," said Modesty. She, too, had left the stairway and was standing next to a pedestal that supported an open book with gilt-edged pages.

I gave in to my own curiosity and followed Pre over to Modesty. Drew fell into step behind us.

"Yes, that's one of our basic magical references." Pre patted the book, then flipped through a few of its pages. "This is the *Necro Name-a-Coin*. It's an index of all the different types of coins that have been recovered using the *To Gather Lost Coins* spell. It's a marvelous book, edited by Johann Necro. It's self-updating *and* self-repairing."

"Self-repairing?"

"If a page tears, it invisibly mends. If a page gets torn out"—Pre grabbed a page and ripped it from the book—"it grows a new one."

We watched, stunned, as a new page spread out from the binding and replaced the one he had taken. He crumpled the page in his hand and tossed it.

"Wow," said Drew. "That's like something right out of *Castle Conundrum*." He looked up at me. "Can we stay longer?"

"Are you out of your mind?"

"We really shouldn't waste any more time," Pre said. "I'm not at all sure how many jars of dragon food Oöm Lout will be able to transfer here; it may only be a matter of days before things become critical."

"You really think this Lout guy is going to help replace the flyer-fries?" I asked as we resumed our climb.

"I don't see why he wouldn't. He said he'd look into it."

"You don't think he might be responsible for your jars going missing in the first place?"

"Oöm Lout's known for being a bit eccentric, but I'm sure he's not out to destroy the world. Are people in the World of Science always this suspicious?"

"We try to be, yes. It's actually what science is all about."

We stepped back out onto the balcony. Modesty was in the lead, and she halted almost as soon as she went through the door. The rest of us bunched up behind her.

"Who are they?" she asked, pointing to the distance.

In a treeless area of the hill below the ruins of Leger-demain, five horsemen were riding down the slope, heading in our direction.

"Well," Pre said, "four of them are wearing the blue uniform robes of Quieters. The one in the middle, wearing the gold robe, would be a board member, so that's probably Oöm Lout. He certainly didn't waste any time getting here. They're less than ten minutes away."

"What about the one in the green robe?" I asked. "The one who's on foot, running ahead of the horses? The horses are having a hard time keeping up."

A sixth figure was visible about a hundred yards ahead of the rest. It was jogging down the hillside, the distance between it and the horses widening with every step it took.

"Judging from the speed at which it's running," said Pre, "that would be a logem." When he saw our puzzled looks, he added, "A logem is a hollow person made from clay."

"You mean a golem," said Drew.

"I'm sure I don't. *Logem* is short for *analogem*—it's an *analog* of a human being. An artificial person. You grow a logem from a single slab of clay taken from the Homunculus Clay Pits—that's a big tourist attraction near the town of Homunculus—and rich people use them as servants. Usually, they mold the faces to look like famous actors or athletes. They're completely hollow, but they're capable of speech and varying degrees of mental activity."

"That's also true of rich people where we come from," said Modesty.

"I can't imagine why they would have brought a logem with them." Pre shook his head. "It's such a waste of magical energy."

"It looks like the logem will be here in a lot less than ten minutes," I said.

"Oh yes," Pre agreed. "They're very fast runners."

"Ring, ring."

The voice I now recognized as that of Delleps came from my pocket. I pulled out my phone and switched it to speaker mode.

"Hello."

"Thank you for using the Congroo Help Line. How may we assist you?"

Pre's eyes went wide. *"Is that—?"*

I held up my hand to keep him from finishing and slapped the phone to my chest to prevent Delleps from hearing anything that might sound like a question.

I thought carefully before I spoke.

"Hi," I said. "You're the oracle known as Delleps. The Congroo Help Line exists to help Congroo. So whenever you call, you have something to say that might be beneficial to your world. *But* because you're an oracle, and oracles have a bunch of bonkers rules, you can't just volunteer the information. You have to be asked a single question, with no follow-up questions, and your answer to the question can't be easy to understand. So I have to guess what the best thing to ask you is and then figure out the meaning of whatever wacky thing you say in reply."

"Was any of that a question?"

"No."

"Good. How may I be of service?"

"Psst." Modesty stuck her head in between the phone and me. "Ask her what the most important thing we need to know right now is."

I examined what she had suggested from every angle. It sounded pretty foolproof.

So I asked it.

"You're a very bright group," Delleps conceded. "Listen carefully: The girl fresh from stitchin' will enter the kitchen and close off the transworldly highway. You better act fast, and Oöm Lout get past, 'cause right now she's out in the driveway."

I waited, in case there was any more. Apparently, there wasn't.

"*Highway* and *driveway* don't exactly rhyme," observed Drew.

"It's a *cryptic prognostication*," grumbled Delleps. "There's no obligation for *any* of it to rhyme!"

"The girl fresh from *Stitchen*," Drew quoted. "Stitchen might be the name of a town here in Congroo." He looked to me to see if I agreed.

"Did you just hear that slap?" asked Delleps. "That was me, hitting my forehead with the heel of my hand."

"Don't make it any more complicated than it is," growled Modesty. "My sister Prudence needed eighteen stitches—she's the girl fresh from stitchin'."

"And *stitchin'* and *kitchen*," Delleps said smugly, "happen to rhyme perfectly."

"Which would be great," said Drew, "if *stitchin'* were a word."

"Delleps is saying Prudence is home," said Modesty, "and when she goes into the kitchen, she'll close the fridge door and break the connection and we'll be trapped here!"

I held up my phone and gave it a quizzical look, which I hoped wouldn't be seen as a question. "That wasn't terribly cryptic," I added.

"No," Delleps agreed. "The more urgent things are, the less mysterious I'm required to be. *Move your tails.*"

Click. Delleps broke the connection.

"I can't believe we've just heard from Congroo's greatest oracle." Preffy sounded overwhelmed.

"Been nice meeting you," I said as I pushed past him to follow Modesty, who was already in motion. Over my shoulder, I added, "We'll get right on the Elwood Davy thing as soon as we're home." I pulled Drew along with me. He had been staring back at the door to the inside of the tower. Modesty was already halfway across the balcony.

A winged gargoyle with a four-foot sword dropped out of the sky and landed on the path in front of us.

"Whoa!" Modesty fell back as the sword swooshed past her face at eye level. We scrambled back ten paces. When the gargoyle failed to chase us, we stopped and squeezed together in a tight, frightened knot. The thing with the sword stayed where it was, blocking our way. It looked like carved gray stone, with horns on its head and sightless stone eyes, but it had an odd shimmer to it, with areas on its chest where you could see through it to its back, as if the whole creature might be hollow. Snowflakes swirled around it and started filling in the holes, and it began to look more solid.

"Fazam!" Pre spat. "It's a Dust Devil."

"A what?" asked Drew.

"Something Oöm Lout must have sent to delay us until he gets here. A Dust Devil's a tiny bit of magical energy, maybe three or four ERGs, that builds itself a visible body by surrounding itself with dust and other bits of debris from the air and ground. This one appears to be using sand and dust and snow, plus maybe some loose garment threads and lint and possibly a few stray nose pickings."

"You're saying it's a whole lot of nothing covered in a thin shell of snot," said Drew.

"A very tiny amount of snot, if any," Pre said defensively. "It's not like we pick our noses that much."

"You don't teleport your snot to Saturn?" I asked.

"No!"

"It would explain the rings."

"We don't!"

"You're saying this thing isn't really here?" asked Modesty, pushing Drew aside.

"Oh, it's here all right," Pre assured her. "But it's mainly air, with a thin layer of dust and snow. Very good for guarding something you don't want people getting into. They're distantly related to logems; Congroo has a lot of hollow life-forms."

"Can't we walk right through it?" I asked.

"You could walk through it, yes, if you kept your eyes closed and didn't inhale," Pre agreed. "Except for the sword. The sword's edge is only the thickness of a dust mote. Do you have any idea how sharp that makes it? Sharper than any scalpel. There's a story about a soldier during the Second Goblin War who walked through a Dust Devil and didn't realize he'd been cut until he leaned over a drinking fountain and his head fell off."

"Ring, ring," said my phone. I slapped my pocket and pulled it out again.

"Hello."

"She's in the house," said Delleps.

"That's...not even remotely cryptic."

"That's how urgent it is." Delleps hung up.

"Your sister's in the house," I told Modesty. "We're out of time!"

Pre took a single step closer to the Dust Devil, which flicked its sword from side to side at the level of our necks.

"There's ice on the floor at its feet," said Modesty. "Maybe we could throw ourselves down and slide between its legs? Like a goal in hockey?"

"Just because it's made of dust," said Pre, "doesn't mean it can't bend at the waist. You'd never make it."

"Okay...then...a party balloon and confetti!" said Modesty. "That's what a Dust Devil is. What happens when you rub a balloon against your shirt and hold the balloon over confetti?"

"Everybody sings 'Happy Birthday'?" I guessed.

"The confetti sticks to the balloon," Drew answered, catching on faster than I had.

"Are you doing *science*?" Pre practically squealed; he was so excited.

"Maybe. If we're lucky." Modesty grabbed Drew and me and pushed us toward the gargoyle. "Distract it. Leave the center of the path clear, but don't get close enough to be cut. Leave the rest to me."

She gave us another shove. Drew and I refused to budge. We both faced her and opened our mouths to protest. She stopped us by shouting, *"Do you want us to be stranded here for the rest of our lives? In a world WITH-OUT TOILET PAPER?"*

I looked at Drew. Drew looked at me.

We launched ourselves at the gargoyle.

The path was six feet wide; I kept the wall of the balcony to my right; Drew stayed to the left. We had maybe a two-foot gap between us. The thing waved its sword from side to side, and we skidded to a halt. It could have taken one step forward and skewered us, but it seemed content to block the way. I got the impression it would kill us only if we refused to take the hint.

I jumped to the top of the wall, made the mistake of looking down, and nearly lost my balance. I briefly glimpsed the green-robed logem sprinting toward the tower's base, and I wondered, very fleetingly, how long it would take it to run up seven flights of stairs.

Not long.

Drew lunged forward in a crouch, putting himself

within sword range, but I waved my arms, shouted "*Nyeah-nyeah*," and pretended I was about to run along the top of the wall to get past.

The gargoyle switched its target from Drew to me and swept its sword at my legs. I jumped with all my might, the sword passed beneath my feet, and I stuck my landing—but just barely. My arms made circles in the air as I fought to keep my balance.

The sword completed its swing.

And came back at me.

I wasn't in a position to jump again. The sword was coming straight at me.

Modesty hurled herself down the alley like a bowling ball, threw herself to the ground, and slid on her back along the icy patch beneath the gargoyle.

She was holding the can of Cling-Be-Gone antistatic spray.

The moment she was directly beneath the monster, she sprayed the can upward. The sword was an inch from my legs when the geyser of anti-cling spray hit the gargoyle in the butt.

It burst like an explosion in a glitter factory.

Sparkly flakes flew in all directions and then cascaded down on the path. The tiny grains stung as they hit our faces, but it didn't hurt anywhere near as much as getting my legs cut off would have.

"Brilliant!" shouted Pre, and ran to us. "That was

like something out of *Mary Potter, Girl Scientist*, during her first year at MIT."

"MIT?" asked Drew as he helped Modesty to her feet.

"The Magicless Institute of Technology. It's the fictitious school of science in one of our most beloved fantasy septologies. I love those books. They're the highlight of the library's STEM collection."

"What's STEM?" Drew asked, adjusting his turkey.

"Stories That Exclude Magic."

"Let's move," I said, dropping down from the wall and pushing everybody forward. Modesty shook off gargoyle dust like a dog shaking bathwater, and we plunged along the path. My longer legs carried me past the others, and I arrived at the doorway first. The refrigerator's interior light was still on, and through the shelves of food, I could see Modesty's kitchen. I stepped forward.

And came face-to-face with a girl who had a bandage wrapped around her head. She had just removed the chair that had been holding the fridge's door open. Her eyes went wide.

She screamed.

And slammed the door in my face.

The refrigerator light went out. It was like sunset on doomsday.

"No!" I shouted. "We're trapped!"

I couldn't help my folks if I couldn't get back to them.

They'd have to sell the farm, all the time wondering what had happened to their younger son. Glen's hand-me-down clothes would go to charity, which, okay, was a silver lining, but still—*I wouldn't be there.* We weren't going to be able to save Congroo—we were going to be stuck in it. I whimpered.

I didn't want to live in a world without toilet paper.

Pre pressed his hands against my shoulders.

"Don't back up!" he ordered. "The door's not closed—you're *standing* in it. The connection will hold as long as you're there. Don't back out. Push!"

He shoved me, and I threw my weight against the inside of the door. I felt a carton of eggs collapse messily on one of the shelves, and then I fell forward and went sprawling on the floor of Modesty's kitchen. Pre tumbled in after me, and Modesty wasn't far behind.

"That was close," she said as she stepped down off the veggie-crisper drawer.

"Hi-yah!" The girl with the bandaged head came out of nowhere and slammed the door shut as she bolted to the opposite side of the room.

"No! He's still in there!" I jumped to my feet, swept the door back open, and threw myself forward. I collided with cold, hard shelving and staggered backward in a shower of soda cans and Tupperware containers.

The connection was broken.

Drew hadn't made it.

We had left him in Congroo.

CHAPTER 15

NO HOUR OF TWELVE

I got to my feet and started shifting the contents of the fridge back and forth, searching for my friend. He wasn't behind the marmalade; there was no sign of him anywhere near the cream cheese—

Preffy pulled me away.

"It's no good," he said. "He can't get through, and I can't go back. Not until we open another door. Which, if what you say about Magic Minutes is true, won't be until sometime tonight."

The girl with the bandaged head was backed into a corner, whimpering. She suddenly found her voice and began to scream. Modesty jumped on her and put a hand over her mouth.

"Prudence," Modesty whispered fiercely. "It's me.

Your sister. You hit your head with a machete. You're hallucinating. I don't know what you thought you saw, but I'm sure it wasn't a bunch of kids falling out of the refrigerator! I'm the only one here. Please be quiet!"

"Pru?" A woman's concerned voice came from the floor above, and a moment later, feet were pounding down the stairs.

Modesty spun Prudence around so she was facing the wall and whispered to us, "Get out the back! I'll meet you as soon as I can at the farm stand. Move!"

The thought that we might be able to save Drew when the next Magic Minute rolled around energized me. I grabbed Pre and dragged him out the back door.

"It's so nice and warm here!" he declared as we emerged into a mild September afternoon. That didn't stop him from flipping his hood over his head, though. I slipped out of the coat Modesty had lent me and left it draped over a bush near the back steps. A gate in the backyard fence led to a path between houses that, eventually, got us to the street.

"I'm sorry about your friend," Pre said once we had gotten far enough from Modesty's place that our voices couldn't be overheard.

"We'll get him back," I assured him—and myself—as we started down a back road with no sidewalks and very few houses. If I hadn't been walking with a kid dressed as a monk, I would have taken the main roads all the way to Sapling Farm. But this seemed like the wiser route.

It wasn't.

We turned the corner onto Elm Street and ran smack into Mace Croyden and his buddy Raymond Chikletts. A hedge had blocked my view; otherwise, I would have turned us around before it was too late.

"Hey, Sap! What's up?" Mace wasn't as tall as I was, but he was wider, and most of it was muscle, especially the area between his ears. Ray stood behind him, moving his jaw around as if he was trying to avoid swallowing something disgusting.

"Hi, Mason," I said uneasily.

"I hear your farm's failing big-time!" Mace gave me a huge grin. "And this is the last time you and your loser family are gonna do the Halloween thing. Same garbage as last year?" He reached over and flicked Pre's hood back. "Whoa!" Mace did a mock cringe. "I expected a skull! Ugly's okay, though. Great mask. Toads are usually a darker green, though." He pinched Pre's cheek. "Oh! It's your face. Sorry about that. I mean, *really*, it's something to be sorry about."

"We have to get going," I told him and started past. He stopped me with his hand.

"You gotta pay the toll, Sap. Both of you. Now... what would be the toll for walking down Elm?" He glanced at Ray, who was still doing cowlike things with his jaw. "Oh yeah. You can only go down Elm if you both have *gum* in your hair."

Mace extended an open palm toward Ray. Ray looked down at it as if he had never seen a hand before.

"What?" said Ray.

"Your gum," Mace prompted.

"What gum?"

Mace turned fully toward his friend. I nudged Pre along.

"The gum you're chewing."

"I'm not chewing gum."

"What have you got in your mouth?"

"My tongue!"

"You were chewing!"

"I'm trying to get jerky out of my teeth."

"When did you have jerky?"

"Last night. No, wait. Night before."

"Well, put some gum in your mouth and start chewing!"

"You've got gum?"

"No!"

"Neither do I!"

And by that time, Pre and I were far enough away that the rest of the conversation was lost.

"Hey!" Mace shouted after us. "Catch ya tomorrow!"

"Am I ugly?" asked Pre.

"Not even remotely," I assured him, and steered us

around the corner onto Crabtree. "And my family aren't losers. At least, most of them aren't."

"It's not your fault your friend got left behind," Pre said, as if he were reading my mind. "He was lingering. I think he wanted to see more of the library."

"Yeah, Drew *loves* libraries," I said. "That's why he's so smart. He's up to level thirty-three in *Castle Conundrum*—that's a game—and that takes a lot of problem-solving. He knew enough to hit the two-headed ogre with the giant tuning fork. He's smart, *and he has his phone.* There's a voice recording of the door-opening spell on it, and he heard you say the spell has to be performed from both sides in order for it to work. So at one twenty-three tonight, I'm sure he'll try it. We'll try it, too, and a door will open, and the two of you will switch places."

"Are Drew's parents living?"

It was such an unexpected question, I paused in mid-step.

"Uh, yeah. Unless something horrible's happened since yesterday. Why would you ask?"

"How are you going to tell them their son is missing?"

Shoot. I hadn't thought of that. But—"Oh! I don't have to tell them for another two days. Drew's supposed to be sleeping over my place tonight and tomorrow. His parents won't miss him until Tuesday afternoon. By that time, he'll be back."

"Convenient."

"Sometimes you get a break. I'll tell my parents he changed his mind." We made a left down Hemlock. "You don't think that golem thing will hurt him, do you?"

"Logem. I'm sure Oöm Lout only sent it ahead to make sure we wouldn't leave the tower. He'll probably be upset that I'm not there, but I don't think he'll take it out on Drew. And I'm sure Master Index will be returning to the tower any time now; you heard Oöm Lout assure me the arrest was a misunderstanding."

I didn't share Pre's opinion of Lout. But for Drew's sake, I hoped I was wrong.

"Is that a flying machine?" Pre stopped dead and stared at a bright-red biplane bobbing over the fields of the Renshaw farm. I noticed, for the first time, a big FOR SALE sign on the farm's entrance road.

"It's a crop duster," I informed him

"You dust your crops! Keeping the leaves clean probably makes them grow better. The World of Science is *so* amazing. What keeps it in the air?"

"The wings are flat on the bottom and curved on top," I said, surprised that I knew. "If the plane is moving fast enough, this makes the pressure of the air greater on the underside, and the air lifts it off the ground."

"Incredible."

"It took us a *long* time to figure it out."

We followed Hemlock to Spruce, then cut through a grove of trees at the far end of the Sapling farm wheat field. It wasn't my favorite part of the farm. High-tension electrical transmission towers stretched power lines north and south down the middle of it; the wheat that grew below the lines never seemed as healthy as the wheat on either side. I hurried us along as we passed beneath the faintly humming lines but then slowed our pace as we approached the section of the field I liked the very least.

"Was that thing struck by lightning?" asked Pre as the remains of the Fireball 50 loomed in front of us. "Or was it hit by some kind of superweapon during a battle between scientists?"

"That damage was done by an eleven-year-old boy," I told him.

"He must be very powerful!"

"Yeah, you wouldn't want to mess with him." I swiped my finger along the harvester's side. It made a streak in the soot. I briefly considered writing BOO! in six-foot letters.

My mom still wrote monthly checks to the bank, paying off something we'd never be able to use again. When my brother, Glen, was learning to drive and he backed over our mailbox, the next day he bought a new box, sank a new post, and it was all repaired by the time the mail arrived. Glen had had it easy. I couldn't just pick up a new harvester at the hardware store. "Hey!" I had a thought. "Do you know a spell that could fix it?"

Pre stopped and gave the hulk a good hard look. Then he shook his head. "Trying to use magic to repair something from the World of Science would be incredibly dangerous. There's no telling what might happen."

"We've used magic to paint some of our rooms," I said.

"Did you get the color you wanted?"

"Uh. I didn't realize I had a choice."

Pre shrugged. "See?"

It was too bad. If we failed to get Elwood Davy to stop making DavyTrons, it would have been nice, at least, to have been able to fix the harvester. That way...I finished the thought and didn't like the ending. That way, Elwood Davy could buy the harvester when he bought the farm. My parents wouldn't be needing it.

We crossed Route 9 to the farm stand. The door of our mailbox was hanging open, and I punched it as hard as I could to close it. Then I punched the side of the box for no good reason.

Modesty was waiting for us.

"Took you long enough," she said. She was sitting on one of the picnic tables. "Now, about Drew. I've been thinking—"

"We're going to get him back at one twenty-three

tonight," I said, "when he and I both play the Magic Bite for door opening."

"Right." She sounded disappointed, maybe because I'd gotten to it first. "That's what I was thinking. You're okay?"

"I'm fine. This will work."

"Good." She pointed to the back of the farm stand. "I towed your bike." My clunker was barely visible behind the boxes of Davy's Deluxe Tomato Juice. Modesty's own bike leaned against a stack of apple crates. "I stowed Drew's in our toolshed so Mum wouldn't notice. I couldn't tow them both."

"Thanks," I said, realizing she hadn't had to do it.

"And..." She tilted her head back and stared at the sky. "Did you see the storm cloud I materialized at two thirty-four?"

I looked where she was looking.

"No," I said.

"No, you didn't," she agreed. "I played the Magic Bite, and nothing happened. If magic works at two thirty-four in the morning—"

"It does," I assured her.

"It *doesn't* work at two thirty-four in the afternoon. We'll check out three forty-five and four fifty-six, but I'm beginning to think magic only works in the morning."

"And twelve thirty-four in the afternoon," I reminded her.

"There's no such time," Pre said quietly.

"What?" I wasn't sure I'd heard him correctly.

"I said, there's no such time as twelve thirty-four," he clarified.

"Of course there is," replied Modesty. "It's right between twelve thirty-three and twelve thirty-five. You can't miss it."

"But there's no hour of twelve," Pre insisted. "There are only the hours one through eight and then the middle one through eight and then the final one through eight."

"I have no idea what you're saying," said Modesty. "It's like the gobbledygook in one of your incantations."

"Wait," I said, working it out. "I think what he's saying is...in Congroo, they've divided the day into three eight-hour segments. Unlike here, where we've divided it into two *twelve*-hour segments. Have I got that right?"

"Yes." Pre nodded approvingly. "The Great Horologist War was fought over whether to divide the day into *four* six-hour segments or *three* eight-hour segments. Oh, with a third group of fanatics who wanted *twelve* two-hour segments, which most historians agree would have been total chaos. The eight-hour segmentists won. Do you really divide your days into two twelve-hour halves? Is there a scientifical reason?"

"Not that I know of," I said. "The first twelve hours are called AM; the second twelve are called PM. Don't ask me why."

"In Congroo, the first eight hours are called BB—Before Breakfast. The second eight hours are BD—Before Dinner. And the final eight hours are BMS—Before Midnight Snack."

"So if it's twelve thirty-four PM *here*," said Modesty, "what time is it in Congroo?"

Pre's brow furrowed as he worked it out.

"Twelve thirty-four PM here would be four thirty-four BD in Congroo."

Modesty thought about that for a moment, then shook her head. "That doesn't help."

"Why would it?" I asked.

"I'm not sure," she admitted. "It just seems to me that Congroo being on an eight-hour clock and us being on a twelve-hour clock might have something to do with why Magic Minutes only work in the four hours following midnight and *not* in the four hours following noontime—except for twelve thirty-four. Twelve thirty-four may be the key to the whole thing, although I can't imagine how. We're missing something, but I can't figure out what it is."

"Let me get this straight," said Pre. "Magic only works here at one twenty-three AM, two thirty-four AM, and twelve thirty-four PM?"

"And three forty-five and four fifty-six AM," said Modesty.

"That's only five minutes each day," Pre said thoughtfully. "That doesn't sound right. *Seven* is a much more magical number. There are seven days in a week, seven seas, seven continents, seven Insights of Irksome—"

"Seven dwarfs, seven samurai, seven swans a-swimmin'," Modesty interrupted. "Yeah, seven comes up a lot. You think there should be seven Magic Minutes? I don't see what the other two minutes would be; there are no other times that match the pattern."

We thought about that for a moment. Then Modesty upended her rhinoceros backpack and spilled an array of clothing onto the picnic table. "Preffy, I brought some clothes for you. These belong to my sister Verity. She lies about her clothing sizes, but you and she look pretty close. Those robes you're wearing might attract unwanted attention."

"They might," I agreed, remembering Mace.

"These blue legging things and the black tunic with the weird rodent creature on it are nice," said Pre, holding up a pair of jeans and a Mickey Mouse sweatshirt.

"They're yours." Modesty stuffed the leftover clothing back in her bag. Pre studied the jeans, looked awestruck when I showed him how the zipper worked, then sat and pulled the pants on under his robe. He pulled the robe off over his head, put on the sweatshirt, and suddenly looked like a typical Disarray middle school student. Except, possibly, for the greenish complexion.

"Thank you," he said to Modesty. "That was very thoughtful of you."

"Yes, it was," Modesty agreed.

"But now," said Pre, rolling up his robe and tucking it under one arm, "we have to figure out how we're going to save Congroo. That's the important thing. We need a plan."

"Already got one," Modesty said, waving her hand nonchalantly. "I came up with it on the way over. We're going to need an electric drill, a piece of wire, and two dozen carrots."

CHAPTER 16

GNICHE VERSUS *NICHE*

O r maybe parsnips," Modesty added after thinking for a moment. "If they're the ones I'm thinking of. Are parsnips the ones that look like carrots, only they're white instead of orange?"

"Yeah," I said. "We've got a whole bin of them. They're not big sellers."

"The veggies can't be from the farm stand," Modesty informed me. "They have to be made in a DavyTron. We really should get started."

Without further explanation, she slid from her perch on the picnic table and headed for the barn, where the sound of power tools suggested it might be a good place to find a drill. Preffy and I trotted after her.

My dad and the high schoolers were up on ladders,

outlining the barn with twinkly orange lights. At the foot of one of the ladders, an open toolbox held a spare recharge-able drill. Since it didn't seem to be needed, I grabbed it, along with a box of drill bits. I tossed a spool of wire to Modesty, and she darted in the direction of the farmhouse.

"Are we doing science?" asked Pre.

"Possibly," I said, not really sure what we were doing. "There's a DavyTron in the farm-stand office!" I shouted after Modesty, and she altered course, retrieving her backpack from the picnic table as she trotted past. Pre paused to study Artie, the chainsaw maniac, for a moment, then took off after her. I glanced up at my dad to see if I needed to wave, which I did, since he was look-ing down at me somewhat quizzically. We exchanged smiles, and off I went.

I broke into a run, arrived at the office door just as Modesty got there, and made sure I went in first. To my relief, the room was empty.

Modesty went straight to the DavyTron.

"I think maybe a mix," she said, bending down to study the control panel. "Maybe a dozen carrots and a dozen parsnips. Holy cow. Your DavyTron can make up to six carrots at once. That's a time-saver!"

She punched in a code, the can of tomato juice on top of the DavyTron went *glug*, and the machine started mak-ing carrots.

"Is that...pie?" Pre asked in a small voice. He was

staring at a stack of clear plastic boxes on the room's central table. I had forgotten he hadn't had anything to eat, other than a bowl of peanut-butter-chicken soup and some watery tea.

"Yes! Here," I said, grabbing the topmost box, popping the lid, and handing the pie to him. "I'll get you something to…cut…it…with…"

My voice trailed off. Pre had the pie out of its metal plate and was devouring it whole. It was apple, which at least was less messy than cherry or blueberry. I grabbed him a bottle of water from the small fridge next to my mom's desk.

"You might want to go easy," I reminded him. "The next Magic Minute isn't for another eleven hours, so we can't…um…send anything to Jupiter."

He stopped short, eyes wide, but seemed to decide it was worth it and continued to wolf down the pie.

"What happens when somebody from your world pukes?" I asked.

He paused just long enough to answer. "We clean it up."

"You don't vomit on Venus? Or something?"

"No. That would be silly."

Ding!

Six completed carrots appeared in the DavyTron. Modesty pulled them out, punched in the code for another six, and threw the first half dozen down on the table in front of me.

"I need two holes drilled in each carrot, one above the other, about an inch apart at the fat end. The holes should be just a little larger than the thickness of the wire." She looked at me expectantly. I flipped open the box of drill bits and started searching for the right size.

Pre came up for air. Modesty handed him a roll of paper towels from my mom's desk, and he wiped his chin. He seemed delighted that the towels had perforations. He kept ripping off sheets, one right after another.

"A perfect tear every time! Science is *wonderful*!"

Modesty rummaged in her backpack and extracted Pre's three-ring binder. She held it up to him.

"How did this get in my gym locker?"

Pre swallowed a final bite and took the binder from her. I removed the second set of carrots from the Davy-Tron and got it started on parsnips, then revved the drill and started punching two holes in each carrot.

"I put it in a gniche," said Pre. When Modesty and I only stared, he added, "A niche is a magical randomizing box, the name of which is sometimes pronounced *gniche*, with a hard *g* sound at the beginning, and sometimes pronounced *niche*, where the *g* is not only silent but missing, in keeping with the box's randomizing nature. One never knows how the word is going to come out of one's mouth or how it will appear on paper. Over the years, this has resulted in the loss of sanity of more than one copy editor. Simply put, a gniche is an anything box."

"An anything box?" Modesty sounded slightly dazed.

"*Anything* can happen to what you put inside. A niche will reject all objects larger than a pizza—that's a circular tomato pie made with cheese and sometimes anchovies—and no niche will accept anything that's alive—in particular, it repels cats very strongly—and that's probably just as well. Sometimes whatever you put into a gniche will be turned inside out. Or changed into a pastrami sandwich or grow a beard or become covered in polka dots. Most usually, though, whatever you put into a niche will disappear. Our scholars think the things that disappear might wind up in one of the Adjacent Worlds, such as Earth or Indorsia. We're not sure. I placed my kindergarten notebook into the library's gniche in the desperate hope it would wind up here in your world and somebody would be smart enough to use it to open the other side of the door that I'd been trying to create on our side almost constantly for the past three weeks."

Pre started in on a second pie. When he noticed Modesty looked particularly dumbfounded, he added, "Kindergartners use the spell to open doors they're too short to reach. I came up with the idea that if the spell was used in two Adjacent Worlds around the same time, it might open a portal between them. There'd only have to be an actual *physical* door on one side or the other."

"You could have included a note explaining all this," said Modesty.

"No, I couldn't have." Pre wiped his chin with a perfectly torn towel. "Obvious attempts at communication get repelled even more strongly than cats. I know it sounds like a contrivance in a poorly written novel, and as a librarian I've seen more than my share, but magic is rife with such things. Gniches are an example of what led Panacea Irksome, our greatest thinker, to say magic isn't arbitrary—it only looks that way."

"What does 'magic is fluid' mean?" Modesty asked, plucking the bookmark with Irksome's Seven Insights out of the binder and reading the top Insight. Pre had turned his attention back to the second pie, only a sliver of which now remained.

"It flows like water," Pre replied after taking a moment to swallow. "Some places in Congroo are like deserts, with very little magic, and other places are like oceans, full of magic. Magic behaves like a liquid—that's why it can drain out of Congroo to somewhere else. We once had an avalanche, and a whole lot of magic got bottled up behind the Delectable Mountains, and we had to use blasting spells to free it. There were wizards surfing on it when it came gushing out. Everything in its path glowed blue for the next three days."

"Done!" I announced, and stepped away from a table that was covered by two dozen carrots and parsnips, each with two holes drilled neatly in their tops.

"Perfect," said Modesty, and shoved me aside with

her hip. She bent over the veggies and began rearranging them.

"When can we go see Mr. Davy?" Pre asked as I took the towels away before there were none left on the roll.

"Not today," I said. "It's Sunday, so the DavyTron factory is closed."

"Tomorrow," Modesty said with her back to us, as she did whatever she was doing to the root veggies. The spool of wire I had thrown her danced around the tabletop. "I'm thinking we sneak out of school during lunch and walk over. The Davy Tower is only about a mile away. We should start thinking about what we're going to say to him."

"One thing we should ask him about is the DavyTron software updates," I said, having given it some thought. "Drew said the machines get updated every twenty-four hours. What if that happens *at the exact same time every night*? And what if it happens to be one of the Magic Minutes?"

"You think the incantation for transmutation might be part of the update code?" Modesty sounded skeptical. "That would be quite a coincidence."

"If we're not doing anything until tomorrow," said Pre, "I'll need a place to sleep tonight. That tower we saw as we approached, the one you and your family watch forest fires from—"

"We don't *watch* forest fires. It's called a fire *watch*-tower because it's part of a system for *preventing* forest fires—"

"Oh. Good. That sounds much less depraved. Anyway, I think I'd like to sleep up there, if you'll permit me. Your world is so nice and warm, I wouldn't mind sleeping in a place with open windows. Especially in a tower. I've slept in one all my life."

"Sounds good to me," said Modesty before I could suggest anything different. "Smuggle him up there, give him some snacks, and lend him a sleeping bag."

"You have bags that sleep?" asked Pre.

"It's a bag you sleep *in*," said Modesty. "And then we'll all meet in the tower around one AM, just in time for the one twenty-three Magic Minute."

"Why... would we do that?" I asked.

"You want to rescue Drew, don't you?"

"I can do that in my room. Just me, my phone, and the Magic Bite for *To Open a Door*. It doesn't need a committee."

"Shortsighted." Modesty sniffed. She looked around. "Are there wire cutters?"

There weren't, but after a moment I found a pair of nail clippers in my mom's desk and handed them to her. She turned back to her project.

"How is it shortsighted?"

"It'll take three seconds to play the Magic Bite for *To Open a Door*. Boom. You've got Drew back. You hug; Drew says thank you, thank you, thank you—and we've still got most of a Magic Minute left. Magic Bites take three or four seconds to play—we could try out a dozen spells before the minute's up."

"Performing that many spells in rapid succession would not be wise," Pre said in alarm.

"*And* we'll have a technical adviser from Congroo with us so we don't blow ourselves up or anything. And he"—Modesty turned and looked meaningfully at Pre—"might have a spell or two of his own to contribute."

"I can't imagine what those spells might be," said Pre, trying to bite into the side of the water bottle. He caught me staring and said, "The cork won't come out."

I took the bottle and unscrewed the cap. I handed both back to him; he studied the cap, said, "It's threaded! Like the lids of the flyer-fry jars. Ingenious!" and gulped down half the water.

"Ta-da!" Modesty trumpeted.

I turned back to her.

She was wearing a crown.

She had threaded the veggies together in a circle, alternating the parsnips with the carrots, the pointy ends sticking upward, and put the whole assembly on her head. As crowns went, it didn't look too bad.

"I don't get it," I admitted.

"This," she said, tapping one of the parsnips, "is absolutely brilliant. We know Elwood Davy poses for pictures with kids who make things with his vegetables, right? Well, tomorrow, when we get to Davy headquarters, we tell the receptionist we made this crown for him, and we'd like to present it to him *personally*. I mean, how could he resist? I look adorable. Then we'll get to talk him out of destroying Congroo. We'll save the dragons!"

"One problem. What makes you think it will fit him?" I asked.

"He's a genius, right?"

"Yeah, so?"

"I modeled it on my own head!"

CHAPTER 17

HIGH-TENSION

"I'm not really all that good at magic," Preffy admitted a little later. It was ten minutes until I was due to start my cashier shift at the farm stand. We had left the office before anyone could walk in on us, and the three of us were hanging out at the Invisible Goat corral. Modesty still had the carrot-and-parsnip crown on her head. Occasionally, she gave a regal wave to passing motorists.

"In fact, I'm terrible at it," Pre continued. "Half my spells are misfires. It's a matter of concentration. I'm usually thinking of something else. For instance, only yesterday, I was levitating a bunch of books back into the celebrity biography section, but I was also working on an invention of mine: a glass jar with a piece of rubber stretched across the top and a straw glued over the center of the rubber but sticking out past the edge of the jar—I think the straw might move when bad weather is approaching, but I haven't tested it yet."

"The books wound up on the wrong shelf?" I guessed.

"The books flew out the window."

Pre leaned over the corral's fence, stretched out a hand, and made the squeaky noise with his lips that many people mistakenly think will attract animals.

"I don't believe there are any goats in here," he said after a moment.

"There aren't," Modesty confirmed.

"But the sign—"

"Yeah, the sign," I said, gesturing to the fence post next to us.

INVISIBLE GOATS

INVISIBLE GOATS (*CAPRA NOSEEUS*)
ARE NATIVE TO PATAGONIA, WHERE THEY
ARE CONSIDERED A TRIPPING HAZARD.
THEY ARE PRIZED FOR THEIR MILK,
WHICH IS UDDERLY TRANSPARENT.

"We *had* goats," I said, "and a pair of llamas and a couple of sheep for a long time. They weren't livestock; they were *pets*, and we kept them out front here so farm-stand customers could see them. But we had to find a good home for them a few weeks ago to save money. My dad made the sign. That's his sense of humor." I glanced across the road and gave the burned-out harvester a dirty look.

"Oh," said Pre quietly.

"Are we all agreed we have to keep the existence of Congroo a secret?" said Modesty, clearly sensing it was time to change the subject. "We don't tell anybody about it except, of course, Elwood Davy, who's the only person who needs to know."

She levered the crown from her head and placed it in a cake box we had found. A strip of cardboard bent into a circle held the crown's shape, and the cellophane window on the front of the box showed it off like jewelry in a display case.

"Oh, absolutely," agreed Pre. "The fewer of your people who know about my world, the better. We can't let anyone with powerful science at their disposal try to breach the barrier between here and there. It would be a catastrophe for both sides. But Mr. Davy must know about Congroo already—otherwise, he couldn't be siphoning magic out of it."

"Okay." Modesty handed me the boxed-up crown. "I'll leave this with you. And I'll be back around twelve forty-five tonight." When I gave her a questioning glance, she added, "I have a window I sneak out of. Leave the tower gate unlocked, and I'll come right up."

Modesty departed on her bike. I waited for our only

customers to drive away, made sure my dad and his high school helpers were still working inside the barn, then escorted Pre up to the top of the fire tower. I left him with a sleeping bag, some water, and a box of Cheerios.

The three of us had agreed we all needed to sleep, since it was possible we might be up for most of the night, so after putting in my four-hour shift at the farm stand, having supper with my folks, and telling them that Drew wouldn't be spending the night after all, I announced I had a math test to study for and went up to bed.

It was eight thirty, which I was pretty sure was four thirty BMS—Before Midnight Snack—Congroo time, which made it feel even earlier.

I couldn't sleep.

Not at first anyway. My head was filled with everything that had happened over the weekend, from stampeding coins to an annoying girl with a notebook full of magic to a gargoyle that exploded if you hit it with anti-cling spray to my best friend getting left behind in the World of Magic. It took me a while to convince myself that we would be getting Drew back in only a matter of hours. He was clever—he had found the keyhole behind Baron Orblacker's eye patch in *Castle Conundrum*—so I was confident he would figure out what he needed to do to reopen the door between the worlds.

Then I started worrying about what we could possibly

say to Elwood Davy to convince him to stop making DavyTrons. I imagined drawing him a chart:

No DavyTrons = No Magic Drain = Congroo Warms Back Up = Flyer-Fries Survive = Dragons Don't Die Out = More Magic Gets Made

I wondered if there would be a blackboard he'd let us use. Then I started wondering if the spell called *To Repair a Chimney* might, at the very least, knock some of the soot off the Fireball 50; the harvester had certainly smoked like a chimney once the blaze got going. Then I remembered I actually *did* have a math test the next day and I should be studying for it....

Which was when I fell asleep.

My alarm went off at a quarter to one. I left the house quietly through the back door, and when I arrived at the base of the tower, Modesty was waiting for me. Together we climbed the zigzag stairs and found Preffy sitting in one corner of the cab, cozily wrapped in his sleeping bag.

"I've thought of a spell that might help," he said. "It's called *To Make an Agreeable Atmosphere.*"

"What...does that do?" I asked him warily.

"Sounds like a spell the people on Jupiter might need," said Modesty.

"There isn't any life on Jupiter," Pre informed her testily as he stood and wiggled out of the bag. "The Sanitation

Commission made sure of that before we started sending our euphemera there. Going ahead without an environmental impact study would have been criminal."

"Oh. Of course. Silly me."

"*To Make an Agreeable Atmosphere* creates the smell of baking bread."

"How does that help us?" I asked.

"According to a study by IBM," Pre said primly, "different smells influence how people behave. The smell of baking bread makes them more agreeable. If there's a smell of baking bread when we ask Mr. Davy to stop draining the magic out of Congroo, he might be more willing to do it."

"IBM?" asked Modesty.

"The Institute for Better Magic. The problem is that the incantation that produces the spell is five pages long. I've memorized it, but there's no way I can *envision* it from start to finish in less than a minute. Things are so much easier in Congroo, where magic works all the time and there isn't a big rush to get things done."

"You don't have to speak the incantation out loud?" I said, not exactly sure what he meant by *envision*.

"No, of course not. You just have to picture each word accurately and hear the correct pronunciation in your head. And if you leave off the final three or four syllables, the spell doesn't work until you finish it, so you can have dozens of spells stored up and ready to go when you need them. They stay fresh for months. That's how wizards used to duel with each other, back before dueling was outlawed. Anyway, the best magicians can envision about two thousand words per minute. I'm not that good; I figure I can manage maybe, oh, I don't know...seven hundred?"

"Couldn't you just envision the spell now," I suggested, "but save up the final syllables and think them during one of the actual Magic Minutes?"

"That's not how it works." Pre shook his head. "I would have to start the spell during one Magic Minute, continue it during the next, and so on, until I finished it in however many Magic Minutes it takes."

"Funny we didn't think to spread out the longer spells like that," said Modesty. "But here's something we *did* try, and it works! Phone, please."

She unpocketed her phone and held out her hand for mine.

Both phones agreed it was 12:53. By the time Modesty finished explaining Magic Bites to Pre and how they could condense a ten-minute incantation into something that sounded like *blippity-blip*, the phones said 1:03.

"It's twenty minutes until one twenty-three, the first Magic Minute of the night," Modesty told Pre. "We don't want to waste it. I'm not saying your smell spell stinks or anything, but—do you have anything better?"

"Yeah," I said. "Maybe something that causes skeletons to rise up out of the floor waving swords over their heads? That might convince Davy to stop making DavyTrons."

"We don't have anything like that," said Pre.

"Oh?" I said. "What about the spell called *To Summon the Forces of Torque*? That's a good one, right?"

"Oh, it's a very useful spell. You know how sometimes you can't get the lid off a jar? When you summon the Forces of Torque, the lid twists right off."

"It's a spell for opening peanut butter?"

"Essentially. And pickles."

To hide my disappointment, I put my face to the pay-per-view binoculars and swiveled them as if I were studying the Davy Tower, four miles away on Gernsback Ridge. I didn't bother to put in a quarter.

"Can you teleport the four of us to Davy's headquarters?" asked Modesty. "Maybe we could sneak around and find out something useful."

"That's not how teleportation works." Pre sighed. "Teleportation breaks something down into its smallest parts—we call them 'atoms'—and sends those atoms somewhere else across a great distance. *But it doesn't put the atoms back together.* Anything you teleport is totally destroyed. That's why the Garbage Magicians use it when they remove our trash from the curb each morning."

"Where does the trash go?" asked Modesty.

"Pluto. We're adding to its mass, trying to make it large enough that it becomes a planet again."

I abandoned the binoculars.

"What about *To Cast a Reflection*?" I asked. "Is that something to do with mirrors?"

"Yes and no." Pre sounded a little embarrassed. "It's mainly used by kids in schoolyard fights, to bounce insults back at bullies. It's also called the *I Know You Are, But What Am I?* spell. Most adults have forgotten the spell even exists. Every kid knows it, though."

"And I suppose *To View Things More Clearly* is a spell for washing windows," Modesty said glumly.

"No," said Pre. "It's a spell that helps you understand things better. Oddly enough, it was invented by a sorceress who was too lazy to wash her windows, but after she used the spell, she realized she didn't *have to* wash them—she just asked the people across the street to paint their house a brighter color."

"It's a spell that makes you *smarter*?" Modesty's voice had an edge to it that set off warning bells in my head.

"Well, sort of." Pre sounded a little uncomfortable. "It would be more accurate to say the spell helps you make better use of the intelligence you've already got. It's for those times when you have a problem to solve but maybe you're tired or not feeling well and you're not thinking as clearly as you usually do."

"My father calls that *coffee*," I said.

"That may be the scientical name for it; I wouldn't know. It only works for a minute or two, and then it can't be used for another twenty-four hours. That's to prevent people from taking unfair advantage during tests and trivia contests."

Our phones said 1:19.

"Let me get this straight," said Modesty. "If, four minutes from now, at one twenty-three, I play the Magic Bite for the incantation *To View Things More Clearly*, it will make me smarter?"

"If you insist on putting it that way. But just a little bit. And only for a minute or two."

"What if Cal plays the Magic Bite for the spell called *To Intensify an Enchantment*?"

"That…might make you even smarter, or it might only make you *mildly* smarter but for a longer period of time. The effect of *Intensify* is hard to predict."

"Either way, it might help me come up with an idea for stopping Elwood Davy from destroying Congroo. I say we try this." Modesty looked from Pre to me.

"Why you?" I asked. "Why do you get to be the one who gets her brain boosted?"

"Because I'm the smartest to begin with."

"Why would you think that?" I squawked.

"Because I came up with the idea, and nobody else did!"

Sometimes she was hard to argue with. Most of the time, actually.

"So right after you play the spell *To Open a Door*,"

said Modesty, "and you get your friend back, then *I* press *To View Things More Clearly* and *you* press *To Intensify an Enchantment*, and I'll become all brainy and figure out exactly what we're going to say to Elwood Davy tomorrow. Agreed?"

"Uh—"

Modesty took my *uh* as a yes.

"All right. We have to be ready. Anything we should know?" She directed the question to Pre.

Pre looked around.

"Close the trapdoor to the stairs," he said. "It's the only door up here, so that will be the one that opens. Make sure you're not standing on it when you play the spell. Unless you want to go flying over the barn."

I undid the hook that latched the open door to the wall and lowered the wooden door until it was flush with the floor.

"Okay," said Modesty. "Now we wait."

I scrolled down to the door-opening spell.

"It only takes three or four seconds for a Magic Bite to play, so we've got plenty of time," Modesty reminded us. "There's no reason to get all tensed up about this."

We got all tensed up about it. We stared at our phones, waiting for the time to advance, and I could tell Modesty was as nervous as I was. My palms got sweaty. Modesty's hands shook a little. She kept flicking the scroll on her phone back and forth between *To View Things More*

Clearly and *To Walk with Stilts*. After what seemed an hour, the phones finally announced 1:23.

I stabbed *To Open a Door*.

Blippity-blippity-blip.

The trapdoor flew open.

I ran to it eagerly and looked down. The stairs were empty.

"He isn't there!" I cried. "It didn't work! I'll do it again—"

"No!" Pre's hand shot out and stopped me from jabbing my phone. "Don't repeat the spell. Your friend may not have tried his side of the spell yet. He has until the end of the minute. Just wait."

We stood, staring expectantly at the hole in the floor.

"While we're waiting," said Modesty, "let's try *my* thing. Scroll up to *Intensify*."

I looked away from the trapdoor long enough to line up the intensification spell. Modesty poised her finger an inch above her phone screen.

DINK-bingle-BONK!

Pre's crystal rang. He pulled it out of his sweatshirt, and the green balloon head of Hemi-Semi-Demi-Director Oöm Lout suddenly loomed over us.

"*Apprentice Arrowshot!*" Lout shouted. "Where are you? I've been trying to reach you all day. I told you to wait in the library. When we got there, the place was deserted! This is insubordination!"

Pre saluted, then stammered, "Hemi-Semi-Femi-uh-Demi-Director Lout. I've made it to the World of Science. My scientist friends and I are working on a way to stop the magic from draining out of Congroo. I'm sorry, but I don't believe it will come back on its own. How many jars of dragon food were you able to transfer from Alkahest's food bin?"

"Alkahest's food bin?" Lout seemed taken aback. "None! That was just a ruse to keep you and your scientist friends where you were."

"Didn't work too well, did it?" Modesty muttered.

"*Return to Congroo at once,*" Lout roared. "The so-called magic drain is fake news. Global cooling is a myth. Colluding with scientists is treason. Listen to me carefully. Magic. Always. Goes. Away. That's my motto. But it comes back! It's a cycle! Return now, and we'll go easy on you. Arrowshot—I have Master Index as my *guest*. Do you understand what that means?"

"You're . . . taking him to dinner?"

"Idiot. It means I have him in my power. If you ever hope to see him again, you'll do as I say!"

Oöm Lout's face winked out. Pre dropped the crystal to his chest as if it had burned his fingers.

"This would be a great time to make me smarter," Modesty announced. She punched her phone—*blippity-brumpity-bork!*—and jabbed me in the ribs with her elbow. I stopped staring at the open trapdoor and pressed my finger down on the intensification spell—*blippity-brap!*

I watched my phone as 1:23 became 1:24.

The trapdoor remained empty.

"I don't feel any different," said Modesty.

"You certainly don't look any smarter," agreed Pre.

The tower shook.

We all froze, as if our movements might have caused it.

Then the tower tilted, and we stumbled across the floor and hit the east wall of the cab. The tower lurched the other way, and the tilt straightened a bit. I scrambled uphill to the west side and looked out.

We were *moving*. My house was gliding by on our right. I jumped halfway down the top flight of the zigzag stairs and grabbed the railing as the tower swayed to the south. Modesty and Pre clambered down behind me.

The tower was walking.

Its four legs—each more than a hundred feet long and made of steel—were taking steps. The two legs on the left bent as if they had knees, and they strode forward together, and all the metal cross braces that linked them to the other legs stretched like rubber bands. Then the two legs on the right lifted off the ground and took their own step, stretching the cross braces again, and moved the tower forward another twenty feet. The zigzag stairway had folded itself upward to half its usual length so it could clear any obstacles. That made it a fifty-foot drop from the bottommost step. Nobody would be getting off.

"Back upstairs," I ordered, and nobody had to be told twice.

"Is this something that Oöm Lout guy is doing to us?" I demanded as we jammed together at the forward-facing window. Pre looked confused.

"You mean the tower isn't supposed to do this? This isn't some scientifical thing?"

"The word is *scientific*, and no, our towers don't do this!"

"*I did this*," Modesty suddenly wailed. She was frowning at her phone. "I must have jogged the screen while Lout-face was talking. I hit the wrong Magic Bite. They were right next to each other."

"What did you hit?"

"*To Walk with Stilts*. And then you intensified it."

"That may be why," said Pre breathlessly, "we're told never to use *Intensify* without adult supervision."

The tower swayed, and its feet, which were blobs of concrete that had been embedded in the ground, made horseshoe-like noises as they clopped across the asphalt of Route 9 and we entered the overflow parking field. For a one-hundred-foot tower wearing cement boots, it moved remarkably quietly. I looked back at my house. The lights were still out.

"I'm sure this is somehow my fault," Pre whimpered. "Magic anywhere near me always goes awry."

"The Magic Minute's over," I muttered. "Why are we still moving?"

"It must be like the coins after the coin-gathering spell," said Modesty as the tower lurched to the right and she grabbed the windowsill. "They keep going until they reach their destination."

"So what's our destination?" I wondered, and it came out shriller than I meant it to.

We peered into the darkness ahead of us. The parking lot gave way to the wheat field. The tower leaned to one side to avoid stepping on the remains of the Fireball 50, then adjusted its path and continued on.

It was the same field Pre and I had walked across that afternoon. Meaning the Fireball 50 wasn't the only unsightly monstrosity in it. Directly ahead of us, a line of latticework metal towers was silhouetted against the distant glow of downtown Disarray.

"Oh *euphemera*!" I said.

"What are those things?" asked Pre.

I gulped. I did a quick calculation in my head. Our fire tower was a hundred feet tall. The power lines… were stretched across our path about eighty feet above the ground.

"They're called high-tension towers," I said. "It's too dark to see, but there are wires strung between them. The wires carry high-voltage electricity."

"High-voltage electricity?"

"Lightning bolts! And we're walking straight at 'em!"

CHAPTER 18

A WALK ON THE WILD SIDE

I f we hit those wires—" I said, but didn't finish. There was no point in stating the obvious. If we hit the wires and they broke, we would be electrocuted. If they didn't break, the tower could easily topple backward and we'd fall a hundred feet.

"Should we jump?" asked Modesty as she leaned too far out the window. I grabbed her by a belt loop and hauled her back, just as the tower started to tilt again. We both staggered to the opposite wall. The rickety table, some loose Cheerios, and the carrot-crown box slid there with us. Preffy clung to one of the roof supports, lost his grip, and landed next to us.

The tower continued to tilt.

"Oh…em…gee!" Modesty screamed, and clutched the window frame. "Hold on! *It's…it's doing the limbo!*"

The fire tower bent backward until the floor of the cab went from horizontal to vertical. The east wall became our floor, and we had to catch ourselves before we fell out the window.

Modesty was right. The fire tower was doing the limbo. It had bent back almost double, and it was taking waddling baby steps to inch its way under the overhanging electric cables. In some places, the tower wasn't quite low enough, and it brushed against the wires, strumming them as if they were guitar strings. They vibrated with weird *twang*s that sounded like calypso music.

Stray Cheerios rolled out the window and fell to the ground fifty feet below, like sweat dropping off an actual limbo dancer. Then the box containing the carrot crown tumbled end over end and followed the Cheerios. Modesty lunged and caught it, but too much of her went out the window, and I jumped and snagged her by the pants before she fell headfirst into the wheat field. Pre and I dragged her back. She clutched the dented box to her chest.

The tower jiggled to and fro and then, finally, returned to its original height after passing completely under the wires and finishing the dance. It started striding forward again. It seemed a little jauntier, as if it had won a contest.

"Where does it think it's going?" muttered Modesty, as if she wanted to have a word with it.

We crowded together at the front window again. The tower picked its way through the trees at the edge of the field, then walked down an embankment to the railroad tracks that ran along the south side of Disarray. It began strolling along the tracks.

"If there's no food for Phlogiston," said Pre, seemingly oblivious to anything being out of the ordinary, "then Phloggie's had her last meal. She'll barely last another day!"

"That's not going to happen," Modesty assured him. "We're going to work this out. No dragons are going to go extinct on my watch!"

"Yeah," I agreed. "If my best friend is going to be marooned in the World of Magic, I want to make sure there's some magic there for him to enjoy."

"I'm sure there's a perfectly good reason Drew missed the Magic Minute," Modesty said.

"Yeah, it would be just like him to get distracted. We'll try again at two thirty-four. At least we know he's not in the hands of Oöm Lout. Lout said the library was deserted when they got there. Drew must have hid."

I knew I might be kidding myself. I knew Lout could have Drew and might be torturing him to find out everything Drew knew about the World of Science. Or Drew might have been injured and was unable to use his phone. Or Drew was hiding out in the library and had gotten engrossed in a good book. If he was reading the Mary Potter septology, I'd probably never see him again.

I would retry the door-opening spell at 2:34.

We came up on the Disarray train station, which was the closest the tracks got to the center of town. The streetlamps beyond the station bathed Main Street in a silvery light, so anybody who happened to be around at one thirty in the morning would have no trouble noticing a fire tower out for a walk along the train tracks. We weren't even leading a doghouse on a leash as a good cover story.

Fortunately, Main Street was deserted. As we strode past, the tower's clunky feet were reflected in the windows of the hardware store, then the bank, then Baba Yaga's Frozen Yogurt Shop, where something in the wavy glass distorted the feet and made them look like chicken legs. Then downtown was behind us, and we were following the tracks into the woods to the west.

In the distance, a train whistle wailed mournfully.

"What was that?" Pre asked.

"Uh..." said Modesty.

"Look," I said after thinking about it for a moment. "It didn't step on the farm stand; it limboed under the electric lines; I'm *sure* it's going to know enough to get out of the way of an oncoming train!"

"You think?" said Modesty. "What if we meet it at Deadman's Curve? The train's hidden by the bend there.

189

By the time you see it, it's on you. There's a reason it's called Deadman's Curve!"

"Yeah," I said. "It was named after Albert Deadman. He used to own the farm where the curve is."

"*That's not the point*," hollered Modesty. "We have to figure out how to control this thing. We can't just let it kidnap us!"

"It *must* be able to hear the train coming," I said as the whistle sounded again, noticeably louder.

"With what?" Modesty demanded. "Where are the ears on a fire tower? Maybe if we all throw our weight to one side, we can get it off the tracks!"

She threw herself against the wall on the right. A moment later, Pre and I did the same. The tower continued to stride purposefully down the tracks, with its two left feet dead center. A hit by a locomotive would shred it and send us falling to our deaths.

"Maybe we can control it by ESP," Modesty said breathlessly. "Maybe if we all *think*, as hard as we can, '*get off the tracks!*' "

There was a moment of silence as we did this. Faint light wavered in the trees to our left, cast by something unseen around the bend. The whistle blew again, much, much louder.

"Sounds like a *very* big owl," said Pre.

The tower didn't deviate.

"*Do something!*" screamed Modesty.

I decided to hurl myself against the left wall, in case it worked better than hurling myself against the right. I turned, took a step, and collided with the pay-per-view binoculars. I staggered back, turned to go around the metal post the binoculars were mounted on, and stopped. Usually the binoculars swiveled easily. I had hit them hard, and they hadn't budged.

Suddenly the light in the trees was very bright, and the hoot of a two-hundred-ton owl filled the night. I grabbed the binoculars on either side and twisted with all my might. They slowly turned.

The tower stepped in the direction I had turned them.

We left the tracks just as the 1:35 from Pratchettsburg came barreling around the bend. The wind from the speeding train buffeted the trees, and the base of the tower trembled.

"This is the steering wheel," I announced breathlessly, and twisted the binoculars a little more to the right. The tower obligingly altered its course.

"How do you put it in *Park*?" demanded Modesty.

"I have no idea."

The tower walked alongside the tracks as the train rumbled past. In less than a minute, the train was gone, and I let go of the binoculars to see what would happen. The lenses swung back to their original position, but the tower continued past Deadman's Curve straight ahead into the trees.

"It still wants to go wherever it thinks it's going," I said.

"We should use the steering thingy and force it to go back to the farm," said Modesty, punching her carrot-crown box back into shape.

"What if we do that," I said, "and once we get there, we stop steering and the thing turns around and comes back here? We have no idea how to stop it." I turned to Pre. "Will it stop automatically when we get to the next Magic Minute?"

"Not if it hasn't reached its destination. The spell has to run itself out."

I checked my phone.

"It's one thirty-eight," I said. "The next Magic Minute is two thirty-four. We've got almost an hour. Now that we know we can steer the tower away from danger, we should probably wait and see where it's going."

"What if it's going to Hawaii or someplace like that?" Modesty grumbled.

"Why would it go to Hawaii?" I asked.

"It did the limbo. Maybe it likes to hula."

I reviewed everything we had done since we had joined Pre in the cab. "The last place I pointed the binoculars at was the Davy Tower," I said, and got the distinct feeling I was onto something.

"You think that's where we're going?"

"Look where we are already," I said.

We were crossing Oakhurst Road, right at the spot where a sign saying WELCOME TO DISARRAY PLEASE DRIVE CAREFULLY used to be before a truck hit it. A mile farther along Oakhurst was Disarray Middle, where Modesty, Drew, and I went to school.

The tower crossed the road and started climbing Gernsback Ridge.

It was a gentle slope, and the tower was easily twice the height of any of the trees on it. The autumn air was crisp, the full moon had risen, and the view was an ocean of treetops. It reminded me of the SAVE THE RAIN FORESTS poster in Modesty's kitchen. At the top of the ridge, the glass rectangle of Davy's Digital Vegetables blocked out part of the star-filled sky. It was probably the way the iceberg had looked from the bridge of the *Titanic*.

"You're awfully quiet," Modesty said to Pre.

"I'm worried about Master Index," Pre replied. He was leaning against one of the four wooden posts that supported the cab's roof, with one arm wrapped around it and his cheek pressed glumly against it. "Ever since my parents died, he's been like a father to me."

"*Both* your parents are dead?" Modesty said softly.

"When I was four," Pre murmured, "something spooked the horse of the carriage they were riding. My mother had the reins, and she was good with horses, but the wheels caught the edge of the embankment, and over they went. I was in an orphanage for two years, and then, after I scored exceptionally low on my SATs—Sorcery Aptitude Tests—I was apprenticed to the Librarians Union."

I suddenly felt that my problem with the Fireball 50

wasn't anywhere near as horrible as I thought it was. There were worse things.

"I've been with Master Index half my life," Pre continued. He sniffed and hugged the post a little tighter.

"I'm sure Master Index will be fine," Modesty assured him.

The tower shifted to the right to avoid a clump of trees, and suddenly the DDV building was directly ahead of us. The central ten-story glass tower, built on the site of the house Elwood Davy had grown up in, was flanked on one side by a four-story wing where they built DavyTrons and on the other by a three-story wing where they made tomato juice. I found myself wishing I had paid more attention during our school trip to the place. All I could remember was not wanting to drink the free sample.

The fire tower stepped, *clippity-clop*, into the deserted parking lot and approached the main entrance.

A big glass greenhouse, five stories high, stuck out from the front of the building and covered the entrance lobby. Through the glass, we could see the reception desk and, behind it, Elwood Davy's parents' house and the garage, where he had invented the DavyTron. A lawn surrounded the house; on the day of my field trip, a tour guide pretending to be Davy's father had been mowing it. He had invited us in and showed us the house, including the apartment above the garage where Elwood had lived and the workbench where he had created his first carrot.

"We're going to hit the glass!" shouted Modesty as the fire tower strode straight for the greenhouse.

But at the last moment, the tower sidestepped and waded into a flower bed. It came within five feet of the sheer glass front of the building and stopped, the lower edge of the cab's windowsill level with the parapet that ran around the building's roof.

"Wow," said Modesty. "If the gap wasn't so wide, we could just step across."

The fire tower settled more deeply into the pachysandra. It tilted forward, and the five-foot gap became five inches.

"Oh," said Modesty. "Yes. Better. Thanks."

The top of the building was a rooftop garden. Trees in huge pots surrounded a central, bubbling fountain, and beyond the fountain, sliding glass doors marked the entrance to a rooftop office, which glowed with a pale-purple night-light that silhouetted a big, important-looking desk.

"So *this* was the destination," said Modesty.

"It's the place the binoculars were pointed at when you played the Magic Bite for walking with stilts," I replied.

"And you *intensified* it," she reminded me, as if she thought we were both responsible. "So the tower's not going to move again until we tell it to?" She looked at Pre.

"Probably not," he said. "But then, everything in your world is so unpredictable."

Modesty consulted her phone. "It's a little after two o'clock. We've got half an hour until the next Magic Minute."

I dug into my pocket and pulled out some coins, ignoring a couple that fell to the floor, and put a quarter into the pay-per-view binoculars. I grabbed the thing I thought of as the *space-alien head* and twisted it by the ears. It moved much more easily than it had when the tower had been in motion. I leaned in to the eyepieces and looked across the valley, adjusting the lenses until I found the Halloween lights of Sapling Farm. I made sure they were dead center.

"If we repeat the spell at two thirty-four," I said, carefully letting go of the binoculars, "it should take us home. And we'll get Drew back at the same time."

"So," said Pre. "What do we do now that we've reached the abode of the evil scientist who's draining all the magic out of my world?"

"Do you think there's an alarm?" Modesty reached out and put her hand on the edge of the parapet.

"I would think," I said, trying to be as logical as I could, "most of the security would be on the first few floors, where it's easier to break in. They might also have some sort of radar, to warn about a helicopter trying to drop somebody on the roof. But I don't think they would have worried much about somebody coming in sideways."

"Good enough for me," said Modesty, tucking the carrot-crown box under one arm, then boosting herself through the window, over the parapet, and into the garden beyond.

CHAPTER 19

SQUISHY FISHY FUN PARK

We watched for a moment to see if Modesty would walk through any laser beams. She didn't, which was encouraging. I gave Pre a boost over the windowsill, clambered over myself, and the two of us joined Modesty at the fountain in the roof garden's center.

"That *has* to be Elwood Davy's office," Modesty said, nodding at the glass doors. "Who else would have a place at the very top of the building? With its own fountain? If we can get in, we've got it made."

"How do you figure?" I asked as I looked around for security cameras.

"We'll leave the carrot crown on his desk," Modesty explained, taking a few cautious steps forward. "With a note, saying it's from us. Then we show up tomorrow, identify ourselves, and he rushes down to the lobby to meet us, because he's so curious about how we managed to leave him such an amazing gift. Then we change the color of the lobby, or, or we open a jar of pickles—no, that's no good—or we...we materialize a storm cloud! Yeah, perfect, we materialize a cloud right there in the lobby and we make it rain on his old house, and that convinces him magic exists, and that we can do it, and if he doesn't help us save the dragons and save Congroo, we'll turn him into a newt."

"That's your plan?" said Pre.

"Wouldn't it be better to ask him nicely first?" I suggested. "Before threatening him with the turning-into-a-newt thing?"

"There's no such spell," Pre informed us.

"He doesn't know that," said Modesty. "I mean, we can't threaten to get gum out of his carpets. What kind of a threat would that be?"

"We probably shouldn't threaten him at all," I persisted.

"And the storm-cloud spell never involves rain," Pre added. "It's mainly to provide shade on a hot day when you're working in the fields."

"You people have the *worst* magic," Modesty muttered.

As she reached for one of the sliding glass doors, my phone said, "Ring, ring."

Modesty paused with her hand outstretched.

"Ring, ring," my phone repeated.

"Uhhh...could you get that? Please? Before I try to open this? It might be...you know...*helpful*."

"Is that Delleps *again*?" Pre couldn't hide his amazement.

"It's her ringtone," I acknowledged. I was stalling before I answered because I needed to get my wits together. My wits, as far as I could tell, were all over the place, like spilled Cheerios.

"How can she communicate with the World of Science when this isn't a Magic Minute?" Pre wondered.

"She's done it before," said Modesty. "It might be because our phones are jam-packed with magic spells. Or it might be because she's the greatest of all your oracles. That's what you said, right?"

"Hello," I answered at the last second. You didn't let the greatest oracle in Congroo go to voice mail.

"Thank you for using the Congroo Help Line," said Delleps. "I would list our options, but we're pretty much out. How may we assist you?"

"What's the most important thing we need to know at this particular moment?" I asked. I was becoming an old hand at talking to oracles.

"I was hoping you'd ask. Listen carefully."

I hit *Speakerphone*, and her voice filled the garden.

"The glass will slide but you'll have to hide and you're starting to alarm me; the quest will fail and wrong prevail if you don't make time for the army."

I waited, as usual, in case there was more. As usual, there wasn't.

"That's...pretty cryptic," I told her.

"It's not as urgent as some of the others," Delleps said. "But I wouldn't dillydally if I were you."

I wanted to get more information from her, but I knew a second question would end the call.

"We're all hoping Master Index is all right," I stated.

"He's been better," said Delleps.

"Can you get a message to him?" Pre asked eagerly.

"Sorry. Only one question per call."

Click.

Pre's shoulders slumped.

Modesty said, "Is she telling us we're not going to be able to handle this ourselves? We're going to have to call in the army?"

"I'm not sure," I said. "Delleps always makes more sense after it's too late."

"That's how oracles work," said Pre.

"She said not to dillydally." Modesty snorted. "And she also said *the glass will slide.*"

She reached forward, inserted her fingers into a slot in the doorframe, and dragged the glass open. If an alarm went off somewhere, we didn't hear it.

"Indoor voices," Modesty ordered as she turned sideways to fit through the narrow slot she had made. Pre and I followed her in, and the lights got brighter.

"I hope that's automatic," said Modesty, "like the hallway lights at school."

"Delleps said we'd have to hide," I reminded her, looking around for possible places of concealment.

The lights revealed an office with a big stone fireplace at one end and an inflatable clear plastic sofa at the other. Above the mantel hung a portrait of Elwood Davy. The portrait didn't show his ears sticking out the way they really did and gave him a little more hair on top than he actually had, but otherwise, it looked exactly like him. Behind the sofa was an elevator, and next to the elevator was a circular hole in the wall with vertical handrails on either side of it. It reminded me of the top of the waterslide at Squishy Fishy Fun Park. I wondered if it was some kind of air vent or if Elwood Davy sometimes left his office through a water-park slide.

"Certainly looks like a boss's office," said Modesty, sidling behind the desk and putting the carrot-crown box in the center. She opened a drawer and rummaged in it, then pulled out a piece of paper and a felt-tip marker. She thought for a moment, then began to write, squeakily.

A second, smaller desk next to the mysterious hole in the wall held a computer screen and a keyboard. The screen saver showed vegetables swimming in a fish tank. A carrot wiggled by like an eel; a cauliflower quivered past like a jellyfish. I sat down, tapped the touch pad, and the veggie fish vanished. The new screen invited me to enter my password and press my thumb to a picture of a fingerprint.

Dead end.

I stood back up.

"There," said Modesty. She held up her note and read it to us.

> Dear Mr. Davy,
>
> We made this carrot crown as a special gift for you.
>
> We hope to see you later today.
>
> Your ~~friends,~~
> Modesty Brooker
> Calvin Sapling
> & Preffy Arrowshot

She placed the note next to the crown.

"Is this a scientifical—uh, scientific—stairway? No steps?" Pre was leaning into the hole in the wall. I walked over and leaned in next to him. The shiny metal tube curved down and to the right.

"Some companies," I said, "try to be fun places to work. So they do things like let their workers ride bicycles in the building, or they have indoor playgrounds or Ping-Pong tables on the roof."

"This slide probably goes down to a lunchroom,"

Modesty decided. She leaned in and sniffed. "Smells like french fries."

"It could also be a trash chute," I said, although I didn't smell anything. Modesty was probably hungry.

The elevator made a noise.

We all looked in its direction. Above the door, a row of numbered lights indicated what floor the elevator was on. The 1 winked out as we watched; then the 2 flickered on and off, followed by the 3, the 4, the 5...

"That's a really fast elevator," I said.

"Hide!" whispered Modesty.

The three of us took a step in three different directions. Then we froze as we all realized the same thing. There was no time to run back to the fire tower and not enough hiding places for all of us in the room. The transparent sofa didn't help.

"Fazam!" said Pre.

"You think this goes to a lunchroom?" I leaned into the pipe.

"It might," said Modesty.

She pushed past me, sat on the edge of the hole, and swung in her feet.

The light above the elevator said 10. Something went *ding*, and the elevator began to open.

Modesty gave herself a shove and disappeared down the tube. Pre leaned in to see where she went, and I nudged him just enough to send him sliding after. I grabbed the handrails, lifted myself up, and followed my feet down the hole.

It was like being swallowed by a big metal snake that had gotten its tail caught in a propeller: It kept corkscrewing. We started to pick up speed, and I realized that if the slide was longer than a floor or two, and our speed continued to grow, we could get seriously hurt when we shot out the bottom.

Especially if the bottom let out in a dumpster.

Dim little lights in the ceiling flickered by, faster and faster. I jammed my hands and feet against the metal walls in an attempt to slow myself. I watched the distance between my feet and Pre's head grow to about a foot.

"Slow yourselves down!" I shouted, and the tunnel acted as a megaphone. Pre started doing the same thing I was, and the distance between him and Modesty began to increase.

There was a small bump, and suddenly the metal tube became a clear plastic tube, and we could see what we were passing through. We spiraled down through a conference room with cauliflower-print wallpaper, then through a laboratory where test tubes overflowed with what looked like spinach, then a cafeteria where the chair legs looked like celery stalks, then a huge room full of cubicles with desk lamps shaped like avocados.

Then we ran out of rooms altogether and spiraled down through the ceiling of the lobby.

The lobby was five stories high. I could see the end of our chute through the clear plastic.

It was only ten feet ahead of us.

Directly beneath us was a three-story drop to the roof of Elwood Davy's house. The roof didn't look soft and spongy. It was all angles and hard edges.

Elwood Davy's house was going to kill us.

Modesty sailed out of the end of the chute first, followed immediately by Pre. I flipped to my stomach and tried to grab the rim around the tube's end as it shot past but couldn't.

We were in free fall.

CHAPTER 20

NOT A MARTIAN DEATH MACHINE

Most of the time we had been in the tube, we had been screaming.

That had only been a rehearsal.

We plummeted and screamed loud enough to be heard back at Sapling Farm. We fell through the open air of the building's huge lobby, and beneath us, the roof of Elwood Davy's old house got bigger and bigger, the way an approaching flyswatter must look to a fly.

But then, somehow, Pre was no longer trailing Modesty—he was suddenly *beside* her—and I was beside Pre. And in the next instant, a giant invisible hand caught me, and all three of us were beside one another. We were all still falling, but much more slowly, until the net we had dropped into stretched to its limit and our noses were only inches away from the shingles on the roof. Some of those shingles needed replacing.

Then the net bounced back, and we rose with it; then the net dropped again, and we fell a bit. We waffled up and down until the net, more or less, came to a halt. It was the kind of net you saw in a circus, beneath the trapeze artists. It was big and stretchy and tied to four tall metal poles that stuck up from the corners of the lawn surrounding the house.

Those of us who had landed on our backs flipped to our stomachs, and the three of us studied the scene below. We were suspended about ten feet above the roof of the two-story house, but I could see a rope ladder dangling from one side of the net, so I wasn't too worried about how we were going to get down. What I was worried about was the guy in the hammock.

He was wearing plaid shorts and a Hawaiian shirt and had a straw hat pulled down over his face. He appeared to be sleeping. His hammock was on a raised deck just outside the house's back door, along with some lawn furniture and a circular table with a bright-red umbrella sticking out of the center.

"That's got to be a dummy," whispered Modesty. "Nobody could have slept through our screaming. Or maybe he's dead. *Eeeep!*"

The guy in the hammock pushed his hat back and looked up at us through dark sunglasses.

"Hi there," he said. "You'll be pleased to hear I'm not dead. And I wasn't in the middle of a nap. To be perfectly honest, I stretched out here to wait for you."

"You were expecting us?" Pre sounded as surprised as I was.

"You're not exactly masters of stealth," he informed us. "Why don't the three of you make your way down the ladder and join me? I'll fetch us some lemonade."

He swung himself out of the hammock and strolled to the back door. In the time it took us to cross the net, with all its wobbling, and descend the ladder, with all its jiggling, he had set out a tray with four tall glasses and a frosty pitcher.

"Do we run?" asked Pre, the last to step off the ladder.

"Where to?" I asked.

"He seems friendly enough," said Modesty. "At least he's not dressed as a security guard."

"How would a security guard dress in a place with a theme-park slide spiraling down the middle of it?" I asked.

We crossed the lawn, kicked aside a stray soccer ball, carefully picked our way through the wickets and mallets of an abandoned croquet game, and joined our mystery man on the deck. As we approached, he took off his dark glasses and removed his hat.

Revealing the face of Elwood Davy.

"So nice of you to drop in," he said, and gestured for us to join him at the table.

We climbed three steps to get to him. The house was dark, except for a light in the kitchen and another in one of the basement windows.

"I sent the elevator up for you." He waved a hand at the three empty chairs across from him. Each had a glass of lemonade in front of it. "But I'm glad you chose the slide; it's so much more fun. Although, to be honest, it was designed more for adults than for kids. It can be a bit frightening. All the employees voted on how it should end. It was either the free-fall drop into the trapeze net or a shorter drop onto a trampoline that would have been angled to bounce you into a swimming pool. Which would you have preferred?"

"Uh…the net was…fine," I said. The others nodded.

"Great! Wonderful! We've tried so hard to make the work environment a fun place to be. Did you know everybody who works for Amazon gets their own pogo stick? And the Microsoft cafeteria has Fudge Brownie Fridays? And the Oompa-Loompas at WonkaCorp get a really nice retirement package? It has a crank on the side, and when you turn it, a clown pops out of the top."

"What does?" Pre asked.

"The retirement package. Do sit down. You have so much to tell me."

Modesty pushed past me to take the seat directly across from our host. Pre and I settled in on either side of her. No one touched the lemonade.

"We brought you a crown made out of carrots," Modesty said proudly.

"You did?"

"Well, *mainly* carrots. With a few parsnips. We left it in the office on top of the building. We didn't expect you to be here. Actually, we didn't expect to be here ourselves. We were sort of kidnapped."

"You're going to have a hard time believing what we have to tell you," I said.

"Oh, you'd be surprised what I'm willing to believe." He took a sip of his drink and smacked his lips. "I already know, for instance, that the three of you are extraordinary children. You are either from some other planet or you've somehow *mastered the powers of magic*."

None of us moved. We stared across the table at him.

"How do you know?" I asked. It came out as a whisper.

"I saw you arrive. Imagine my surprise. I was sitting at the reception desk, reading a book, when I happened to look up, and I saw the trees shaking at the far end of the parking lot. I assumed, maybe, it was the work of a particularly large squirrel, and I returned to my book— I'm reading Mr. H. G. Wells's *The War of the Worlds*. It's the one where Martians invade Earth and walk around in three-legged towers destroying everything with heat rays—then I glanced up again, and a Martian death machine was walking across the parking lot straight at me. I wasted no time falling off my chair."

"When was this?" asked Pre, sounding alarmed.

"Just now."

"*The Martians invaded Earth?*" Pre jumped out of his chair. "Are they still upset about Jupiter? They said they were cool with it!"

Our host stared at him. "You really aren't from around here, are you?"

I tugged on Pre's shirt. "*War of the Worlds* is fiction."

"Oh. *Fictional* Martians. That's all right, then." He plopped back down.

"As I was saying, I thought a Martian was after me, but when I peeked over the desk in abject terror, I realized it was just a forest-fire lookout tower—the fourth leg gave it away, along with the cabin at the top with the three of you leaning out of it. I said to myself, this is either science unknown here on Earth or an example of powerful magic." He reached forward and twisted his lemonade glass a quarter of a turn. "So. Which is it?"

"*Magic!*" the three of us shouted simultaneously.

"That's three votes for magic." He twisted the glass back the way it had been. "I've always suspected magic might exist. Please tell me all about it."

"Well, this is certainly going to be a lot easier than we

thought." Pre sighed with relief. "I guess the best place to start would be Congroo. That's where I come fr—"

"Hold on!" Modesty's hand shot out and gripped Pre by the wrist. "Before we tell you anything, I have a question."

"Certainly. If you'd like to borrow *War of the Worlds*, I'll be happy to lend it to you as soon as I've finished reading."

"That's...not my question. My question is, let's say you're running a big company, and the company makes, oh...*croquet mallets*, and one day you find out that every time you make a croquet mallet, a tree in a rain forest dies. And you make so many croquet mallets that all the trees are dying and the rain forests are drying up and everything that lives in them is going extinct, including plants and dragons and, well, maybe not *dragons* but *animals* that help the entire world because they're sources of medicine and oxygen and, and, well, *beauty* just for beauty's own sake. They're all going to die. Because you're making croquet mallets. What do you do?"

The man sitting across from us stroked his chin.

"Why would it take an entire tree to make a single mallet?" he asked.

"They're very big mallets," Modesty replied crossly. "Answer the question."

"Well, morally and ethically..."

"That's a good start."

"Morally and ethically, if I were running a company that was doing this, I would have to stop production of croquet mallets. Maybe...I'd start making baseball bats."

"*No*," shouted Modesty. "You don't have an alternative. You either make mallets or you go out of business. The rain forests are dying."

"Then...I guess...I go out of business."

"Good answer. Okay, we tell him."

We told him.

Not in any straightforward way, and not without interrupting one another and correcting one another and repeating, using different words, something that one of us had already said. Pre described Congroo and the idea of Adjacent Worlds and why there are so many books about librarians—which I thought was a little off topic—and how DavyTrons were doing *transmutation* and draining all the magic out of Congroo. Then Modesty told about finding the notebook and our first meeting with Pre, with special emphasis on how she destroyed the Dust Devil with a can of anti-cling spray. And I—finally—summed it all up by saying how important it was that all the Davy-Trons be shut down and no new ones be made.

Not one of us mentioned how magic worked for only five minutes each day. In fact, the way we had told our story, we sort of *implied* we could do magic anytime we wanted. Apparently, each of us had decided that the fewer people who knew which minutes were magic, the better. We were thinking as one.

Which was a little scary.

The last thing I said was, "And I know this might sound selfish, what with the fate of an entire world at stake, but if the DavyTrons stop making digital vegetables, it would also save my family's farm. We're getting less and less customers, and we're going to have to sell the place. To *you*."

"Oh," said our host. "If your family's farm is about to be purchased by Davy's Digital Vegetables, that must mean your last name is... Alvarez?"

"Uh, no—"

"Bonheur?"

"No—"

"Chung? Denovich? Fujiwara? Gupta? Horowitz? Littlefeather?"

After each name, I shook my head.

"MacDonald? Nnamani? O'Keefe? Papadopoulos? Renshaw? Sapling?"

"Yes! Sapling!"

"Ah, yes. Sapling. I should have started with Zefferelli and worked my way back."

"All those families are losing their farms?" I asked.

"This week. Yes. And while it's a pity that this is happening to so many of you, you have to admit, compared to what's happening to this world of Congroo, your misfortunes are nowhere near as bad."

"They're bad enough," I said angrily.

"So you believe us," said Pre, sounding hopeful.

"Oh yes. Of course I do." He stared into his lemonade and frowned. "Although I wouldn't have believed a word of it if I hadn't seen you arrive in an ambulatory fire-watch tower."

"Not ambulatory," I corrected him. "State Forestry Service."

"It *walked* here," he replied.

"It sure did," I agreed.

"So?" Modesty pressed her fists down on the table and leaned halfway across it. "Are you going to shut this place down? *Or…* are you going to put a lot of farmers out of work and force the population of an entire world back into the Dark Ages?"

"Oh, I would shut this place down in a heartbeat—I understand everything you've told me, and I agree it's a terrible situation—but I can't. It's not mine to shut."

"What do you mean?" I squawked. "This is your company."

"It's not."

"You're Elwood Davy."

"No."

"We've seen you on television," said Modesty. "There's a picture of you in your office."

"It's not my office, and that's not my picture. I am *not* Elwood Davy."

I was getting tired of being on the wrong side of the looking glass. Just once, I wanted people—and inanimate objects—to behave the way I expected them to. I understood life could be random, but things were getting ridiculous.

"Then...*who are you*?" I demanded.

He stretched his arms out to either side and grinned a grin that would have reached to his fingertips if his cheeks hadn't been there to stop it.

"*I...am an impostor!*"

CHAPTER 21

HOUSE TOUR

"We really should have introduced ourselves right off the bat," said the man who wasn't Elwood Davy. "I have you at a disadvantage, and it's entirely my fault. I apologize. I learned *your* names as you told your story—it was inevitable, since you thought it was so important that I should know who did what and who said something especially stupid—but I was remiss in not identifying myself the moment we met. My name is"—his eyes flicked across the lawn—"Spalding Wicket."

"Are you a Quieter?" Preffy asked suspiciously, apparently forgetting our word for *police.*

"A quieter what? I'm more of a blabbermouth than anything. I find conversation absolutely fascinating. I portray Elwood Davy when tour groups come to the house. Actually, I'm supposed to portray him the way he was four years ago, just before he invented the DavyTron, but he looked pretty much the same then as he does now. That's my job. Have any of you ever taken the tour?"

"You're saying you're *not* Elwood Davy?" I stared him in the eyes. He didn't blink.

"I assure you, I am not."

"You say your name is *Spalding Wicket*," I said. "Really? You're sure about that? Spalding, as in…the name on the soccer ball out there on the lawn? Next to the *wicket*?"

"Life would be awfully dull without coincidences." He shrugged.

"*I've* been on the factory tour," said Modesty. "When I was in fifth grade. After they took us through the factory, we came here to the house, and a woman pretending to be Elwood Davy's *mother* took over from the tour guide and led us through the house."

"Ah! That would have been Mildred Pinkerton. Such a dear. She's so sweet, hummingbirds hover around her head, trying to get at her earwax. If you saw Mildred, that means you were here on a Tuesday. Tuesday is my day off."

"I was here last year," I said. "There was a guy mowing the lawn, pretending to be Elwood Davy's *father*. He stopped mowing and took the group through the house." That school trip had been three days after I had incinerated the harvester, so the details of the tour were a blur. But I remembered the guy with the mower.

"That would have been Vern Wilson. Very cautious man, Vern—he *staples* sticky notes to things, just to be sure. So if you saw Vern, that means you were here on a Thursday. Thursday is my *other* day off. It's a pity, really. I do a much better tour than either of them. In fact— follow me!"

He pushed his chair back so suddenly it fell over, and he headed for the kitchen.

"That's a very strange scientist," said Pre.

"Not everyone in our world is a scientist," Modesty told him. "They're actually few and far between."

"Then I'm very fortunate to have found you two."

"True," said Modesty. "But about that—"

I glanced at my phone.

"Ten past three!" I was so upset I jumped up, and my chair went over, too. "We missed the two thirty-four Magic Minute! We didn't try to open a door for Drew! He might have been trying from his side. I screwed up again!"

"Set your alarm," said Modesty.

"What?"

"Set your alarm for the next Magic Minute. So we don't miss it. And...don't just set it—change your alarm tone from whatever it is now to the Magic Bite for the door-opening spell. That way, the spell will be cast even if you forget."

"Scientifical," Pre said approvingly.

It took a moment for me to absorb what she had suggested. Then I hugged her.

"Modesty! You are brilliant!"

She looked completely taken aback but then said, "Yes. I am. Please let go."

"Are you coming?" Spalding Wicket leaned back out the door. "I've turned on the animatronic grandfather. He's been updated to say more than four hundred possibly appropriate things!"

He disappeared back into the house. I set my alarm to three forty-five and changed the alarm tone. Then I jammed the phone into my pocket, and we followed Spalding into the kitchen.

The table was set for a family of three. Spalding pointed to one of the chairs and said, "It was here, twenty years ago, that five-year-old Elwood Davy first realized he liked broccoli. None of the other guides include *that* in their tours."

"I can't imagine why," said Modesty.

"Is this you?" Pre asked, squinting at a photograph stuck to the fridge.

"No," answered Spalding. "That's the real Elwood, on the day he graduated from MIT."

"MIT?" Pre's eyes lit up. "Is it truly magicless?"

"That, I imagine, would depend on the instructors.

Those are Elwood's parents on either side of him. That picture was taken only two days before he invented the DavyTron."

"The tour guide who pretends to be his mother doesn't look *anything* like her," I said, leaning against the fridge to study the photo. "And the guy who pretends to be his dad doesn't look like his dad. But *you* look *exactly* like Elwood."

"Weird, isn't it?" said Spalding as he fished a powdered doughnut out of a ceramic jar shaped like a cabbage. He took a bite of the doughnut and continued to talk as he chewed, getting white powder down the front of his shirt. "When Elwood first appeared in the news, after he announced his brilliant invention, all my friends and neighbors said, 'Hey, Spaldy, you look just like this guy. Maybe you should travel to Disarray and see if he'll give you a job.' So I did, and it turned out I didn't look *exactly* like him, but then I got my nose fixed and my hair dyed, and you couldn't tell us apart."

"Getting your nose repaired caused your hair to die?" said Pre, sounding appalled. "Is that why it's so thin?"

Spalding winced. "You're using humor to chide me for the extremes I went to. I understand."

"No, he's just taking you too literally," I explained. "You get used to it."

"Oh." Spalding seemed confused. He blinked several

times as he held the ceramic cabbage out to Modesty. She looked inside and shook her head. Spalding recovered and continued. "Whether you approve or not, the things I did to my appearance worked. Elwood hired me, at first to stand in for him at things he didn't want to attend, like appliance-store openings and that pesky Nobel Prize ceremony, but then, once the factory was in full operation and he decided there were going to be guided tours, he made me the official Elwood Davy for tour groups."

"And you *live* here?" I asked. "In his old house?"

"Of course not. That would be silly." He offered me the jar. I started to reach for a cinnamon doughnut, then thought better of it and pulled my hand back.

"I'm only here tonight because Bert, the security guard, took a sick day," Spalding continued. "I sometimes fill in for him. Elwood has complete trust in me. I think he likes my face."

"Where is Mr. Davy now?" asked Pre.

"Currently, he's away on business in the Champagne region of France."

Spalding offered the jar to Pre, who pulled out a plain doughnut, sniffed it, and took a tentative bite.

"What's Mr. Davy doing in France?" I asked.

"He's buying up all the vineyards so he can tear out the grapes and plant tomatoes. The world will need more and more tomatoes, as more and more DavyTrons go online. Assuming we can't talk him into shutting down his multibillion-dollar company to save a bunch of people he's never heard of."

Spalding plunked the cabbage down on the table, spun on his heel, and darted through the door to the living room. We trailed him. A lifelike mannequin sitting on the sofa swiveled its head as we walked by. Its jaw moved, and it said, "Howdy," which was what I expected it to say, but then it added, "young girl with a determined look," and Modesty stopped in her tracks.

"It can see me?"

"Well enough to see you're a girl who shouldn't be messed with," simpered Spalding, as if it were all his doing. "Granddad here is now hooked in to the mainframe. He can analyze what's in his field of vision. It's cheaper than hiring a tour guide to play Elwood's grandfather. If we had more time, you could actually engage him in conversation."

The animatronic grandpa, who had a face molded to match the face of an old man in a photo hanging on the wall behind him, leaned to one side and looked directly at Pre. "Hi there, youngster in a Goofy sweatshirt!"

Pre stretched out the fabric and stared down at it. "My shirt's goofy?"

"He means the picture," I said.

"Which happens to be *Mickey*," Modesty pointed out.

"Oops," said Spalding. "That's a glitch. He's *supposed* to be able to recognize all six thousand four hundred and

fifty-two copyrighted cartoon characters. *Granddad!*"
The mannequin's head swiveled toward him. "Access code
2-MATE-2. Perform a self-diagnostic. Search for possible
error in cartoon-recognition subroutine. Make all necessary corrections."

"Sure thing, kiddo." Granddad's eyes crossed, his
head bowed, and he started rummaging around in his
inner self.

"Grandfathers only say *kiddo* in old movies," said
Modesty.

"Yes," agreed Spalding. "Elwood's granddad watched
a lot of old movies when he was a boy. He also sometimes
says *daddy-o* and *peachy keen*. Let me show you where
Elwood invented the DavyTron. It's the highlight of the
tour."

He brushed past us, and we followed him down a hall
that connected the house to the garage. A flight of stairs
took us to an apartment with scribbled diagrams stuck
to its walls, tomato plants on the windowsills, and a
desk crowded with a grubby, old computer and loose
electronic parts. A sofa sagged under blankets and what
looked like a pair of leopard-print pajamas, but when you
looked closer, the leopard spots turned out to be pictures
of potatoes.

"This is where he did it." Spalding spread out his
arms and spun around once. "This is where he invented

the hardware. And over here—" He leaned in a doorway, flipped on a light, and revealed a bathroom. "This is where he came up with the computer code to turn tomato juice into turnips!"

"Did he write down the code on that scroll?" Pre asked.

"That's a roll of toilet paper," I said.

Pre's eyes popped. "You need that much?"

"Not usually," said Modesty. "It depends on what Fidelity's put in the chili."

"We think," I said to Spalding, "the nightly Davy-Tron updates might contain a magical incantation for something called *transmutation*. How can we find out?"

"What an extraordinary notion." He gave me a quizzical look. "I *suppose* we could look at the code." He flicked a pair of undershorts off the computer chair and sat. He fumbled with the computer's mouse, then leaned over the keyboard so we couldn't see what he was typing.

"This is the oldest processor on the network," he explained. "They keep it connected for sentimental reasons. But it should still be able to access the mainframe. And...here we go. Easy as pi. Provided you're calculating pi to the four millionth decimal place. There—the code for tonight's DavyTron software update!"

He grabbed a rag and wiped dust off the screen, then moved aside so we could see. Filling the display from top to bottom were lines and lines of stuff that looked like this:

```
( _ ,T,"@N'+,#'/*{}
W+/W#CDNR/
+,{}R/*YAM}+,/*{*+,/W
{%+,/CARROT,/#{L,+,/N{N+,/+
#N+,/#;\#Q#N+,/+KALE#;*+,/'
R:'D*'3,}{W+KW'K:'+}E#';
DQ#'SOY#'+D'K#!/+K#;\Q#'R}E
KK#}WK'RK}PEAS{NL]'/#;#Q
#N')(W'){){CHIVES]'/+#N';D}R
W'I;#){NL]!/N{N#';R{#
TARO{N
L]'/#{L,+'K{RW'IK{;[{NL]'/W
#Q#\ \ TAT SOI# IWK{BEANS{NL]!/
W{%'L##W#' I;;{NL]'/*{Q#'LD;
R'}{NLWB!/*DE}'C;\ {LEEK'-{
}RW]'/+,}#'*}#NC,',#NW]'/+K
D'+E}+;\ #'CHARD#W! NR'/')}
{RL#'{N' ')(!!/"): T<-50?
```

I took the mouse and scrolled down the screen.
And scrolled.
And scrolled.
And scrolled.

"How long does this go on?" I wondered as the same sort of gobbledygook kept rolling past.

"For about half a mile," said Spalding. "At the speed you're scrolling, it will take two hours to reach the end."

I let go of the mouse. "It would be easy to lose an incantation in something that long." I turned to Pre. "You wouldn't happen to *know* the transmutation spell, would you?"

Pre leaned in to study the screen. "Only our master mages know it by heart—it's forty pages long. But every Congruent schoolchild knows the opening lines." He put his hands behind his back, straightened his shoulders, and recited, "Kimbo scalawag fluffernutter yeep; antiphon epsilon bedder cheddar fleep."

"It goes on like that for forty pages?" I asked.

"Pretty much."

"No wonder nobody here ever got magic to work."

Spalding moved back in front of the screen and typed *fluffernutter yeep* into a search field, then tapped the *Return* key.

The transmutation spell was suddenly on the screen.

"That's it!" Pre confirmed.

"So the incantation goes out every night as part of the DavyTron updates," I said. "Does it go out the same time every night?" I turned and looked at Spalding.

"That's…not something I've ever been asked by a

tour group," he said. "But wait a sec—I'll check the tour guide manual." He stood up, pulled a phone from his pocket, and skated his fingers over it. "Ah. Here we go. In the IAQs—the Infrequently Asked Questions—it says the updates are transmitted *every* night, whether there are any changes to the code or not, at *exactly* the same time. It takes forty-five seconds to send the entire update, which, by computer standards, is a huge amount of time."

"What time is *exactly the same time*?" I was positive there were only four possibilities—1:23, 2:34, 3:45, or 4:56, the four Magic Minutes that occurred after dark. Magic wouldn't work at any other time.

Spalding squinted at his phone again.

"Twelve minutes past midnight," he said.

CHAPTER 22

PACIFIST ENFORCEMENT AND CONTROL ENCHANTMENT

*T*welve *twelve?*" Modesty yelled. "That can't be. It makes no sense."

"Why does it make no sense?" Spalding blinked. I didn't blame him for being confused. I knew I was.

"Because—" Modesty caught herself. She couldn't tell him 12:12 wasn't a Magic Minute without explaining Magic Minutes to him, and that was information we had all decided to keep to ourselves.

"Because," I said, "you'd think the updates would go out at a time that was, uh, neat and tidy."

"Neat and tidy?" Spalding shifted his attention to me.

"Like midnight or one AM or maybe even two thirty. Nothing with odd, freaky minutes in it."

"Oh, definitely," Spalding agreed. "I've always thought that times like three oh nine or eleven forty-six were very sloppy. And ten seventeen? A total mess. Still, it says here that the time the updates go out is twelve minutes past twelve. Every night. Who knows how scientists think or why they do the things they do?"

"Scientists are very mysterious people," Pre agreed.

"*So!*" Modesty drew the attention back to herself. "If we delete the transmutation spell from the DavyTron updates, will it stop the magic from draining out of Congroo, warm up the place, and keep the dragons from going extinct?"

"Yes," said Pre eagerly. "I'm *sure* it would do all that. Prevent the spell, prevent the effects!"

"Unfortunately," said Spalding, "we *can't* remove the transmutation spell. The password I entered grants read-only access. We can look at this stuff, but we can't make changes. The only person who could do that is Elwood Davy himself."

"*What?*" Modesty sent Spalding spinning away in his swivel chair and stepped up to the keyboard. She typed frantically. The screen remained unchanged.

"Fazam!" She kicked the table leg.

"But," said Spalding cheerfully, "here's the good news: Elwood will be back tomorrow night around nine o'clock.

He always comes straight to headquarters after his trips—he has a secret luxury apartment on the other side of one of the giant tomato-juice tanks in the factory wing—and I will be there to meet him. I will tell him everything you've told me, about how his life's work is destroying an entire magical world—no offense, but he'll be more apt to listen to a grown-up than to a bunch of children, even if they *have* made him a crown out of carrots—and then, after I've told him *everything*...he'll refuse to believe me."

"That *is* good news!" said Modesty archly.

"How does that help us?" I asked.

"Because *then* you'll come along, oh, let's say around eleven o'clock—a nice neat and tidy time—and you'll do some genuine magic to convince him. You should definitely bring your fire tower. Then, as soon as he's convinced magic exists and Congress is a real place—"

"Congroo," Pre corrected him.

"Congroo, yes. Once he's convinced Congroo is a real place and the DavyTrons are destroying it, I'm sure he'll stop the updates and save your world. He's that sort of guy. An absolute prince."

I gave Modesty a sideways look, and she responded by shaking her head. We were thinking the same thing. We couldn't do magic at eleven o'clock at night. The nearest Magic Minute was more than two hours later at 1:23. Unless 12:12 *was* a genuine Magic Minute, but I wasn't at all sure about that.

"That sounds great!" said Pre. "We'll be here. Congroo is running out of time—delaying any longer than tomorrow night would be fatal. At the very least, I don't think Phlogiston can hold out beyond that. We should get going now"—he waved at a clock on the wall, and I was shocked to see it was already 3:39—"young folk such as ourselves need our sleep. How do we get back to the top of the building? Is there some sort of fun catapult thing?"

"The elevators are behind the reception desk," said Spalding. "I'm not sure how fun they are, but follow me."

He left the room with us right behind him, and a short stroll over the lawn and across the tiled floor of the lobby took us to the elevators.

"You should plan on something spectacular, magic-wise, in addition to arriving in a walking fire tower," Spalding advised us as he ushered us into an elevator, came in behind us, and punched the 10 button. The doors slid shut, and the elevator shot upward.

"Ooh," said Pre, pressing one hand to his stomach and the other to the wall. "Scientifical levitation."

"What I'm saying is," Spalding continued, "you'll have to lay it on thick if you're going to convince Elwood as quickly as possible. Can any of you make balls of fire shoot from the palms of your hands?"

"No," said Modesty, "but I can tell which card's been picked from an ordinary poker deck. As long as it's my deck."

"Um…I might work on that a bit," replied Spalding as the doors opened and we spilled out into the office. The fire tower waited patiently for us at the far side of the roof garden, right where we had left it.

The night had gotten cooler, and it was a relief to get back into fresh air. The three of us clambered over the parapet and dropped into the cab. I kicked the trapdoor shut as soon as I got in.

"I'll see you all tomorrow, then?" said Spalding once we were aboard. "Promptly at eleven PM?"

We nodded.

"And don't come to the main entrance," he added, stepping back from the parapet as if we were about to blast off and he didn't want to get scorched. "Go to the factory wing on the north side. Come in the door marked SERVICE PERSONNEL ONLY. I'll leave it unlocked. That's the closest entrance to Elwood's secret apartment."

My phone was mostly hidden in the palm of my hand. I glanced down at it and discovered it was 3:44.

The clock advanced to 3:45.

Blippity-blippity-blip.

The trapdoor flew open as my phone's alarm automatically played the door-opening spell. I eagerly looked into the opening.

Only stairs.

No Drew.

"Time to go," Modesty announced, and turned her

back on Spalding. She nudged me with her elbow, and I put aside my disappointment—I was still hopeful I would see Drew before the minute ended—and turned the same way she was facing. We pressed ourselves together side by side to form a wall that Spalding couldn't see past, and Modesty took out her phone.

We repeated what we had done the first time we had animated the fire tower. Modesty cued up the stilt-walking incantation and played it—*blippity-brumpity-bork!*— then I hit the intensification spell—*blippity-brap!*—and we waited, knowing it took a few seconds to work.

"Is it something I said?" asked Spalding behind us.

I looked over my shoulder.

"No offense. For the magic to work, we, uh, have to be facing in the direction we want to go."

"Which is away from *you*," Modesty felt compelled to add.

The fire tower lurched. It took a step forward and immediately opened a ten-foot gap between the top of the building and us. We hid our phones and whirled to face Spalding. He looked properly impressed, even if he had seen the tower walk before.

"Bye!" said Pre, and gave a little wave.

"Tomorrow!" Spalding shouted as the distance increased. "Eleven o'clock! At the north entrance!"

His voice dwindled as the tower reached the far edge of the parking lot and plunged into the trees.

I watched my phone as 3:45 became 3:46. I hung my head, and Modesty put a hand on my forearm.

"Reset your alarm for the next Magic Minute," she advised me. "We'll get him back one of these times. I know we will."

I did as she suggested and tried to think of other things.

After a moment, she asked, "Any way we can get back to your farm *without* going through Deadman's Curve?"

I nodded and grabbed the pay-per-view binoculars by the ears, then swiveled the space-alien head to the left. The more I tried to force it, the more resistance it gave; the tower really wanted to go straight to its destination, but it grudgingly altered course enough to go where I pointed the lenses. I found it felt good to actually be in control of something.

"There," I said. "That should take us across the grounds of the middle school and over Campbell Hill to the opposite side of town, where it's all farmland and there'll be less danger of being seen. Then we can cross the tracks at Baily Road."

"That still leaves the power lines," said Modesty.

"Nothing I can do about that. We'll just have to hold tight when the tower dances under." I turned to Pre. "*To Walk with Stilts*!" I said, and he took a step back, as I'd said it rather accusingly. "That's the spell we used, and the tower started walking. We didn't use a spell called

To Make a Tower Walk. Getting the tower to move was an accident. It only happened because the tower's legs are a little like stilts. Am I right?"

He shook his head. "I really don't know. It never would have happened in Congroo. Magic is much more focused there. You usually get what you expect. Except when I use it...."

"Do you remember the burned-out machine you thought had been hit by lightning?" I asked.

He nodded. "Yes—"

"When it burned, it smoked like a chimney. You could see the cloud for miles. If I were to sit in its driver's seat during a Magic Minute and play the Magic Bite called *To Repair a Chimney*, do you think that might fix it? It wouldn't have to be as good as new, just so long as it became a working harvester again."

"I have no idea." Pre looked perplexed. "It might, I suppose, fix it. Or it might turn it into a *real* chimney or a pile of bricks, or it might start the fire all over again. It would be a very dangerous thing to do, especially if you're sitting in the middle of it."

"But it's something I'm going to have to try," I said, feeling hope for the first time since I had set fire to the thing. Maybe I could finally make it up to my folks.

"Anybody besides me think Spalding Wicket might actually be Elwood Davy?" asked Modesty. She had yawned during my conversation with Pre and had now planted her elbows on the forward windowsill and was peering out into the night.

"You think that might have been the *real* Mr. Davy we were talking to?" asked Pre as the tower lurched across the football field behind Disarray Middle. "Why would he pretend to be someone else?"

"He may need time to think about everything we told him," said Modesty. "Claiming to be somebody else could be his way of buying time before he has to make a decision. I mean, if he shuts down the DavyTrons, it saves Congroo, but it also puts him and everyone who works for him out of business."

"It's not a decision he should need any time at all to think about," said Pre defiantly. "It's affecting both our worlds."

"Or," I said, "he may have told us he's an impostor as the best way to hide the fact that *he's an impostor.* He might know we wouldn't believe him and we'd assume he's the real Davy. So he could be messing with our minds bigtime. Anybody else think that returning at eleven tonight and going to the factory entrance sounds a little fishy?"

"What do small fish have to do with it?" Pre inquired.

"He means *suspicious,*" Modesty enlightened him, "and yes, it is suspicious, but I think we're going to have to do it. As Preffy says, Congroo is running out of time. We'll sneak back tonight, earlier than he expects us. Only this time, we'll ride our bikes."

"Yeah," I said. "Nothing says *master magicians* better than three sweaty kids on bicycles."

"Once we're sure we're with the real Mr. Davy," continued Modesty, "all we have to do is keep him talking until one twenty-three rolls around. Then we'll knock his socks off with an intensified *To Materialize a Storm Cloud* spell."

"That spell has nothing to do with removing stockings," Pre informed us. "You're thinking of *To Undress the Feet*, a spell invented by Prince Goldbric the Lazy so he'd never have to bend over again."

The fire tower shifted direction, again lining itself up with Sapling Farm. I threw all my weight at the binoculars, swiveled them, and forced the tower away from its destination. It crossed the rock-strewn gully that separated Gernsback Ridge from Campbell Hill and headed up the slope. Once we were over the hill, I could let it set its own course. We'd be on the less populated side of town.

"Tell us about this Oöm Lout guy," said Modesty. "What makes him such a creep?"

"I've never thought of him as a creep," said Pre. "Although his treatment of Master Index is worrisome, and his shortsightedness with regard to Phlogiston's feeding is vexing. I'm sure he's reconsidered since we spoke."

"Didn't sound like he would." Modesty snorted.

"No, Oöm Lout isn't necessarily *bad*," Pre continued.

"He's just somebody you can't argue with. Of all the Louts, he's the biggest."

"There's more than one?" I asked.

"The Louts have been a powerful family for decades. They made most of their money building livery stables, slaughterhouses, and casinos. Oöm Lout himself, though, isn't much interested in those things. When he's not at Weegee Board meetings, he spends most of his time doing Goblin War reenacting. He dresses up like one of the original Goblin War generals and commands a bunch of volunteers who dress up like his troops. They run around on some of the original battlefields and pretend to fight with cardboard replicas of the old shields and swords. It's a silly hobby, but at least it keeps him out of the Weegee Board a few days each week."

"Goblin War?" I asked.

"Named after Beatrice Goblin, usurper of the throne of Congroo nine hundred years ago. The Goblin Wars were fought shortly before the people of Congroo mastered magic and created PEACE. That's the Pacifist Enforcement and Control Enchantment, an ongoing spell that prevents troops from using lethal weapons. The Second Goblin War was our final war. We've had PEACE ever since."

The tower tottered a bit as it made its way around a rocky outcropping halfway up Campbell Hill. We all steadied ourselves.

"How many reenactors does Oöm Lout play soldier with?" I asked, feeling it might be important. Fearing it, actually.

"Oh, it varies, but according to the last thing I read, there's about a quarter million of them."

"That's a lot of troops," said Modesty.

"I guess a lot of people like to dress up and run around waving cardboard weapons."

"What happens to the Pacifist Enforcement and Control Enchantment when all the magic disappears from Congroo?" I asked.

Pre was silent. One of the tower's concrete feet scraped against a tree trunk, and a bunch of bats flew out.

"I guess..." he said slowly, "that would be the end of the enchantment. Anybody who survived the increased cold and the scarcity of food would also have to face the possibility of the first real war in almost eight hundred years."

"Anybody other than Oöm Lout have their own army?" I said as gently as I could. Part of me wanted to scream it.

"No, of course not. Lout and his people are only playing. It's not like all their fake battles are training exercises or serious military drills...." Pre trailed off. Modesty and I stared at him.

"No," he said at last. "I can't believe Hemi-Semi-Demi-Director Lout is planning to benefit from the loss of magic. He's not that clever. The only reason he was able to get elected sixty-fourth assistant head was because my mother died two days before the election, and he ran unopposed. My mother would have won in a landslide. Everybody says so."

"Your mother was running against him in an election?" Modesty's voice got shriller as she spoke. "And she died—in an *accident*—two days before? You don't think that's...*suspicious*?"

"I try to think the best of people," Pre said, an uncertain quaver in his voice. "Oöm Lout may be overbearing and a bully, but I can't believe he's evil."

"I say he is!" declared Modesty.

"He isn't."

"Is!"

"Isn't!"

I S

Huge block letters—an *I* and an *S*—suddenly appeared in the forward window of the cab. The tower stopped moving.

"What the—?" said Modesty.

We had reached the top of Campbell Hill. In front of us, the town of Disarray's water tower stood on the crest. Our fire tower had come up beside it, until the cab was level with the water tower's huge tank. The name of the town—

DISARRAY

—curved around the tank, with spotlights shining up at the letters. We were only a few feet away from the *I* and the *S*.

"Then again," said Pre in a tiny voice, "maybe I'm wrong."

CHAPTER 23

HYPOTHESES

Why are we stopped?" I wondered.

The tower was no longer going forward. But that didn't mean it was completely motionless. The cab was swaying from side to side, as if it were trying to look around the curving tank of the water tower. After a moment, it started walking again, but instead of continuing down the hill in the direction of Sapling Farm, it strode slowly around the Disarray tower, keeping the same window of the cab always turned toward the tank, as if the two towers were having a staring contest.

"This must be the first other tower it's ever met," said Modesty. "I'm sure it doesn't get out much."

"It's *out* all the time," I said. "It's a *tower.*"

"I meant socially."

"The tower moves because of *magic*," I replied. "Not because it's alive. It doesn't have a brain in its head."

"Actually, it has three," said Modesty. "If you think of this cab as its head."

Our tower completed its circle around the water tower. When it got back to the point it had started from, it stopped and leaned forward until the edge of its roof touched the side of the tank.

"No, no, no!" shouted Modesty. "You're a *fire* tower. This is a *water* tower. It'll never work!" She kicked the wall below the window to get the tower's attention. "Fire and water do not mix. There can only be heartache." She kicked it again. "Forget this. Take us home!"

The tower straightened. Its side legs became its front legs, and it started down the hill, but not without one final twist of the cab to look back at the other tower. One of the spotlights on the water tank—the one shining up at the letters

R R

—flickered.

"What was that?" asked Pre.

"Short circuit," I said.

"Possibly," said Modesty. "Or maybe it's warning us to be careful crossing the railroad tracks."

The fire tower picked its way slowly through a grove of tall pines. The pay-per-view binoculars swiveled until they were aligned with the distant Halloween glow of the lights that outlined my barn.

"How is it possible," Pre said quietly, "that it never occurred to me that Oöm Lout might have had something to do with my parents' deaths?"

"Because," said Modesty gently, "if you had been born into *my* family, they would have named you something like Innocence, and you would have been the first of us ever to live up to your name."

"Your mother, Hope, lives up to her name," I pointed out.

"No, she doesn't. We call her 'Mum.' She never shuts up."

"What did the Congroo police say about the accident?" I asked.

"The Quieters? They said…it was an accident." Pre shrugged. "I only read the reports years later, when I was old enough and Master Index was willing to show them to me. The Quieters, as detectives, aren't very good. They're much better at locking people up for disturbing the peace. They rarely solve a mystery, unless the answer's really obvious."

"I'm guessing the people of Congroo aren't big on the *scientific method*," I said.

"What's…the scientific method?"

"You make a guess at the explanation for something you don't understand. The guess is called a 'hypothesis.' Then you come up with ways to test your hypothesis. You set up experiments. You gather evidence. If your hypothesis turns out to be wrong, you chuck it and you think up a different hypothesis and test that. Until you come up with the answer. Any good police detective uses the scientific method."

"So," said Pre, "our *hypothesis* is…Oöm Lout somehow caused the accident that resulted in my parents' deaths, because it was the only way he could win a place on the governing board. How do we test that?"

Neither Modesty nor I had an answer. Our silence said so.

"We have a second hypothesis," said Modesty, reaching down and yanking a handful of pine needles from the top of a passing tree. "If Oöm Lout has an army that can only fight in a world without magic, and the magic will be gone from Congroo in a day or two, then Oöm Lout will be able to start conquering Congroo by the end of the week!"

She tossed her pine needles in the air. They fell on us like thin, undernourished confetti.

"That's actually a syllogism," I said.

"There's nothing silly about it," Modesty snapped. "And I'm not finished. *Therefore*, if what I said about Lout is true, he may have had something to do with the DavyTrons' draining Congroo's magic. Because he would profit from it—he'd get something he wants. That's the hypothesis. Somehow, Lout may have been responsible for the transmutation spell winding up in the DavyTron computer code."

I raked pine needles out of my hair and asked Pre, "Is that possible? Could Lout, or somebody working for him, have come here and messed with Elwood Davy's computer code?"

"Impossible."

"But *you're* here," said Modesty.

"I'm only here because I had somebody here who could open the door for me. And that only happened because I put a notebook into a niche, the gniche sent it to your locker, you figured out the incantation, and you created the other side of the door. Do you know what the odds of that happening even *once* are? Almost impossible. Do you know what the odds of it happening *twice* are? Beyond possibility."

The tower stopped.

"Now what?" muttered Modesty.

We leaned out the window.

The tower had paused on Baily Road where the railroad tracks crossed it. The tower leaned cautiously forward and turned the cab so we could see down the tracks to the left. Then it turned the cab so we could see down the tracks to the right. No trains were coming. The tower straightened and walked assuredly across the tracks, continuing down Baily a little way before it again waded into the woods.

"It's learning safety," said Modesty.

"H-how can it learn?" I sputtered. "How can it even

think? Its head is hollow, except for three kids riding around in it."

"Maybe that's enough," she said.

"Some things with hollow heads think pretty well for themselves," said Pre. "A logem is hollow from head to toe, but some of them think well enough to pass for human. We believe their brains are spread through their outer shell."

We rode in silence for a moment. Then Modesty said, "A logem is a magical robot made out of clay?" She spoke very slowly, as if she was working something out in her head, "*Grown*...from a slab of clay...from the Humpty Dumpty Clay Pits?"

"*Homunculus* Clay Pits," Pre corrected her. "What's a robot?"

Modesty ignored Pre's question. "How big is the slab of clay?"

"Oh, it's about the size of that *wonderful* apple pie I ate. In fact, the trendier stores, like the Logemporium, actually sell them in the shape of a pie. You put it on your windowsill, let the sun hit it for a few days, and the third morning there's a full-grown, life-size logem sitting in your window, ready to work. Usually, the first thing you tell it to do is, *wash the window.* They come pre-enchanted."

"Pre-enchanted?" I asked.

"With a set of tasks they already know how to do."

"Programmed," I said.

"Is that the scientifical word for it?"

"I think it might be."

"I've only seen logems at a distance," said Pre. "They're ridiculously expensive. Only the very well-to-do have them."

"Do logems sleep?" asked Modesty.

"Well, they become motionless for thirty minutes each day. Nothing can get them to do anything during those thirty minutes. For them, that might be sleep. Nobody's sure."

"Thirty *consecutive* minutes?" Modesty said. "Or thirty individual minutes spread out over the day?"

"Consecutive." Pre nodded emphatically. "And always at the same time each night. Seven thirty BMS until midnight. In your time, that would be...eleven thirty DM."

"PM," I corrected him.

"PM. The logems become unmoving statues during the final half hour of each day."

"Well," said Modesty despondently. "There goes *that* hypothesis."

"What hypothesis?" asked Pre.

"I was thinking maybe we were right when we called Spalding Wicket a dummy. I was thinking that maybe he's one of these logem things. But he can't be."

"No, he can't," I said, surprised that I was following her logic. "Why would he want us to come back to

Davy headquarters at eleven o'clock tonight if he's going to go off-line half an hour after we get there? He certainly didn't invite us back just to watch him sleep. The moment he turned into a statue, Pre would realize he's a logem. Even you and I would be a little suspicious."

"That was a very good hypothesis, though," said Pre.

"*Power lines!*" Modesty announced. "*Limbo positions!*"

We grabbed the posts that held the roof to the cab and braced our feet against the walls. The tower slowly bent backward, took eight or nine sliding steps forward, and righted itself after it had passed under the wires. We swung our feet back to the floor as if we did this every day.

It took another minute or two for the tower to cross the wheat field, clomp across Route 9, and bury its concrete boots in the four holes it had created when it had uprooted itself and gone for a walk. I glanced at my phone. It was 4:03.

Modesty departed immediately, hoping to get a few hours of sleep before school. I left Pre hidden in the fire tower and descended to the farmyard, intent on getting to my own bed.

I found it hard to believe that less than two full days had passed since Drew and I had first seen coins move by themselves in Onderdonk Grove. That had been Saturday afternoon. Now Monday's sunrise was less than three hours away. As I got to the house, I paused and looked across Route 9 at the carcass of the Fireball 50.

It was 4:07. Briefly, I considered trying to stay awake until 4:56. I wanted desperately to see if a door would open into Congroo and Drew would come tumbling home. And if that happened—*when* it happened—I wanted to see if *To Repair a Chimney* might restore the harvester to the way it had been before the fire.

But I decided I couldn't stay up for either of those things. At 4:56, my phone would automatically play the Magic Bite for *To Open a Door*, and either Drew would come through or he wouldn't. If he didn't, it would mean it was becoming less and less likely that he was ever going to. Repairing the harvester would be nothing compared with the loss of my friend. My hesitancy when coming back through Modesty's fridge would have doomed him to life in a cold and hostile place.

I kept putting off thinking about that, using each upcoming Magic Minute as an excuse. When I did finally allow myself to think about it for more than a passing second, I knew it was going to hit harder than my guilt over the harvester ever did.

I went to bed and slept through the 4:56 Magic Minute. When I awoke, the door to my room was open, but nothing, not even my alarm going *blippity-blippity-blip*, had disturbed my sleep.

Drew was still in Congroo.

CHAPTER 24

A MIDDLE SCHOOL IN DISARRAY

I took Preffy to school with me. I couldn't leave him in the fire tower—my dad hadn't photographed this year's maze yet, and chances were good that he would climb the tower before the end of the day. So I hid the sleeping bag, brushed some stray Cheerios out of the cab, looked for the spare change I had heard fall from my pocket the night before—found nothing—then took Pre along when I went to the bus stop.

The morning was chilly, so I lent him a windbreaker. It belonged to my brother, with the word *SAFE* in big block letters across the back, and Pre had to roll up the sleeves before it came anywhere near fitting.

"What kind of animal skin is this?" he asked, feeling the rubbery fabric.

"It's just cloth." I shrugged. "It's waterproof. Rain beads up on it."

"Scientifical textiles! Does it repel lightning?"

"It's not Iron Man's underwear. It's just a raincoat."

The school bus turned out not to be the problem I had dreaded. The driver was too busy blotting spilled coffee off her blouse to notice an extra student get on with the usual group. The kids on the bus, one of whom had worn green hair for at least a week, found Pre's green skin unremarkable. Half of them were in the habit of painting their faces different colors in support of their favorite sports teams, and one—Celia Berringer—found Pre's color "totally unconvincing."

When we arrived at Disarray Middle, Pre shuffled through security with the rest of the throng, and we met up with Modesty in the lobby.

"I figured out where we can hide him," Modesty announced, without so much as a *hello* or *how'dja sleep?* We had been texting back and forth while we rode our separate buses, working out our plan for the day. One of the hurdles was finding a place for Pre. He couldn't attend class; even our most self-absorbed teachers would eventually notice a new face.

"Science Lab C," said Modesty. "It's only used Tuesdays

and Thursdays. And it's got a periodic table of elements taped inside the door's window, so you can't see in from the hall. It's perfect."

"I'm going to spend the day in a room full of *science*?" Pre looked as though he might start jumping up and down.

"Touch nothing," Modesty warned a few minutes later as we slipped inside the room and Pre ran immediately to a locked glass cabinet full of jars of chemicals. A full-size human skeleton dangled from a hook next to the cabinet, wearing a fedora on its skull and a name tag saying MR. PALMERI on its clavicle.

Only eighth graders used the room. Ten slab-topped tables, each with a built-in sink and a pair of Bunsen burner gas hookups, faced a blackboard that currently had the words *marine biology* and a diagram of an Aqua-Lung scrawled across it. The Aqua-Lung was a cross section, with only two things labeled: SEAWATER (on the outside) and AIR (on the inside), pretty much confirming my suspicion that eighth graders, despite their attitudes, weren't much smarter than sixth graders.

"I packed you a lunch." Modesty plunked a brown paper bag down in front of Pre, who was barely listening, so engrossed was he in reading the titles of the books on the teacher's desk. "The red things in the coleslaw are gummy bears."

"Anybody comes in," I said as Modesty and I were

leaving, "tell them you're a new student, and you came in here looking for the restroom."

"But I don't need—"

"I know. Just pretend."

Modesty and I kept our phones on us, which was against school policy—normally, we were required to leave them in our lockers—but we had a Magic Minute coming up at 12:34, and we had no intention of wasting it. Modesty would be in gym class; I would be at lunch: We had both decided to use *To View Things More Clearly* and attempt to boost our brainpower so we could figure out how we were going to convince Elwood Davy to give up his DavyTron business.

When I got to the cafeteria at twelve thirty, I took a seat in the far corner, near a door labeled CUSTODIAL, which I made sure was unlocked. I put my phone on the bench beside me, hid it under a bag of chips, and waited as patiently as I could.

"Hey, *Sap!*"

I cringed as I realized I was on Mace Croyden's side of the cafeteria. He had seen me as he was about to sit down several rows over; now he was working his way down the aisle with an overflowing tray of food, some of which I was pretty sure I'd be wearing within a minute or two. He reached the end of the aisle and started along the wall in my direction.

"*I've got something for you!*" he shouted.

My phone alarm played the Magic Bite. The CUS-TODIAL door flew open, hit Mace full in the face, and knocked him and his heaping lunch tray head over heels onto the floor. The lunchroom erupted in thunderous applause. At least one teacher forgot himself and joined in.

I leaned forward and determined, as I had feared, that there was no sign of Drew or Congroo through the open doorway: only the mops, brooms, and buckets of vomit-absorbing sawdust essential to any school cafeteria. I moved the chip bag, scrolled to the Magic Bite for *To View Things More Clearly*, and played it.

Almost immediately, I felt my thinking grow sharper.

"Sapling!" A Mace Croyden covered in spaghetti sauce with strands of pasta dangling from his ears shoved my shoulder. Two of his cronies, Scoops Hernandez and tongue chewer Ray Chikletts, stood on either side of him. "I saw you laugh. You think that was funny?"

I hadn't laughed; I'd had far more serious things on my mind.

"You know what you are, Sap?" Mace leaned around to get in my face. With a clarity of mind that surprised me, I reached down, flicked my phone until *To Cast a Reflection* came up, and stabbed it with my middle finger.

"You're *much* better than I am." Mace sneered. "I'm a gangly, pencil-necked scarecrow who shouldn't be allowed to walk the streets! I am pus!" He pointed at himself proudly with his thumb. "I am walking diarrhea!" He held his head in place by wrapping one arm around his neck, made a fist with his other hand, and gave himself a noogie. Ray and Scoops took two steps back. "I. Am. A. Steaming. Pile. Of. Puke." With each word, Mace slapped himself on the chest, sending drops of spaghetti sauce flying. *"And don't you forget it!"*

He turned and stalked away. Out of the corner of my eye, I could see at least two contraband phones being held up, presumably filming the presentation for posterity. I looked at my own phone. The Magic Minute was over, and even though I hadn't had time to try any additional spells, it had been one of the best minutes of my life.

"How did it go?" Modesty asked me, two periods later, when we had our first chance to meet in the hall.

"Not bad," I said. "Although I didn't think up anything to help us with Davy." My sharpness of mind had faded as quickly as it had come.

"Me neither." Modesty shook her head. "But for a minute, I understood algebra completely. All those letters in the equations are actually *numbers*."

"Really?"

"Yes! And there are ways of figuring out which letters are what numbers. And then it was gone." Modesty waved her fingers at her head, indicating thoughts turning to vapor. "Preffy was going to try some spells he had memorized. I wonder how that went."

A stampede of screaming middle schoolers rounded the corner, followed by a walking skeleton.

"Apparently not well," I said.

Pre came running from behind and tackled Mr. Palmeri a few feet from where we stood. The skeleton crashed to the floor and stopped moving. A dozen terrified eighth graders had pressed themselves against the lockers on the opposite side of the hall; one—Mace Croyden—appeared to have wet his pants. Mace was not having a good day.

I grabbed the skeleton by the neck, held it up, and said, "Sapling Farms Halloween Spooktacular! Opening this Friday! Great new special effects! If you come—wear a diaper!"

The eighth graders scattered.

"Sorry about that," said Pre, working hard to catch his breath. "At twelve thirty-four, I envisioned the final four syllables of *To Cure a Numb Skull*, which is a lesser-known version of *To View Things More Clearly*, but, as usual, I messed things up. Instead of making me think better, the spell animated Mr. Palmeri, and he started dancing on his hook, and the clicking noise drove me crazy for a couple of hours, until five minutes ago the hook broke, and he ran out the door. I'm so glad he finally wound down." He patted the skeleton on the rib cage. "Oh, and it turns out I *love* cold sores with grumbly bears, and guess what? *Scuba* isn't just the first two syllables of the incantation *To Fold a Napkin Neatly*. In *your* world, it stands for Self-Contained Underwater Breathing Apparatus. I learned that in a book about undersea life. Science is so wonderful. I should have been born in your world!"

We sat the skeleton on the bench where sick students usually waited to see the school nurse—I hoped it might inspire her not to be out of her office for such long periods of time—then we tucked Pre into the back row of the empty auditorium. Modesty and I finished off school's final period—she in social studies, me in math (failing the test I hadn't had time to study for; the letters *may* have been numbers, but I didn't have a clue what those numbers might be)—then we collected Pre and made our way home.

All in all, the school day hadn't been too bad.

I found myself wishing every day could be more like it.

CHAPTER 25

TANKED

If anyone had been standing in the parking lot of Davy's Digital Vegetables at 10:52 that evening, they might have noticed some of the bushes along the edge of the parking lot shake and a flashlight beam or two flicker through their branches.

So we were lucky there was no one in the parking lot.

We had arrived later than planned. We had wanted to get there an hour before the agreed-upon time of eleven so we could hide and keep an eye out for anything suspicious—neither Modesty nor I fully trusted Spalding Wicket—but instead, we reached the edge of the lot only a few minutes before we were expected.

It had taken three hours for Pre to learn how to ride a bicycle.

"We have something like this in Congroo, really we do, but without the pedals and the chain thingy," he kept assuring us, usually just before tottering sideways and falling over. I had dug my brother's bike out of the garage for him and lowered the seat as far as it would go. "It's one of many things we have in common with the World of Science," he said during a break in the bike-riding lesson while he applied a bandage to his knee. "We have the wheel and arithmetic and three-ring binders and mayonnaise and other things that don't require magic, although I will say our wheels work much better when they have *seven* spokes, which doesn't seem to be the case here, but it's another argument in favor of there being *seven* Magic Minutes instead of five. We really should give more thought to what the remaining two might be. This scientical bandage is sticking to my fingers and not my knee."

"Face it the other way," said Modesty.

"Oh."

Pre finally mastered the bicycle and the art of applying a self-sticking bandage, and the three of us, dressed for a chilly autumn evening, pedaled up Gernsback Ridge. Modesty and I both wore hoodies; Pre had on the SAFE windbreaker, which he seemed to have grown quite fond of. ("*Safe* is the final word of *To Make a Sweater Cozier*," he told us.)

We departed the road about a quarter of a mile before

the entrance to the DDV property, hid our bikes in the woods, and crept up on the side of the building where the Service Personnel Only entrance was. We pocketed our flashlights—Pre had been thrilled when we gave him his very own "scientific wand"—and we crouched down and studied the place through gaps in the shrubbery.

"That's a *very* empty parking lot," I whispered. "Shouldn't there be at least one car here? The one that brought Elwood Davy back from his trip?"

"Maybe his secret apartment has a secret garage," Modesty whispered back. "Or maybe a helicopter dropped him off on the roof. Or he took a taxi."

"Oh," I said. "Okay. I suppose there are other possibilities."

"That's what makes *me* the great detective that I am," Modesty said in her normal, far-from-whispering voice.

"Why, exactly, do they call you *Modesty*?" asked Pre. He sounded sincere. I waited for Modesty to take his head off.

"That's a good question, isn't it?" Modesty surprised me by saying. "It's part of a long tradition our world has of naming girls things like Patience or Prudence or Charity or Désirée and naming boys things like *Joe*. From the moment we're born, girls are expected to behave in specific ways, and while there's nothing wrong with being patient or charitable or exercising a little caution when you're waving a machete, my sisters and I just do what we want. I know I sound arrogant sometimes. Get over it. If you think this is the part of our adventure where I start sounding a little less braggy because of everything we've been through together—*forget it.*"

Modesty looked from me to Pre as if daring us to argue.

"I'm fine with that," I said.

"I was only wondering if you were named after a relative," said Pre.

A rectangle of light appeared in the side of the factory as the door marked SERVICE PERSONNEL ONLY scraped open and a man's silhouette appeared in it. He took two steps forward, looked across the parking lot directly at the bushes where we were hiding, and called out, "Are you coming in or not?"

"So much for sneaking up," I said.

Modesty grimaced and pushed through the shrubs. Pre and I stepped out after her.

"Where did you park your tower?" The figure in the doorway looked down the length of the parking lot, and light from the door hit the side of his face. It was Spalding Wicket. Or possibly Elwood Davy pretending to be Spalding Wicket. Or possibly a logem pretending to be Spalding Wicket pretending to be Elwood Davy. It bothered me that we didn't have a clue.

"We gave the tower the night off," I said. "It didn't seem necessary."

"But...I've told Elwood all about it." Spalding sounded genuinely upset. "He's looking forward to seeing it. He was hoping you might invite him for a ride." He held the door open for us, and we trooped past him into a gray cinder-block corridor. "I told him it was irrefutable proof you were magical children and everything you had told me was true."

"Why is *magical* a word but *scientifical* isn't?" Pre asked him.

"I have no idea. Is it important?"

"No..."

"We'll prove to Mr. Davy we're magical when we see him," I said, although I didn't have much confidence in the deck of playing cards Modesty had brought. She knew only two tricks. We were hoping we'd be able to keep Davy talking until 1:23, when we'd be able to play a Magic Bite and impress him with our sorcery. Until that time, in addition to Modesty's tricks, we were hoping he might be willing to play Go Fish.

"Well...I hope you don't disappoint him. Follow me." Spalding stepped in front and led us down the hall.

The corridor opened up into a vast room full of cylindrical metal tanks that towered from floor to ceiling. Each had a number painted on it, starting with the closest, which was number one.

"We want tank thirteen, way down at the end," Spalding informed us. "These are the tomato-juice holding tanks.

Each one stores more than one hundred thousand gallons of juice; imagine ten backyard swimming pools stacked one on top of the other."

"That's a lot of juice," I said.

"It all comes in through the TJP—Tomato Juice Pipeline—which passes through three different states and eight separate processing plants north of here, where the tomatoes get juiced. Once the pumping starts, one of these tanks can go from empty to full in less than fifteen minutes."

"Is there any time when you're *not* giving a tour?" Modesty asked.

"Am I in tour mode?" Spalding faltered, then regained his stride. "I suppose I am. I have to admit, I'm a little nervous. I want this to go well. I did, after all, go to bat for you. Mr. Davy was a little tired when he got back from his trip, but I told him about the three of you, and your walking tower, and about how his DavyTrons only work because they're draining the life out of someplace magical, and he perked up—seemed very eager to talk to you—but then he said he needed a nap. He went into his private apartment, and I haven't seen him since. That was more than an hour ago. Ah. Here we are."

Spalding stopped in front of a three-foot-square hatch in the side of tank number thirteen. The hatch had a wheel in the center. He twiddled a keypad next to the hatch, and the wheel turned on its own and made unlocking noises. Then the hatch swung open. He took a heavy-duty flashlight from a hook above the keypad and shone it into the tank.

"After you," he suggested.

"I don't think so," I said.

"Are you trying to tell us there's no *light* in the entrance to Elwood Davy's secret luxury apartment?" Modesty asked.

"There is, but the bulb burned out just as I was leaving earlier."

"Life would be awfully dull without coincidences," said Modesty, repeating what Spalding had said the previous day. I understood she was being sarcastic. Spalding did not.

"Exactly!" he said, and threw a leg over the hatch's high threshold. "I'll go first, then, and put your minds at ease."

He ducked through the opening, took a few steps into the tank, and turned back to us.

"Look," he said, waving the light around. "It's completely clean inside. If this were a *real* tomato-juice tank, there'd be sticky residue all over the walls. There's even a carpet." He shone the beam at his feet. A narrow red carpet ran from the hatch, across the floor of the tank, to another hatch on the opposite side. "And that's the door to Elwood's apartment." He threw a circle of light at the second hatch. "I can't imagine why you're so hesitant. You told me Congroo is dying, and only you can save it, and time is running out, and one of you wants to save your farm, and another's keen on dragons not going extinct, but you're acting like a bunch of frightened children."

"He's right," said Pre. "We have to save Congroo! Scientifical wands out!" He drew his flashlight, muttered something that sounded like "Lumos," and clicked it on.

Pre pushed me aside and levered himself through the opening. Modesty and I pulled out our own flashlights, and Modesty straddled the threshold, then turned back to me and whispered, "One of us should stay near the hatch and make sure it doesn't close."

"Yeah," I agreed, and followed her through. Once inside, I sat on the edge of the opening with my butt sticking out. Modesty joined the others.

Spalding rapped on the far hatch with his flashlight.

"*Hello?*" he shouted. "Mr. Davy? I'm sorry if we're waking you, but the magic kids are here. They have a world to save. They say it's urgent." He rapped again. He turned and shone the light on me. "Are you just going to sit there?"

"Um," I said. "I, uh, have Overheated Butt Syndrome. It feels better if it's out in the cool air."

Modesty pointed her flashlight at the ceiling. There was a third and final hatch at the very top of the tank, about fifty feet over our heads.

"So," she said, "where's this burned-out bulb?"

"Oh. Well," said Spalding. "There you've got me."

And the hatch behind me swung in, whacked me in my overheated butt, and knocked me into the tank. I scrambled to my feet and turned back to the hatch just as it thudded closed and made noises like bolts sliding into place.

"Oh, thank goodness," said Spalding. His shoulders sagged, as if a great weight had been lifted from them. "This has been so stressful. I've been practically out of my mind all day!"

He walked to the center of the tank and sat down on the rug. He folded his legs beneath him as if he was going to meditate, balanced the flashlight upright on the floor in front of him, let go of it, and regarded us sadly.

"I really do apologize for this," he said. "I am *so* sorry."

"For what? Doing yoga?" asked Modesty.

"No. For everything I'm about to tell you. I'm sitting, to make myself shorter than the three of you. That will make me less intimidating. I don't want you to panic. Almost everything I've told you has been a lie." He sounded nothing like the fast-talking Spalding Wicket we had first met. His voice had become soft and sorrowful. "I'm not *supposed* to be feeling guilty. I'm not supposed to *feel* anything at all. But being on my own for four years seems to have caused certain *abnormalities*."

"Your name isn't Spalding Wicket," Modesty told him.

"Actually, it is. My name is whatever I say it is at the time. Names are irrelevant."

"You're not Elwood Davy," I said.

"I've already told you I'm not."

"You're a logem," said Pre.

"Yes." He gave Pre a woeful look.

Bam! Bam! Bam!

Modesty pounded on the hatch that led to Elwood Davy's apartment.

"Yoo-hoo! Mr. Davy! Time to wake up! Hello!"

"There's no one there," said Spalding. "There's no apartment. That hatch is locked, as is the one we came in through. They're both on timers. They won't unlock for another hour. The overhead hatch isn't automatic, but it has a crowbar jammed through its outside wheel so the inside wheel can't be turned. I'm sorry it had to come to this, but..."

"But what?" I growled.

"The three of you are my prisoners."

CHAPTER 26

SEVEN THIRTY BMS

I'm calling the police," said Modesty, and whipped out her phone. She tapped it, then scowled.

"You're inside a giant metal jar," said Spalding. "There's not going to be any reception. That's why I brought us here. No distractions. You'd never let me get through my story otherwise."

"We outnumber you three to one," said Modesty.

"Yes, you do. But there's nothing you can do to me."

Spalding gripped his flashlight and gave himself a tremendous whack in the face. He put the flashlight back on the floor. His face was undamaged, but the metal flashlight now had a dent.

"*We saw you eat a doughnut!*" I shouted, not convinced

he wasn't human. I still wanted him to be the real Elwood Davy.

He grabbed the middle button on his shirt and pulled a drawer out of the center of his chest. He removed the drawer completely, turned it upside down, and dumped a pile of gooey crumbs onto the floor. Then he reinserted the drawer, and it became impossible to tell where it was.

"I eat and drink. It helps convince people I'm Elwood Davy."

"Does *anybody* here have phone service?" Modesty demanded.

I was the only other person with a phone. I checked. I didn't.

"All right," I said. "We'll give you one last chance."

"One last chance? Really?" said Spalding. "For what?"

"To let us out," I bluffed. "If you don't, we'll use *magic* and get out on our own. You know we can do it. You saw what we did with the fire tower. And right now, I'm using tremendous willpower just to prevent my teeth from shooting out laser beams. They do it all the time. It's how I...*floss*. And if you force us to resort to magic, we won't go easy on you. We'll...we'll..."

"You'll what?"

"We'll turn you into a bobblehead doll!" snapped Modesty.

"I have a cousin who's a bobblehead," said Spalding. "She's very agreeable. Nods yes to everything."

"Really?" asked Pre.

"No, of course not. It's about as true as the idea that the three of you can do magic whenever you want. I know you tried to give me that impression yesterday, but I'm fully aware that magic only works in the World of Science at very specific times. And I can name both of them."

"*Both?*" said Modesty.

"Twelve past midnight and three forty-five," Spalding replied smugly. "I know this because I was present when magic was successfully performed at both those times."

Preffy stepped in front of Spalding.

"Are you working for Oöm Lout?"

"I suppose I must be," Spalding replied. "Yesterday was the first time I ever heard his name, when you told me about him. I said to myself, *Oh, I bet he's the one behind this.*"

"You don't *know?*" I asked.

"No, I don't. That's part of my story. The sooner I tell it, the sooner the three of you can move on. I really need to clear my conscience. It would make me feel so much better."

"You're a logem," said Pre. "You don't *have* a conscience."

"Don't tell me what I do or do not have. You're not

me. All I can tell you is, thinking about what I'm about to do makes me feel all empty inside."

"You *are* all empty inside!"

"I am speaking metaphorically."

"Oh, *well*, then," said Modesty.

"Once we listen to this story of yours, you'll free us?" I asked.

"Trust me. Within minutes of what I have to say, you will no longer be prisoners."

"Then your story better be short, and you better tell it quickly." Modesty plunked herself down in front of Spalding and leaned forward, until her nose was only inches from his face. "We're listening."

She eased back a bit. Pre settled down next to her. I remained standing, the better to spring into action, should anything occur to me. Which didn't seem likely.

"Okay, then," said Spalding. "The first thing I remember is falling out of a tree."

"Like a nut?" said Modesty.

"This will go faster if you don't interrupt. We're on a somewhat tight schedule. The first thing I remember is falling out of a tree. That was four years ago. Two angry squirrels rolled me out of a hole halfway up the trunk. This was at three forty-five in the morning. I couldn't have arrived in your world during a time when magic wasn't working here, so this is how I know three forty-five is one of the two Magic Minutes. I landed on top of some mossy roots; when morning came, it was a very sunny spot. The tree is about a mile from here. It's a lovely oak. I visit it every Mother's Day."

"The hole in the trunk must have connected with a gniche," said Pre. "The way Modesty's gym locker did. And if squirrels *rolled* you, you may have been in the shape of a pie."

"I couldn't say. But three days after I arrived, I had grown large enough, with the requisite number of arms and legs, that I was able to get up and walk. I molded myself to appear fully clothed and completely human. I have no recollection of anything before that. So I have no knowledge of who sent me." He nodded to himself. "This is good. This is what I wanted. To be able to confess but still fulfill my mission. Yes.

"I assumed the shape of a young man—generic but passable—and the first place I came to was Elwood Davy's house, and Elwood was out mowing the lawn. He stopped to empty the grass catcher, and I leaned over the fence and asked him what all the stuff in his garage was. The garage was open, and there wasn't any room for a car; it was so full of electronic equipment and computer parts. He said *that* was where he'd rather be, fooling around with that stuff, instead of mowing, and I said I'd be happy to mow for him if, after I was done, he would explain all the garage stuff to me. We got to be good friends. I worked for his family doing yard work; he taught me about computers and computer code. I told him I lived in town. I told him my name was John Deere."

"Which...was the name on his lawn mower," I guessed.

"Yes. We both had a good laugh over that. Anyway, it turned out I had arrived pre-enchanted with the words to all the most powerful, magic-intensive spells. And as soon as I met Elwood, I knew my mission. I was pre-enchanted to create some sort of colossal, ongoing magic project in your world that would drain all the magic out of Congroo. I couldn't do the magic myself, of course—logems, being products of magic, can't perform magic—"

"Of course not," said Pre, as if everybody knew this.

"So I had to get somebody here in the World of Science to do the magic for me. At first, I had no idea what my project could be. Then I noticed how much computer code resembles magical incantations. Elwood was working on a program to get a 3-D printer to make a plastic toy he called a Mister Zucchini Head. Imagine his surprise when it made a *real* zucchini instead. I had typed the transmutation incantation right into the middle of his code. He pushed the *Enter* key to run the program, so he was the one who did the magic. He had tried running the program a number of times without success, but when he hit *Enter* at precisely twelve minutes past midnight, it produced a genuine vegetable. This is how I learned there were *two* Magic Minutes. Ever since, I've deliberately made zero hour plus twelve the standard time to send out the DavyTron updates."

I could hear a faint noise from somewhere. I pressed my hand against the wall of the tank.

It was vibrating.

"I worked for Elwood doing different jobs," Spalding continued, "until the company started making lots of money. Then, when Elwood built his headquarters around his family home, I locked him in the basement of his own house, remolded my appearance so I looked like him, and took his place. The house's basement is soundproof, and I don't have to feed him—he has his own DavyTron. I just keep him supplied with tomato juice. I need him in case I have technical questions only he can answer. I visit him every day. Sometimes he attacks me with a frying pan. Sometimes we play chess. It's complicated."

He stopped talking.

The faint noise became a distinct rumble.

"Is that it?" said Modesty. "That's your story?"

"Pretty much."

"And now you'll let us go?"

"I said nothing about letting you go."

"You said—"

"I said you would no longer be prisoners. Which, in a few minutes, you won't be."

"Why is the wall shaking?" I asked.

"I am *so* sorry about this." Spalding ignored me. "I truly regret it. You have to believe me. Until my mission ends, I have no volition. That means I can't do what I want. I can't make my own choices, even when I know what I'm doing is wrong. I'm pre-enchanted to do the things I'm doing. It's not me. At least I was able to confess. And it *has* made me feel better."

"You're not supposed to have feelings," Pre said. "You're a logem."

"I've been on my own for four years now, living with human beings. Why shouldn't I have feelings? But I can't do anything that contradicts my pre-enchantments, and I'm pre-enchanted to eliminate any threat to my mission. The three of you are a threat to my mission. I should have eliminated you yesterday, but I didn't want to see your faces when I did it. This is better. I don't have to watch. That's why I brought you here just before I shut down for the day."

The rumble got louder.

"What's that noise?" I had to raise my voice to be heard over it.

"It's an ocean of tomato juice coming down the pipeline. It will be here in a moment, and when it hits, it will only take twelve minutes for the tank to fill to the top. The liquid will force all the air out through tiny screened vents—you won't be able to escape through the vents; they're too small—and it won't leave even an inch of breathing space. As I say, I am *so* sorry about this. *Good night.*"

Spalding's eyes closed. He stretched out like a corpse, turned the color of red clay from head to toe, and became completely rigid.

"Seven thirty Before Midnight Snack," said Pre. "Eleven thirty your time. Bedtime for logems."

The entire tank shook as, with a deafening roar, hundreds of gallons of tomato juice came blasting down from an overhead pipe.

CHAPTER 27

THE TOMATO JUICE OF DOOM

The spewing juice knocked us off our feet. We floundered, then slipped and sloshed until we were no longer directly beneath the deluge and shakily stood up. The combined light from three flashlights—along with Pre's "scientific wand"—showed us our situation clearly. We were up to our ankles in tomato juice.

"Twelve minutes, he said, until it reaches the top!" I shouted to make myself heard above the roaring downpour.

"Can we all swim?" Modesty hollered just as loudly.

I nodded. Pre wagged his hand in an iffy motion.

"I can tread water. I'm not sure about tomato juice."

Don't panic, I told myself, even though my heart was

hammering harder than it had when the fire extinguisher ran out of foam and the flames rose higher on the Fireball 50. I couldn't let this be a repeat of that. Our lives were at stake. There had to be a way out.

I told myself to calm down and *think*.

Something bumped the back of my legs. I turned. It was Spalding, still frozen in sleep position but buoyed up by the juice.

"Logems float?" I shouted at Pre.

"They're hollow. He shut up before he shut down, so his mouth is closed. So yes, a tight-lipped logem would float."

"Good!" Modesty snapped. "We have a raft!"

She boosted herself up and sat on Spalding's chest. The logem sank a little but remained on the surface.

The tomato juice rose another six inches.

"If we could only manage to stay alive until twelve twelve, we could use the Magic Bites on our phones to get us out of here!" Modesty held up her phone to keep it from getting wet. My phone was still in my pocket. I fumbled it out.

"The big gush started at eleven thirty," I said. "There's no way we're making it until twelve past midnight. Eleven forty-two rolls around, this glop will be up to the ceiling. We've only got ten minutes!"

"What if we did something to slow down the flow?" asked Pre. "Something scientific?"

"If we could block off the pipe, that would help," I said.

"We could wad up some clothing," said Modesty, "but there's no way to get it up there. By the time the juice raises us high enough, it will be too late!"

The tomato juice surged to our waists. Pre lost his footing, and Modesty hauled him up next to her. A moment later, my own feet left the floor, and I put one hand on the logem's shoulder to steady myself as I floated beside them. I pointed my flashlight at the ceiling and jammed it into a convenient gap between Spalding's arm and the side of his chest.

"Spalding's full of air; could we crack him open and get the surplus?" Modesty asked.

Pre rapped on Spalding's forehead with a knuckle. It made a brittle *klonk-klonk* sound.

"When a logem's at rest, it's all hard ceramic," he explained. "Unbreakable. You saw what happened when he hit himself with the scientifical wand. Whatever air is inside is going to stay inside."

"That's just as well," I said. "We don't want to kill him."

"We don't?" said Modesty. "He's trying to murder us. He isn't even human. He's a *thing*."

"He knows the difference between right and wrong," I said. "He apologized for not being able to ignore his programming. He can't help what he's doing."

I turned around slowly, treading tomato juice, studying the walls of the tank. They were smooth with no handholds.

The tank was already half full. As the tomato juice got higher, the cascade had less far to fall, and the noise of the splash got quieter. We didn't have to shout quite so loudly.

It got a little easier to think.

"We should have called in the military, the way Delleps told us to," said Modesty. "They could have saved us by blowing this thing open with a bazooka."

"What's a bazooka?" asked Pre.

"It's an anti-tank weapon. We're in a tank. It's what they'd use."

"Delleps never said we should call in the military," I reminded her. "She said we should...make time...for the army..." I trailed off. Something was nagging at me. "What time did Spalding say the DavyTron updates go out?"

"Twelve minutes past midnight," said Pre.

"No," I said, "he didn't say *midnight*—"

"He said *zero hour plus twelve*," said Modesty, and her eyes went wide as she realized the same thing I had. She reached across Spalding and grabbed my wrist. "That's it, isn't it? That's why twelve past twelve is a Magic Minute!"

"*Yes.*" I was glad she saw it, too. "Twelve twelve

isn't twelve twelve; it's zero twelve! It's zero, one, two—consecutive numbers! *Magic is on military time!*"

"Military time?" asked Pre.

"It's time for the army. You know how Congroo divides the day into three eight-hour segments? And in this part of our world, we divide it into two twelve-hour segments? The army doesn't divide it at all."

"They're bad at arithmetic?"

"Who knows? But if you're on military time, one o'clock in the afternoon isn't one o'clock—it's thirteen hundred hours. You hear it that way in war movies all the time. So one twenty-three *isn't* one twenty-three; it's thirteen twenty-three: Those numbers aren't consecutive, so that's why magic doesn't work at one twenty-three in the afternoon but it works at one twenty-three in the morning!"

"Okay," said Pre, "so zero twelve is a Magic Minute. *How do we live long enough to use it?*"

"Maybe we don't have to," said Modesty excitedly.

"No," I agreed, catching her excitement. "We're in the final hour of the day, but the final hour didn't start at eleven o'clock. It started at—"

"Twenty-three hundred hours!" Modesty thrust her phone at my face. She had been rapidly tapping it as I spoke. Her time readout was 23:37.

"How'd you do that?"

"*Settings. General. Date and Time.*" She rattled it off in fluent phonespeak.

I followed the trail on my own phone and immediately got an option called *24-Hour Clock*. I tapped it, and suddenly my phone also read 23:37. Except, as I watched, it changed to 23:38. I glanced at the walls. We were more than three-quarters of the way to the top.

"I have a hypothesis," Pre declared happily. "Your world has *more* than six Magic Minutes. It has *seven*, and the seventh is—"

"*Twenty-three forty-five!*" Modesty and I shouted at once.

Then we all got very quiet.

"Even that's too far away," I said. "According to Spalding, the tank will be full by twenty-three forty-*two*. We can't hold our breath for three minutes."

"*I* might be able to," said Modesty. "I'm on the swim team. The coach says most healthy people can hold their breath for about two minutes. Provided they're not, you know, *stressed* or anything—"

Pre started wiggling out of my brother's windbreaker.

"I'm not at all good at holding my breath," he announced. "Maybe I can manage a minute—"

"What are you doing?" I asked him.

He had the jacket off and was zipping it up the front. "I'm…getting ready to test a hypothesis," he said vaguely as he tied a knot in one of the sleeves.

I looked up. The top of the tank was only five feet above us. Around the hatch, I could see the vents Spalding had mentioned, the ones that allowed the juice to force the air out of the tank. The vents were tiny two-inch squares with screening over them. They were too small to offer any means of escape. You couldn't even stick your nose into one.

Pre glanced at the approaching ceiling and worked faster. He had only moments before he'd be forced from his perch on the logem's stomach, and his project, whatever it was, would become much more difficult. He yanked on the cord that ran around the windbreaker's waist until it cinched the bottom closed; then he used the excess cord to tie the bottom even tighter. He went to work on the drawstring in the hood, even as he slid off into the rising juice and found a way to support himself with his elbows against Spalding's chest. Modesty slid off next to him.

The pipe spewing the juice went *GLOOP*, and the flow slowed down to about half what it had been. The splash got quieter, but the juice level continued to rise. It was a sure sign we were almost full.

I checked my phone: 23:39. I went to my list of Magic Bites and started scrolling.

"So which incantation will get us out of here?" I asked.

"*To Open a Door*, obviously!" Modesty was studying her own phone.

"No," said Pre. "That only works with doors that aren't locked."

"It only—?" Modesty glared at Pre. "*What is WRONG*

285

with you people? What do you use to open a door that's locked?"

"A key."

Modesty clutched her phone as if she was about to throw it. The light coming from it winked out.

"No! Don't! Not now!" Modesty shook her phone. She drummed her fingers all over the screen. She pushed every button on the side. A couple of drops of tomato juice leaked out. "It's dead. No, *no, NO!*"

"It's all right." I tried to sound reassuring. "We've still got mine." I made my phone's display as bright as I could. I suddenly realized I would have to read it through tomato juice.

"Maybe this will help," said Pre, holding up his project. He had tied off the neck of the jacket. He gripped the unknotted sleeve tightly in one hand.

He had made a bag of air.

"Aqua-Lung," he said. "Or maybe a Tomato-Juice-Lung. I figure it might keep some of the air in here with us. We can take turns breathing through the sleeve."

"That's...very scientifical," said Modesty.

Pre flashed her a grateful look.

The airbag, if it didn't collapse from the pressure of the liquid around it, would prevent the air inside it from being forced out through the vents. It might contain about a minute's worth, shared out among the three of us. That wasn't much, but it might do the trick. I turned my attention back to the list of Magic Bites.

"What about *To Sop Up a Spill*?" I suggested eagerly.

Pre shook his head. "The spill goes into the rag you're holding."

"*So what good is the spell?*" Modesty blurted.

"You don't have to bend down."

"Invented by the same guy who came up with *To Undress the Feet*?"

"Yes."

"None of these is going to help us, then," I said, reminding myself to stay calm but finding it more and more difficult. I flipped frantically up and down my list of Magic Bites. *To Change the Color of a Room, To Tidy a Drawer, To Cast a Reflection*...

I looked up and realized the overhead hatch was within reach. I handed my phone to Modesty, put a knee on Spalding's face, extended my hands upward, and grabbed the wheel in the hatch's center. I twisted it with all my might. It refused to budge.

"He said he put something through the other side," Pre reminded me.

"Yeah. A crowbar."

I dropped back into the juice.

"How about this?" said Modesty, handing my phone back to me. She had cued up the Magic Bite called *Egg*.

"That's—?" I couldn't remember what *Egg* was short for.

"*To Empty an Egg without Breaking the Shell*," said Modesty. "I figure this tank is like an egg, and we're what's inside, and if you follow it up with *Intensify*, maybe it will get us out of here." It wasn't any more desperate than my hoping to fix the harvester with *To Repair a Chimney*. I looked at Pre for his reaction. He shook his head again.

"That's a *teleportation* spell. It's only good if you want your eggs *scrambled*."

"Well, I think it's the best chance we've got. You find something bet—*Blah! Pooie! Yuck!*" Modesty spat; tomato juice had sloshed into her mouth.

My phone said 23:41. We were within inches of the top of the tank. We all sank down as far into the juice as we could go and tilted our heads back. Pre centered himself between Modesty and me and held up his improvised airbag. We squeezed together so we'd be able to take turns sucking air out through the sleeve. I really wondered if that would work.

My phone advanced to 23:42.

"Everybody take a final deep bre—" I didn't have time to get it out. I inhaled as much as I could, clamped my eyes shut, and then all our heads were under juice. It had risen all the way to the ceiling, without leaving an inch of space.

I wondered how accurate Modesty's swim coach was. Could we really hold our breath for two minutes? I figured after a minute, we'd all be trying to get a gulp from Pre's windbreaker.

I cracked my eyelids.

Tomato juice stung!

I forced my eyes open anyway. I brought my phone as close to my face as I could and saw a blob of light, without any details. I blinked. Then I blinked again. Fuzzy numbers appeared in front of me. It looked like they might be 23:43.

Two minutes to go.

My lungs started to ache. I fumbled at the phone screen and brought up the list of Magic Bites. I was pretty sure *Egg* was selected. I changed it. I didn't think Modesty was right. *Egg* might get us out, but we'd be a pile of scrambled euphemera. I scrolled until I found what I was looking for. At least, it looked a little like what I was looking for. Then again, it might change the color of the room from tomato to cerulean.

My head hurt, and my chest felt about to burst. My jaw was clenched, and I was seconds away from trying to breathe. Suddenly someone grabbed my shoulder and forced something over my mouth. It was rubbery. It was the sleeve of the windbreaker. I reached up, held it more tightly around my lips, opened my mouth, and inhaled. Some liquid came in, and I almost gagged, but then I pulled a greedy lungful of air into myself. As I did, I felt the airbag *collapse*.

I had emptied it.

We had whatever air was in our lungs and no more.

Was I the last one to take a breath? Or was one of us still waiting for their turn? If one of us hadn't already taken a breath, they weren't going to make it.

I brought my phone back to my face.

23:44.

Was I about to make the right choice? Should I go back to *Egg* and trust Modesty's judgment? Or should I stick with my decision? Why was it getting so hard to think? My lungs were about to explode.

Pre started thrashing violently.

Then he went limp.

That wasn't good.

23:45.

I jabbed my thumb against the phone—

—and summoned the Forces of Torque.

CHAPTER 28

"I'M SO SORRY!"

Nothing happened.

I had guessed wrong.

Unless—

I wiggled my thumb against the face of my phone, trying desperately to move down the list of Magic Bites, but the list didn't budge. I pressed harder. The list slid sluggishly upward. I squinted at a tiny blob of light that might have been the word *Intensify* and jabbed it.

A grinding, scraping noise made the top of the tank shudder. It grew louder until an earsplitting, metallic *KA-BLANG* ended it. I reached up blindly, trying to find the wheel on the hatch, and my fingers got knocked aside. The wheel was turning on its own.

Another moment, and a crescent of light appeared

overhead. I gripped the shoulder of the sleeping logem and launched myself toward the light, hitting my head on the underside of the hatch but knocking it open at the same time. I grabbed the rim, pulled myself up, and I was out.

And dizzy. Hitting the hatch with my head hadn't been a good idea. I clutched my chest and gulped air, then spun back to the hatch on all fours. Modesty's face broke the surface. She opened her mouth and inhaled, then went under again. I reached for her, fished around frantically, and suddenly Pre was thrust into my hands. I got him under his chin and pulled him up while Modesty pushed from below.

Pre was deadweight.

I dragged him from the hatch and stretched him out on the floor.

"Hand!" hollered Modesty, and I caught her by the wrist and helped her out. She tried to get to her feet, staggered, and went down on her knees next to Pre. She jabbed her fingers against his neck, feeling for a pulse, said "Call 911!" and started performing CPR, rhythmically pushing her clenched fists up and down on Pre's chest.

I looked at my empty hands.

My phone was somewhere at the bottom of the tank.

Along with my chance to call for help.

Along with my hope of opening a door for Drew.

Modesty broke off her compressions, pinched Pre's nose shut, and pressed her lips over his. She blew hard enough to make his chest rise. It fell back. She tried again. Then she went back to pressing her fists into his chest.

Pre convulsed, spitting up a fountain of tomato juice. He heaved himself to one side and spewed more juice across the floor. He gave a final retch and started coughing.

"*Yes!*" I shouted, then knelt to one side and helped him sit. Modesty rubbed his back until the coughing finally stopped.

We were covered in red goop. We looked like the posters at the Disarray drive-in movie theater during the annual Gore-Fest-A-Rama. The main movie would have been *The Kids Who Dripped Blood*.

"How do you feel?" I couldn't tell if a healthy green had returned to Pre's cheeks.

"I've felt better," he said wheezily. He lifted a hand. He was still clutching the SAFE windbreaker by one of its arms. "My Tomato-Juice-Lung worked!"

"Yes, it did," I said. "Your idea saved our lives."

"Do you think it was...*science*?" Pre looked at me hopefully.

"You bet it was science." Modesty leaned in between us. "You came up with a hypothesis and you tested it. Fortunately for us, the results were positive."

"Wow!" Pre looked impressed. "I've never in my life thought I'd be able to do *science*."

"You've done it before," I assured him. "That thing you came up with to measure air temperature—we call that a 'mercury thermometer.'"

"Scientifical?"

"Highly. And I'm not sure, but I think you may also have invented a barometer. It's a thing that measures air pressure and helps predict the weather. Not that you'd really need that in Congroo."

Pre grabbed my forearm, and I helped him lever himself to his feet. "Oh, we could use it. We control the climate—mainly the temperature range—but the daily weather always takes us by surprise. Do you think I might be a scientist? Like Mary Potter? It would explain why I'm so lousy at magic."

"Maybe," I said. "Maybe you were just born in the wrong place."

"What Magic Bite did you use to do this?" asked Modesty. She was studying half of a crowbar embedded in one of the concrete pillars that held up the catwalk we were on. The end of the crowbar was jagged. She held the other half in her hand. "It twisted the wheel so hard, it snapped the bar. The pieces went flying."

"*To Summon the Forces of Torque*," I said as Modesty brushed past me, kicked the hatch shut, and jammed the remaining half of the crowbar through the spokes of the wheel, catching one end on a knob at the hatch's rim.

"That should keep Spalding in the tank until the lower hatches unlock," she said. "Spalding said they were set to open after an hour, which I'd guess would be about a quarter past midnight. What time is it now?" She directed the question at me.

I looked away.

"Where's your phone?"

I pointed downward.

"So you didn't dial 911?"

"Only in my head," I admitted sheepishly.

"Great. Okay—we have to get to Davy's house in the lobby, free him from the basement, and get him to stop the DavyTron update from going out at twelve twelve. Whatever the time is—we don't have much of it. Let's go!"

We didn't exactly run. None of us, not even Modesty, felt up to it, but we moved as swiftly as we could.

The catwalk stretched across the tops of the tanks, all the way back to tank number one, where a spiral staircase took us down to ground level. Once there, helpful signs on the walls guided us to the lobby.

We passed a restroom, and I asked Pre, "You've been here two nights; how come you didn't realize eleven forty-five was a Magic Minute?"

"Why would I have?"

"That first day, you ate two apple pies. I'm thinking about the Jupiter thing. Wouldn't you have, uh, felt something?"

"Maybe I did." He shrugged. "But both days, I was sound asleep. Hey, there's a clock!"

A digital display at the reception desk said 11:56.

Four minutes until the logem woke up.

Sixteen minutes until the DavyTron update.

Nineteen minutes until the hatches on the tomato-juice tank unlocked.

We clambered up the front steps of the house and let ourselves in. It had taken us maybe five minutes to get there—Pre kept lagging behind; he was easily winded—but once in the house, we wasted no time finding the door to the basement. It was around a corner, hidden from visitors who might be on the house tour. The door had no knob and no hinges.

We pounded on it.

The soundproofing was good, but when we put our ears to the surface, we could hear faint knocks answering us from the other side.

"How do we get this open?" asked Modesty.

"Why don't we ask the logem in the parlor?" suggested Pre.

"The logem in the—Oh!" It'd taken me a moment to get it. "You mean the animatronic grandpa? You think he would know?"

"He's connected to the computer network," said Modesty. "It's worth a shot." She wheeled around and led us back the way we had come.

"Howdy there, blood-soaked children," said the robot figure when we stood before it. "Rough day?"

"It's not blood; it's tomato juice," I explained. "How do we open the basement door?"

"I was born eighty-seven years ago," Granddad recited.

"That's not what I asked."

"I used to tell my grandson, little Elwood, all about my adventures running a cucumber ranch. Those were the days, by cracky." Granddad slapped his left knee.

"All he's doing is repeating his house-tour spiel," I said, disappointed. "We're wasting our time!"

"Wait," said Modesty. "Granddad! Access code TOMATO."

"I always knew Elwood would grow up to do great things," Granddad droned on.

"That wasn't the password," I said, casting my mind back to what Spalding had said. "Granddad! Access code 2-MATE-2."

Modesty shrugged. "You say 2-MATE-2, I say TOMATO—"

Granddad's head swiveled in my direction.

"How do we open the basement door?" I repeated.

"Press your thumb on my face."

"Excuse me?"

"Press your thumb on the face of Elwood Davy's grandfather in the photo hanging next to the basement door. The photo of the family picnic from ten years ago. It's a fingerprint reader."

"Will it work for anybody?"

"Anybody, so long as they have Elwood Davy's fingerprints."

"Oh. Could you open the door for us? We're kind of pressed for time."

"You wish me to override the lock?"

"Yes."

Something down the hall went *clonk*. A scraping sound followed, then running footsteps, then a wild-eyed man, hairier than anything in a werewolf movie, appeared in the doorway.

We screamed.

He screamed.

Everybody jumped back a foot.

The hairy-faced man shakily stretched his hand toward us and said, "Did he kill you? Are you ghosts? Or am I hallucinating again?"

"It's...tomato juice," I said, remembering we all looked like something out of Sapling Farm's monster barn. "Are you Elwood Davy?"

"*Yes, yes*, of course I'm Elwood Davy." He raked his fingers through hair that would have reached to his shoulders if he had ever taken the trouble to comb it in that direction and yanked at a beard that covered his chest like a furry lobster bib. He stepped into the light, and we could see Elwood Davy's face peering out of all the shagginess. He was barefoot, wearing blue jeans and a ragged T-shirt.

"He didn't kill you? Where is he? He's got the strength of ten men, you know!"

"He's in one of the tomato-juice tanks," said Modesty. "At least, I hope he is. He's awake by now. Listen, *listen*—we don't have much time, and you're probably not going to believe us—"

"Never mind all that!" he snapped. "I have to stop the twelve twelve DavyTron update from going out, otherwise Congroo will become a wasteland!"

"Well, that was easy," said Pre.

"You *know* what's going on?" I asked.

"Of course I *know* what's going on. I can't help but know what's going on. Every night I've been imprisoned, John Deere's been telling me everything he's been up to! Then he apologizes over and over. *I'm so sorry! I'm so sorry!* What's the time?"

He spun around to see the clock on the mantel.

It was 12:11.

"Whoa! Follow me!"

He dashed out the door, and we ran after him, racing

up the stairs to his old apartment over the garage. He threw himself into the chair in front of the computer. He flexed his fingers above the keyboard.

"Now—"

He typed furiously. Then he sat back and slammed his fists down on the desk.

"*He changed the password*. I can't get in!"

The computer's clock advanced to 12:13.

We were too late.

CHAPTER 29

MAGIC AMOK

What could he have changed the password to? Maybe he wrote it down somewhere." Elwood started rummaging through the papers on the desk. "Help me look!"

"It doesn't make any difference," Pre cried. "It's past time! The update thingy's gone out. Congroo is doomed!"

"What?" Elwood glanced up. "Oh, that. This computer's clock has always been fast. We've got, oh, at least thirty seconds. What could he have used as a password?"

"Only Ye Who Speak Wisely May Enter Here," I said.

"What?" Elwood glanced up at me and frowned.

"It's a quote on a locked door in the video game *Castle Conundrum*," I explained. "It only took my friend Drew half a second to figure out the password. It was obvious. I'm trying to think the same way he did."

Elwood considered for a second. "The password was…*wisely*?"

"No—the password was *obvious*."

I leaned past him and typed ten characters into the keyboard.

I'M SO SORRY

The screen remained locked.

I added an exclamation point.

!

The screen cleared.

"That's it!" Elwood crowed, and reclaimed the keys. His fingers flew, and in a moment, the mind-numbing gibberish of computer code appeared before us.

"Select all," Elwood barked. *"Delete!"*

Everything on the screen vanished.

"There!" Elwood raised his arms over his head in triumph. "Three seconds to spare. That'll show that Oom-pah-pah guy. Mess with me, will he?"

"Oöm Lout," Pre corrected him, and a strange blue— possibly cerulean—light came in through the window.

"Does anybody else feel strange?" asked Modesty, and hugged herself.

My skin prickled, and I was suddenly light-headed.

"You're getting it, too?" Elwood got shakily to his feet. "I thought it might be the altitude. This is the first time I've been out of the basement in years. But if we're all feeling it—"

"Are the trees supposed to be glowing?" asked Pre from the window. "Is it something scientifical?"

We crowded around him. Through the front of the lobby, we could see the trees on the far side of the parking lot. They were the source of the eerie blue light. They were covered with it.

"Like St. Elmo's fire," said Elwood.

"Did we do that?" Modesty wondered. "When we stopped the update?"

"I don't know. Maybe." I suspected we had. "We should get a closer look."

We turned for the door and crashed into a wall in the middle of the room that hadn't been there a moment earlier. The wall was stone, covered with moss, and almost reached the ceiling. It had a hole in it where a window might once have been.

"I *know* this wall," said Pre. "It's part of the ruins of the Abbey of Legerdemain. You've seen it—looking across the valley from the top of the library tower. It's part of Congroo!"

"What's it doing here?" I asked.

"Getting in our way," growled Modesty, and she clambered through the hole. Once through, she gestured impatiently for us to follow.

"The abbey's in the same location in my world as Mr. Davy's factory is in yours," said Pre as he slid over the sill. "Somehow, our two worlds are drawing closer together. They're overlapping."

We got out of the house. Broken stone walls jutted out of the lobby's tile floor. A withered tree loomed over the reception desk.

"Let's see how far this thing extends." Elwood ran for the elevators, dodging around the rocky remains of the former home of Congroo's foremost dragon expert. At the elevator, we helped him pull a vine off the door. The elevator seemed sluggish on the way up, but it finally opened on the top floor, and the office didn't look any different from the last time we had been there. We sprinted out through the roof garden, stopped at the parapet, and gazed across the valley.

The entire forest that surrounded Gernsback Ridge was glowing with the eerie blue light, and the glow was spreading out in all directions. As we watched, it engulfed downtown Disarray—the buildings began to shimmer— and then it rolled like an ocean across the far side of the valley and lit up Sapling Farm.

"Somebody's bound to notice this," I said.

"Ring, ring."

I fumbled at my pocket, then realized I didn't have my phone.

And Modesty's phone wasn't working.

"Ring, ring."

The voice came from behind us.

We turned.

A large lady in a lavender dress and a matching hat with a swooping brim that hid one eye was sitting on the edge of the rooftop garden's fountain, knitting a sweater. The strand of yarn she was using ended in midair, as if the ball it came from were invisible or located somewhere else.

"You're all quite revolting; are you aware of that?" she said. "Even the adult, who should know better. I really can't talk to you while you're looking like this."

She waved a hand at us, said one word—it sounded like *xylophone*—and I shuddered as something rubbed itself all over my body, yanked my hair in every direction, and flapped my clothing around me as if I were standing in a hurricane. It lasted only a moment, then I stretched out my arms to see they were no longer covered in tomato juice. My clothing was clean and dry. I had a sneaking suspicion my hair had been combed.

The others were equally neat and tidy, wearing what looked like freshly washed apparel. Elwood had been shaved and given a haircut. He looked like the Elwood Davy in the photos.

"That's better," said the woman.

"Delleps." I stated it, just in case she'd disappear if I asked a question.

"Yes, of course. Who else would I be?"

"You can do magic here," said Pre.

"So can you." Delleps put aside her knitting and stood. "At least for the next hour or so. That's what I have to talk to you about. I tried calling, but *somebody* isn't answering his phone." She glared at me.

I hunched my shoulders and studied my feet.

"I lost it."

"Careless."

"We saved Congroo!" I reminded her, hoping that would make it better.

"That's just it. *You didn't.* You were too late."

"*What?*"

"I deleted the DavyTron update code," Elwood protested. "That should have made everything all right!" He turned to me. "Who is this woman?"

"She's an oracle. Her name is Delleps."

"Delleps?" Elwood pondered for a split second. "That's *spelled* backward."

"Your quick and unnecessary word analysis tells me you *must* be the nerd genius who started all this." Delleps sighed. "I would say I'm pleased to meet you, but I'm not. Not even remotely."

"I didn't start all this," Elwood protested. "I only

wanted children to be able to design their own Mister Zucchini Heads. And I've just undone the damage. I deleted the code."

"Yes, and that was well done." Delleps nodded. "But what's happening now is, any unused magic stored up in those machines of yours is leaving the machines and rushing back into Congroo, and there's too much of it. It's like a bathtub that can only drain a little water at a time trying to deal with thousands of gallons."

"Like the time the landslide dammed up the magic behind the Delectable Mountains," said Pre, looking awestruck. "*That's* what all this blue light is!"

"Exactly," Delleps agreed. "A huge puddle of magic is forming. It's draining here in this building, but the puddle extends a good four miles in every direction. For the next hour or so, magic will work within that puddle."

"Without it being a Magic Minute?" said Modesty, her eyes lighting up.

"Without it being a Magic Minute, yes," agreed Delleps.

"And this is a problem?" I asked.

"It's not, in and of itself. Congroo will have its magic back within the hour—but it won't do any good. It may give us a few extra months, maybe even a year or two— but it won't last."

"But—but the magic will raise the temperature and keep the last of the flyer-fries alive, and dragons eat flyer-fries, and dragons exhale magic." Modesty sounded like

307

she was pleading. "So it'll start up again. Life's a web. My father always said so."

"It *would* start again." Delleps's face became grave. "Except for one thing. *Phlogiston is dead.*"

"Phloggie died?" Pre said in a small, broken voice.

"*No!*" Modesty yelped. The rest of us were stunned speechless. "She can't be! It's my mission to keep her alive! It's what my dad would have done! He would have dropped everything and risked everything to do it. She can't be dead!"

"It happened only moments ago," Delleps said crisply. "Leaving only her mate, Alkahest, as the last surviving dragon. A single dragon is not a breeding population. Congroo will use up its magic, the Pacifist Enforcement and Control Enchantment will fail, and petty warlords like Oöm Lout will enslave the land. Congroo will return to the Dark Ages."

Pre shuddered. I stood silently. Modesty paced rapidly back and forth, as if she was looking for something to hit.

"Wait," I said, thinking it through. "You're not... being *cryptic*."

"No, I'm not here in my capacity as an oracle. I'm here on my own as a concerned citizen of Congroo. If I had been able to reach you on your phone, *then* I would have been cryptic. I had a nice ambiguous limerick all worked out, rhyming *airborne* and *forlorn*. And a third word. Now I'll never get to use it."

"You didn't come here just to make us feel bad," I said, knowing I was onto something. "You came because you must think there's still something that can be done. Something...involving whatever it is Verbena discovered about dead dragons!"

"Viridis, and yes—there is a slim hope. And you're the only ones in a position to do anything about it. I've taken the liberty of calling you a cab. It should be here any minute."

Pre stepped forward.

"What can we do?" he demanded.

"Phlogiston is dead. But Phlogiston's anima—her spirit—has yet to go wherever dragons' spirits go when they die. No. Phlogiston's spirit has entered the receptacle that this young man's father so thoughtfully prepared for her."

She pointed at me.

"*My* father?" I leaned forward as if I hadn't heard her correctly. "My dad hasn't made any *receptacles*. He's getting ready for Halloween. He painted some signs; he decorated the barn; he made a...corn maze...."

"Exactly. The labyrinth. In the shape of a dragon. Phlogiston's spirit fled there when our two worlds became even more *overlapped* than usual. I hope your father didn't make the maze too simple, because once the spirit finds its way out, there will be no bringing it back. You must track it down and give it a good slap in the face."

"A slap in the—"

"Or a kick in the butt. If the three of you could tackle it from three sides and give it a good simultaneous whack, that would be ideal—a sudden jolt *should* send it back into its body, unless you take too long and the body grows cold. Do you understand?"

"*No!*"

"Good. That's exactly what an oracle likes to hear, even if she is off duty."

A loud *thud* came from behind us. We turned. The fire tower was pressed up against the parapet.

"There's your cab." Delleps walked toward us, fluttering her hands as if she were shooing geese. "Let's not dillydally. Off you go. Get in. Get in! *Not you, Mr. Davy!*"

Elwood had been eagerly following us. Delleps caught him by the shoulder and spun him around. "You've got sixteen hundred employees and no product to sell. There's work to do, young man, if you're going to treat those people fairly. Stay here and get to it!"

Elwood looked like a five-year-old who had been denied ice cream.

"But—"

"No buts."

"These children need a responsible adult with them," Elwood protested.

"And how is that you? Besides, I've found these three do very well without supervision."

She brushed past him. The rest of us had straddled the parapet and dropped into the fire tower's cab. Delleps leaned in the window.

"A couple of things before you go. Once the magic drains out of here, the suction that follows it will slam shut all the conduits between the two worlds. Magic will cease to work here, even at the times you call Magic Minutes."

"*No!*" shrieked Modesty. "Permanently?"

"That, I can't predict. Certainly for a while. You should check back periodically. My point is, one of you is going to have to decide which world you'd prefer to be stranded in." Delleps gave Pre a piercing glance. He staggered back a step. "And the rest of you should realize that if this puddle of magic made it possible for *me* to cross over from Congroo, then nothing is stopping *others* from doing it." She glanced at me. "Including your friend, provided he wakes up to the fact in time. And"—she turned her attention back to the three of us—"I'm sure by now Hemi-Semi-Demi-Director Oöm Lout has figured out his plan is in jeopardy. *Be on your guard.*"

She rapped her knuckles twice on one of the cab's roof posts, and the tower lurched away from the building.

"And oh," she called after us, "don't underestimate how fast a logem can run!"

The fire tower crouched and hurled itself forward.

"Whoa!"

We each grabbed a post for support. The cab rocked back and forth as the tower galloped, no longer picking its way carefully but barely missing obstacles as it dodged from side to side, sprinting straight for Sapling Farm. If there was any doubt that we were in a puddle of magic, it vanished the moment the water tower atop Campbell Hill leaned forward and turned its tank to watch us go.

Pre moved to one corner of the cab and began mumbling to himself.

"What—?" I started to ask him what he had said.

He held up a hand. "I'm envisioning spells," he explained as the tower *jumped* across Oakhurst Road and we nearly bounced out of the cab. "Magic is working here now; even if I'm not much good at it, I should have a few spells set up, ready to go, just in case. After all—*sometimes* I get it right." He bowed his head, turned away, and continued to mumble.

The tower hopped and leaped and sprinted past trees and houses that glowed with the ghostly light of surplus magic. When it got to the high-tension wires, it skipped the limbo in favor of leaning to one side and ducking under, which was quicker but nearly hurled us out the window. We hugged the roof supports, and a few moments later, we arrived at the Sapling Farm corn maze. The tower bent to within a few feet of the ground, and the three of us slipped out. It straightened to its full height, took two dignified steps to the left, and resumed its normal place. I noticed dew was clinging to it. Then I realized it wasn't dew: It was *perspiration*.

I looked across Route 9 to the wheat field. Once all the magic drained back to Congroo, there would be absolutely no way I could fix the Fireball 50.

Even if I had my phone.

"The entrance to the maze doesn't look right," said Modesty.

I turned, and a chill ran down my spine.

"Yeah," I agreed. "Artie's missing."

"Artie?" said Pre.

"The chainsaw maniac."

The cornstalks at the maze's entrance rustled. Artie, the roughly carved ten-foot-tall chainsaw maniac, lumbered into view. It was holding its wooden chainsaw high over its wooden head.

It turned to face us, crouched with its legs solidly apart, and blocked our path.

CHAPTER 30

THIS DRAGON'S ON FIRE

The onetime stump lowered the wooden chainsaw and twisted it sideways, as if it were getting ready to cut down a tree. Which was pretty ironic, for a stump. It tilted its head to one side and stared at us.

"I don't think it realizes that's not a *real* chainsaw," said Modesty.

"And what, exactly, *is* a *chainsaw*?"

The familiar voice came from inside the maze. A moment later, Oöm Lout strutted around the corner and stood next to Artie. The hemi-semi-demi-director was wearing a black robe and a purple cape with a collar that fanned out behind his ears like a cobra's hood. He might as well have been wearing a T-shirt that said EVIL WIZARD.

"Chainsaw? Anybody?" He looked at each of us in turn.

"That thing in its hands," I said. "*That*'s a chainsaw."

"That's what *you* may call it," Lout purred. "I call it a massive wooden club with nasty sharp teeth. Capable, I would think, of inflicting bone-crushing damage. And my magically animated friend here knows how to use it. Show them!"

Artie took one step forward and slashed the saw through the air—up, down, forward, and back—like an enormous ninja doing a sword demo. Then it shouldered the saw and snapped to attention.

"It's here to stop you if you decide to do anything foolish, like running into the maze in search of dragon ghosts." Lout looked me up and down, a growing frown on his face. He waved his hand at the ground in front of him, said "Sarcophagus," and a two-foot-high fluted Greek column rose out of the dirt like a mushroom. He stepped on top of it, and it made him taller than I was. He stopped frowning.

"*You! Librarian!*" He pointed an angry, quivering finger at Pre. "I don't care about the rest of them, but for the trouble you've caused me, *you must pay!*"

"What have you done with Master Index?" Preffy demanded coolly.

"Oh, your head librarian is fine," Lout assured him jovially. "His bones will heal. Although not with any help from magic. And they'll have plenty of time to do it as he languishes in my deepest dungeon."

"Did you kill my parents?"

Oöm Lout drew back. He waved one hand dismissively.

"No. The overturned carriage killed them. I only sent the hornet that stung the horse."

I caught Pre as he started to lunge. I knew he would never get past the chainsaw. He struggled with me and screamed at Lout, "They were wonderful people, and you took them from me! Master Index says that only a monster would separate a child from their parents! *You—are—a—monster!*"

Pre twisted out of my grip and began a suicidal charge. But before he could take more than a step, he was shoved to the ground by a bloodred figure that sprinted past us from behind. The figure, covered in tomato juice, ran up to Oöm Lout and took a place at his side.

It was Spalding Wicket. He bounced on his heels and drove one fist into the palm of his opposing hand. He looked ready to get back at us for making a fool of him.

"And now we are three," crowed Lout. "An example of how my power will grow in the future. Welcome, my faithful analogem. Now—*twist the head off the one you just knocked down*! You may do with the others as you see fit."

Spalding sprang forward with outstretched hands,

reaching for Pre's throat. He hesitated. "I'm so sorry," he said.

"Hurry it up," growled Lout. "Redeem yourself for failing in your mission! It's the least you can do!"

Spalding froze.

"I failed in my mission?"

"I wouldn't be here if you hadn't."

"Then…my mission has ended? It's over?"

"It was a total disaster. Yes, it's over!"

Spalding turned his head sideways and gazed up at Lout.

"Mission terminated?"

"How many times must I say it?"

"Thank you!"

Spalding stood, spun, and slammed his fist so furiously into Artie, the chainsaw splintered and went flying through the air, taking one of Artie's hands with it. Spalding tackled the statue around the waist and forced it back into Oöm Lout, knocking the hemi-semi-demi-director off his pedestal.

"Run!" shouted Spalding. "Do what you have to do. I'll keep these two busy. My pre-enchantments have ended. *I can make my own choices at last! And this* is what I choose!" He drove an uppercut into Artie's jaw that sent splinters flying like knocked-out teeth. The former stump's bite was now worse than its bark.

Pre got to his feet and sprinted for the maze. Modesty and I chased after him.

As I rounded the bend, I glanced back. Spalding had Oöm Lout by his cape and was twisting it around his throat. Artie was down on the ground, crawling toward the remains of the chainsaw, but Spalding's right foot was pressed solidly on its back, and the statue wasn't making much headway. I wondered how long Spalding could keep up the fight.

Two turns into the maze, we caught up with Pre, who was mumbling nonsense syllables as he ran. I took the lead and headed for the center, thinking that might be the best place to start looking for Phloggie's anima. The cornstalks were glowing in the same way everything else was, so the path was easy to see. I took the shortest route, glancing every which way as I ran, searching for something that might be the soul of a dragon.

But by the time we reached the center, we had found nothing, and the center turned out to be empty, too. We padded to a halt and started searching the surrounding vegetation.

"Quiet!" Pre held up a hand.

We listened. At first, I heard nothing. Then I noticed a rapid *thip-thump*, *thip-thump*, *thip-thump*, like—

"The beating of a heart," said Pre.

The plants nearest us began trembling.

Suddenly the cornstalks were thrashing to and fro,

and the taller ones began braiding themselves together. They whipped back and forth as if they were caught in a twister; then they uprooted themselves and came flying at us, like missiles launched by an angry Mother Nature.

"Look *out*!" I shouted as the stalks hit us and started to cluster. In only a moment, we were chest deep in writhing, flailing snakelike plants.

"Climb!" yelled Modesty as she wiggled out of the hole we were being buried in and clawed her way to the top of the rapidly growing mound.

We struggled to stay on top as plants came hurtling at us from all directions. The entire labyrinth was uprooting itself, and the stalks were converging, pressing themselves together, the same way the snow and the dust—and possibly bits of snot—had joined together to create the Dust Devil on the library tower's balcony. The mound we were desperately trying to stay on top of suddenly sprouted a long tail in one direction and an equally long neck in the other. The neck collected more twining cornstalks and grew a head.

"The maze is *sculpting* itself," I cried. "It's becoming a—"

"*Dragon!*" Modesty shouted.

Enormous wings unfolded on either side of the mound, and the cornstalk dragon reared back on two legs. Its head came up to the cab of the fire tower. Somewhere I could hear my mom and dad shouting and the sound of wood splintering. The dragon crouched. It shuddered.

"Oh no!" I feared what might be coming. *"Hold on!"*

We dug our hands and feet into the braided stalks and secured ourselves as best as we could to the dragon's back.

It leaped into the air, and something that big and ungainly should never have been able to fly, but fly it did. The dragon made of cornstalks soared above the fire tower, broke through a low-hanging cloud, then wheeled and started circling the farm.

"We're supposed to slap her in the face," said Pre.

"You think this is Phloggie's anima?" I bellowed over the rapidly increasing breeze.

"What else could it be?" Modesty shouted back.

"We could also whack her in the butt," Pre added. "Or just somehow give her a jolt. That's what Delleps said. That's supposed to send Phloggie's spirit back into her body in Congroo. Where, I'm hoping, things will change enough to keep her alive. Help me!"

He began flailing his arms against the cornstalk body, slapping it with all his might. When we saw what he was doing, we copied him, behaving like little kids having a tantrum.

"We have to work together!" shouted Modesty. "Hit her at the same time. Count of three—one, two, *three*!"

We struck the dragon simultaneously, giving it every-thing we had. Once we got into rhythm, we kept it up, slapping the cornstalks with all our strength.

It had no effect.

"She's too big, and we're too small," shouted Mod-esty, angrily yanking a cornstalk out of the creature's body and shaking it. Phloggie's anima had done a nice job of creating the look of scales by using ears of corn to cover her outer surface from head to tail. They looked like little green pillows.

"There must be *something* we can do!" Pre wailed.

Phloggie dropped through the clouds and dove for the farm. I suddenly had a dragon's-eye view of the Hallow-een barn. The twinkling orange lights reminded me of something.

"The holiday lights!" I shouted into the up-rushing wind. "They look like—"

"*Flyer-fries,*" Pre finished for me. "She's going to feed. Hold on!"

I was sure we were going to hit the barn. But at the last second, Phloggie pulled up and sailed over it, skim-ming the roof. She opened her cornstalk mouth and scooped up the strings of lights that outlined the build-ing. Electrical cords snapped, sparks flew, and the lights went out. Phloggie gained altitude and whipped her head from side to side, spitting out tiny light bulbs.

"The magic glow is getting dimmer." Modesty pointed below us.

The weird light that had bathed everything within miles of Elwood's factory was getting softer. Even the glow from the cornstalks of Phloggie's body was starting to fade.

"The magic's almost gone," cried Pre. "We're running out of time. I'm going to crawl along the neck and try to slap her in the face!"

He stood up and took a step forward. I gave one regretful look at the burned-out harvester below and started after him.

A hand burst out of the cornstalks at Pre's feet and grabbed him by the ankle.

Pre fell backward. Another hand broke through, and Oöm Lout clawed himself out of the stalks. He swung Pre by the leg, let go, and Pre would have gone over the side if Modesty hadn't thrown herself forward and caught him in time. She dragged him back to us.

Oöm Lout struggled furiously out of the plant fiber and stood at his full height, blocking the path between the dragon's neck and us. He was covered in corn silk and scratches, as if his fight to the top hadn't been easy. Since it didn't seem right to face him on our knees, the three of us let go of the stalks we had been gripping and got to our feet. We swayed a little, but at least it didn't look like we were groveling.

"*Oo effling iddel onthders!*" Oöm Lout shouted, and

I thought it might be part of a deadly incantation until he spat a baby ear of corn out of his mouth and tried again. *"You meddling little monsters!"*

His cape flapped in the wind from the dragon's flight. He raised his hands over his head and clawed his fingers, as if he were getting ready to pull down lightning bolts.

Pre stepped forward and put his hands up, palms outward, like a shield.

"I'm not sure I can do this," he whispered fiercely to us. "You may have to jump!"

"You can do it!" Modesty assured him. "Whatever he throws at us, you can beat him!"

"We're not in Congroo!" Lout announced, his eyes blazing. "There is no Pacifist Enforcement and Control Enchantment here. The World of Science is a world without PEACE! I can use the ultimate forbidden warfare spell and send you all on the longest journey of your pathetic little lives! One that will end in your deaths!"

Pre shivered and appeared to lose courage. I leaned forward and whispered, "I've had pretty good luck with *To Cast a Reflection.*"

Pre's spine straightened. Lout made complicated weaving movements with his hands and fluttered his fingers at us. He shouted three syllables.

"Lava tree!"

But at the same instant, Pre shouted back, *"Doomerang!"*

Oöm Lout doubled over and clutched his stomach. He looked up at us in surprise. Then the look turned to one of pure hatred.

"*No! You can't do this to me!* This isn't a schoolyard. It's a battlefield! Oh, what a world! What a world!" He bared his teeth. His eyes crossed. He reached one trembling hand toward us. "*At least throw me a magazine!*"

He disappeared into his clothing. One moment his head was surrounded by his collar and his hands were outside their shirt cuffs, and the next moment his head and hands were being sucked into his wizard's outfit. Another instant, and his empty clothing fell in a heap in front of us.

"What just happened?" asked Modesty, sounding as stunned as I felt.

"What would have happened to me if I hadn't been quick enough," said Pre. He turned to us. All the green had drained from his face. "Oöm Lout may have thought it would happen to you, too. I think he forgot, in all the excitement, that the two of you are different."

"What are you talking about?" I asked.

Phloggie was circling lower and lower, her glow getting dimmer and dimmer.

"The ultimate forbidden warfare spell," said Pre. "He tried to use it on us. I used *To Cast a Reflection* and sent it right back at him."

"So what was the spell you reflected?" I asked.

"Oh. Well. It's not even nice to talk about it."

"Talk about it," Modesty suggested.

"It...removes the filters from an enemy's IT."

"From their Information Technology?" Modesty said.

Pre looked uncomfortable.

"No. Their Intestinal Teleportation. The spell removes the filters, expands the scope, and increases the urgency. It's a terrible weapon."

"*What happened to Oöm Lout?*" I demanded.

"He...pooped himself to Jupiter."

Well.

There wasn't too much anybody could say to that. We just stood in shocked silence.

"Heck of a way to meet your end," Modesty decided. "I mean. You know. So to speak."

Phloggie pitched to one side, and we were suddenly reminded we were on the back of an airborne dragon made of cornstalks. We flailed our arms to keep our balance and twisted our feet more deeply into the corn. Pre stepped carefully over Oöm Lout's empty cloak and studied the dragon's neck, trying to figure out the safest places to put his feet.

Suddenly, he froze. "Anybody smell smoke?" he asked.

I sniffed, smelled it, then saw it: gray tendrils rising from Phlogiston's back. I looked more deeply into the body of the dragon and saw a red glow. It brightened even as I watched. I knew at once what had happened. I had seen it before.

"There were sparks when she tried to eat the string of lights," I cried. "The cornstalks are starting to burn. When that fire takes off, this dragon's gonna fry, just like the harvester!"

We were flying at twice the height of the fire tower. Jumping wasn't an option.

Modesty stepped back from the neck. "Maybe the fire will knock Phloggie back into her own body," she said excitedly.

"No!" Pre shook his head. "Fire doesn't *jolt*—it *eats away*. Flames won't save Phloggie. I have to stop this. I've almost finished the incantation *To Put Out a Fire*—" He started chanting some typically nonsensical syllables from a Congroo incantation. "Chim chiminny go Bimini banana phana foe fiminny; skeetches, peaches—"

Phlogiston spiraled downward. She began a tight circle around the top of the fire tower, her left wing grazing the roof of the cab. I thought she might be doing it intentionally, as a way for us to save ourselves if we had the courage. With a *whoosh*, the smoldering fire inside her became a full-fledged blaze that sent tongues of flame up through her body to lick at our feet.

"*We're not going to be able to stay airborne*—" I shouted; then I heard the word *forlorn* in my mind as I said *airborne*, and I remembered Delleps talking about a limerick that rhymed *airborne* with *forlorn*. And one other word...

"Stop! Don't put out the fire!"

I threw myself at Pre and clamped my hand across his mouth. Then I remembered that all he had to do was *think* the words of the incantation, and it would work. I distracted him the only way I could think of.

I threw us off the dragon.

We tumbled down the left wing, dropped off the tip, and landed on the roof of the fire tower. We caught ourselves before we rolled off and dodged Modesty as she slid down the wing and landed next to us.

"I can still put out the fire!" said Pre, scrambling to his feet and pointing his hands at the blazing dragon.

"*No,*" I shouted, and got in his face. "We need the fire! Some fires you put out—*some fires you let go!*" From the direction of the dragon came a few small noises—*pip! pip! pip!*—and I was almost certain I was right. Then a few white things like soft hailstones rained down on us, and I was positive.

"How do you know?" demanded Pre.

"Because I know what rhymes with *airborne* and *forlorn*. Do you?"

"Uh—foghorn?"

"*No.* But Panacea Irksome knew. Seven hundred years ago, she foresaw this very moment! She made it one of her Seven Insights!"

WHUMP!

The sound of a muffled explosion came from overhead

as every kernel in every ear of corn erupted at once. The shock wave hit us with the force of the grand finale at a fireworks show. The flying dragon became, briefly, a fuzzy white cloud; then the cloud disintegrated, and fluffy, spinning particles whirled through the air around us.

"Do you think *that* was enough of a jolt to send Phloggie's spirit back where it came from?" I asked.

"I . . . I would think so!" Pre broke into a grin. A fluffy button landed on his nose. He crossed his eyes to look at it. "This is—"

"Yes! *POPCORN!*"

CHAPTER 31

V FOR VICTORY

Doorway," said Modesty.

Pre and I turned. Modesty was on the other side of the fire tower roof. Behind her, hanging in midair about five feet from the roof's edge, was the faint, ghostly outline of a stone arch and the open doorway beneath it.

"That looks like—" I said.

"The door to the balcony on top of the library in Congroo," Pre said without hesitation. "Remember how parts of the Abbey of Legerdemain started showing up in Mr. Davy's house? The same thing's happening here. Your tower and the library tower are *congruent*—they occupy the same place but in different worlds. Our two worlds are still joined—but just barely."

"It's starting to fade!" cried Modesty.

"Delleps warned me about this." Pre shook his head. "She said I'd have to choose." He turned to me. "Do you really think I could be a scientist?"

"Well..." I thought for a second. "You certainly *think* like a scientist."

"He's *already* a scientist!" Modesty stepped between us. "He made a barometer. He made an Aqua-Lung out of a windbreaker!"

"Then, that's it," said Pre.

"You're staying," I said, thinking it was obvious.

"No. I'm going back. If I stay here, I'll be one more scientist in a world of scientists. But if I go back to Congroo, I'll be the only scientist there. If I have a different way of seeing things, then I owe it to my world to contribute the new ideas. I know who I am now. And—I have to rescue Master Index!"

He hugged me, reached out, and dragged Modesty into the hug. After a final heartfelt squeeze, he broke the embrace, got a running start, and sprang from the roof. For a split second, I thought the stone doorway would disappear before he got there and he would plummet to the popcorn-covered ground, but he landed solidly in midair, turned, and waved at us. The doorway rapidly faded around him.

And vanished. So did Pre.

I realized, with a pang, that with him went our last connection to Congroo.

"*Drew!*" I shouted at the empty space where the doorway had been.

"What?" said Drew behind me, and I staggered forward, slipped on the sloping shingles, and went over the side. I twisted and grabbed the edge of the roof, and my feet found the windowsill beneath me.

"Didn't mean to scare you," he said, bending down to offer me a hand. I refused it.

"We should all get off the roof and into the cab," I said, my voice shaky with the scare I'd just had and my joy at having Drew back. "It'll be safer."

He and Modesty wiggled their way off the overhang on either side of me, and a moment later, we were all securely inside. I hugged Drew, just as Modesty had predicted I would.

"How'd you get back?" I asked.

"Just now. Through there." He pointed at the open trapdoor. "Everything around the library starting glowing blue about an hour ago. Then I heard Phlogiston roar—I had thought she was dead, so that was good news—"

"*Yes!*" Modesty turned her face heavenward. "We did it, Dad!"

"But," continued Drew, "I decided maybe I *shouldn't* wait until four fifty-six to come back—that was my original plan—so I tried opening a door right then and there, and it worked."

"*Calvin!*" My dad's voice bellowed from somewhere below.

"*We're up here!*" I leaned out the window. "*We're all right!*"

"*The fight between the statue and whatever that other thing was took out the bottom zig of the zigzag stairs,*" he shouted up at me. "*I'm fixing it! But it's gonna take a few minutes before you can get down!*"

"*Take your time!*" I shouted back. "*We're fine!*"

So the logem's fight with the chainsaw maniac had caused some damage. I knew, if I analyzed it, that I would turn out to be somehow responsible. My eyes traveled across Route 9 to the harvester's hulk. Was that a trace of blue light lingering around it? Or only reflected moonlight? I whirled on Drew.

"Is your phone still working?"

"Barely. Battery's down to two percent—"

"Gimme! Quick!"

He fished his phone out and jammed it into my hands.

I zipped through the list of Magic Bites, found the one I wanted, and pressed it; then I pointed the phone at the harvester, as if it were a magic wand channeling my energy. I concentrated on the way the harvester had looked when it was new.

Blippity-blork.

"*To Repair a Chimney?*" asked Drew as he craned his neck to see what I was doing.

"It's gotta work," I muttered. "Gotta, gotta, *GOTTA*."

It didn't work.

"Don't forget *Intensify*," said Modesty.

My hands trembled. I skimmed to the intensification spell and jabbed it with my thumb.

Blippity-brap!

Blippity-brap! Blippity-brap! Blippity-brap!

I kept stabbing the screen with my thumb, but I could see, even at that distance and through some thin filmy tears, that the Fireball 50 wasn't changing. If anything, it looked more charred and blackened.

"The magic is gone," said Modesty, gently easing the phone from my fingers and handing it back to Drew. "It's too late, Cal. You tried your best."

I slid to the floor of the cab. Modesty plunked herself down next to me.

"We've put an end to digital vegetables," she said. "Farm stands—and farms—will start making a comeback. And I can guarantee you, the real Elwood Davy isn't going to be interested in buying yours. You saved your farm. Or, as I like to think of it, you helped *me* save your farm. And keep dragons from going extinct."

"You don't understand," I said. "None of *that* was my fault. The harvester burning, *that* was my fault. And for a couple of days, I could do magic. I could have fixed it. But I screwed up again. I wanted to make it up to my folks."

"'So what happened to you, Drew, after the door slammed in your face and you were stranded in Congroo?'" Drew asked himself as he sat down next to us. "'We certainly missed you.' Well, I'm glad you asked."

"We *were* really worried," I assured him, leaning past Modesty so he could see my face. He held up his hand.

"I got off the balcony in time to hide from Oöm Lout's logem (I found a cupboard), and then Oöm Lout himself arrived with his posse of Quieters, which, let's face it, is a really *disturbing* thing to call your police force—and Lout was furious that the library was empty, so he decided to close it permanently, and when they left, they chained and padlocked all the exterior doors and windows on the lower levels."

"So you've been trapped in the library all this time?" Modesty asked.

"I wouldn't say *trapped*; I pretty much enjoyed it. It was like being in a real-life *Castle Conundrum*. I knew you guys were smart enough to play *To Open a Door* whenever a Magic Minute rolled around, and I knew I wouldn't be missed at home until Tuesday evening, and I really wanted to avoid my parents while they were trying to renovate the bathroom, so I pretty much made up my mind *not* to open a door from the Congroo side until four fifty-six on Tuesday morning, which would have given me time to go to school with Cal and be back at my folks' in time for supper. And here's a surprise: It turns out, *I like porridge.* I found a kettle of it in one of the back rooms."

"You were in a world without toilet paper," said Modesty.

"Yeah, but I was also in a world where one of the books grows its pages back whenever you tear one out, so it wasn't all that bad. Although it would be nice if books, in general, were printed on softer paper. Which reminds me—" He pulled a folded sheet from his back pocket and spread it out against his knee. "I brought this back for you, Cal. Since you still think that you, personally, have to make up for what happened to the harvester."

He shoved the page in my face. I reared back so I could focus.

"What?"

"It's a page from the *Necro Name-a-Coin*, the book that lists every type of coin ever found by the *To Gather Lost Coins* spell. The book updates itself every hour. Surprisingly, it doesn't matter what world the coin was found in." He pointed to one of the pictures on the page. "That's one of the coins you found in your house, right? With a 1913 date, capital *V* on the back?"

"Yeah. *V* is the Roman numeral for five, so it's a nickel."

"Yes, it is." Drew nodded. "But in this case, I think we could say *V is for victory.* Did I ever tell you my dad has a 1904 penny worth one hundred dollars?"

"Lots of times. What's my nickel worth?"

"Three."

"Three hundred? Well, that's...nice."

He pointed to the small print next to the picture.

"Three *million*. Actually, three-point-seven million. Dollars. And I know that's accurate, because I remember my dad getting all excited the last time a similar nickel sold at auction, and it sold for something pretty close to that. I didn't realize you had the same type of coin until I saw the picture."

I grabbed the page from him.

It was the same coin.

"You...what...that can't be..." I didn't know what to say. Three million dollars could buy *thirty* new Fireball 50s. With change left over for a hundred leaf blowers.

I jumped up and turned my pockets inside out.

They were empty.

I'd *had* the nickel. I knew I had. It had gone into my pocket the night I found it. The nickel *had* to be on me. There wasn't anywhere else it could be. I felt frantically around in the cuffs of my jeans.

Nothing but lint and a piece of popcorn.

Had I spent it? Had I bought a three-million-dollar ice-cream cone in the school cafeteria? No—I hadn't allowed myself ice cream since I destroyed the harvester.

Wherever the nickel was, I didn't have it.

I'd screwed up again.

"*I've lost it!*" I wailed as Drew hauled himself to his feet, plucked the piece of popcorn from my fingers, and ate it.

"Porridge is nice, but you get tired of it," he said.

"Are we talking about *this* nickel?" asked Modesty, waving a coin in my face. I grabbed her hand and held it steady. The *V* on the coin was like two fingers jabbing me in the eyes. I shot her a quizzical look, and she shrugged.

"It flew out of your pocket when you put money in the binoculars. So you had something of great value all along. You just didn't realize it. If I had a nickel for every story I've read that ends that way…" She squinted at the five-cent piece appraisingly.

I reached for the coin, but she closed her fist around it.

"*You* found it," she said, "*I* saved it, and *Drew* figured out what it's worth. Sounds like a three-way split to me."

My parents believed everything.

Or, at least, most of it.

It took them a day or two to wrap their heads around it—I couldn't blame them—but in the end, even though magic no longer worked in the World of Science, there was too much of our story that couldn't be explained any other way. How the corn maze had vanished, where the lights on the Halloween barn had gone, what exactly my parents had seen when they had rushed out in the middle of the night and a mysterious figure was pounding Artie into toothpicks while the silhouette of something that looked like a dragon circled overhead. How the mysterious Artie-basher had vanished down Route 9, breaking the speed limit and doing it on foot.

And, of course, why the farm was covered in popcorn.

The 1913 nickel sold at auction in New York City for 4.3 million. If my dad had had any doubts about our story up until then, he was a true believer once the auction ended. We split the money evenly with Drew's family and with Modesty's, and my parents made some interest-free loans to neighboring farmers until everybody had time to recover from the damage the DavyTrons had done. There was still plenty of money left over for a brand-new Grain Gobbler 500, which was a bigger and better harvester, made by an entirely different company than the Fireball 50.

Drew's family used part of their share to renovate their entire house—including the addition of a second bathroom—and Modesty donated huge amounts in her father's name to organizations dedicated to protecting wildlife and the environment. Drew and I gave some money to those, too. You didn't spend time with Modesty without her enthusiasms rubbing off on you.

Davy's Digital Vegetables announced that DavyTrons

would no longer work and that anybody who had kept their receipt could get their money back. The company also announced it was no longer a company. It was going out of business, but all the money it had made would be shared equally among the former employees, which gave everybody an estimated two years of income during which to find new jobs. The company's "genetically modified" tomato plants withered the moment all the magic went back to Congroo. There had been nothing *scientifical* about them.

About a week after our adventure, I received a package in the mail from Elwood Davy. Inside the padded envelope was a note—*I believe this belongs to you*—and my cell phone. It had been cleaned, charged, and the operating system updated. I turned it on and stared at the background photo of the burned-out harvester.

I deleted it and replaced it with the photo that had been there originally, of my mom and dad and Glen and me having a cookout in Onderdonk Grove.

It was a better picture than I remembered—it gave me a warm feeling just to look at it.

And that, I realized, was magic that would work *any* time of the day.

Acknowledgments

In what has to be the wildest coincidence ever, these are the exact words of the Congroo incantation *To Express the Warmest Gratitude*:

To my editor, Deirdre Jones, who helped me get the manuscript down to a manageable length, and who was willing to defer to the CMS (*Congroo Manual of Style*) over the CMS (*Chicago Manual of Style*) if it helped a poor struggling joke land a little better. (The Comic Comma really should be accepted by *both* manuals, a point I intend to raise at this year's Comic Comma Con.)

To my managing editor, Lindsay Walter-Greaney, and copy editor, Stacy Abrams, who wrote funnier things in their marginal comments than I had written in the novel, and noted that this was one of the few books they had seen that actually mentioned a copy editor in the text, a situation I intend to remedy with my next book: *Lucida Bright, Mountain Climber Copy Editor.* (The title of which LBYR marketing will no doubt change to something like *What We Found in the Landslide and How It Saved a Bundle on Car Insurance.*) (Just wait.)

To my agent, Hilary Harwell, whose initial reading of the book fleshed out a number of characters, and who proved to me the Rocky Mountains are only a block or so away from the Avenue of the Americas, despite what Google Maps may say.

To my daughter, Elyse, and son-in-law, Adam, without whom my wife and I would still be stuck in our very first Escape Room and this book would never have been written, unless, of course, I used a piece of coal from the overturned scuttle and wrote on the lining of the Mysterious Lighthouse Keeper's raincoat.

To my wonderful wife, Kathy, who tolerated my disappearing into the basement for days on end, even though our house doesn't have a basement. (This is how fantasy gets written. She understands that.)

To lifetime friends Terry Hunt and Paul Feldman, who joined me all those years ago at the Uniondale Mini Cinema, where all three of us memorized dialogue from classic movies, and who will therefore recognize that this book references—in the same paragraph—my two favorite 1930s film icons: the Wicked Witch of the West and Rufus T. Firefly. ("Throw me a magazine" is my favorite line in the book, and it isn't even mine.)

And finally...to all those readers who wrote in to tell me they found all *eleven* vegetables hidden in the "computer code" in Chapter 21.

I had thought there were only ten.